# LIVING THE DREAM

Sharon Thomas
Does love
conquer all?
Nancy

First Published in Great Britain 2018 by Mirador Publishing



First edition: 2018



A copy of this work is available through the British Library.

ISBN: 978-1-912601-15-8

Mirador Publishing
10 Greenbrook Terrace
Taunton
Somerset
TA1 1UT
UK

# Living the Dream

Nancy Chapman

**June $27^{th}$ 1969**

# *CHAPTER 1*

"I am so relieved and so excited," Maddie told her aunt as the plane touched down at Prestwick International Airport. "I hate flying and I can't wait to meet Jack Buchanan… and Bob too."

Other than a little turbulence, the flight from Ottawa had been uneventful but Maddie had been anxious throughout it.

"For someone who hates it, you do a lot of flying," her aunt replied.

Fifteen-year-old Maddie frequently flew to dance competitions and highland games in Canada, the US and Europe. She was a world class highland dancer. Her success at highland dancing competitions and her status as the youngest ever World Champion was the reason she had been offered the job of lead dancer in a Scottish summer variety show.

"I'm so glad you came with me this time instead of my mother. You're much more fun."

"Just because you're working doesn't mean we can't enjoy ourselves too. We'll do some sightseeing, some shopping, maybe a few day trips if you have a day off."

Maddie's Aunt Joan was a very upbeat person. She was always ready for a good time. Indeed her constant smile was an indication that she loved life and was enjoying it to the fullest. The family resemblance between her and Maddie was obvious in looks and temperament. Joan was a short woman, just 5', but she had a big personality. Always open to new adventures, she was the opposite of her sister, Maddie's mother. Maddie and Joan were more like friends than niece and aunt.

Customs and immigration were cleared with no trouble. Walking towards the exit, Maddie stopped dead in her tracks. There was a man walking directly towards them and not just any man. It was the one man Maddie was dying to meet, the handsome singer of the legendary duo Bob and Jack Buchanan.

"Jack Buchanan!" she said.

"Maddie Campbell!" he replied.

As her hand touched his in a handshake, she felt a jolt of electricity run through her. He held her hand for what was only seconds but seemed like an eternity.

"You're not here to meet us? This is my aunt, Joan Kerr. She's my chaperone." The words tumbled out of Maddie's mouth in an embarrassing rush. "Joannie, this is Jack Buchanan."

"Nice to meet you, at last. I've heard so much about you. Maddie's been very anxious to meet you." Maddie blushed at her aunt's words.

"A pleasure to meet you too," he replied, shaking her hand. "If you'd like to come this way, my car is just outside."

"You didn't come to meet us?" Maddie repeated, feeling herself blush again.

"Oh," he said. "I did. It's not every day I get to meet the youngest ever World Champion Highland Dancer."

Maddie was beginning to think a blush was going to be her permanent colouring around this man. As they followed him, she said, "But we would have met at the hotel."

"That's where you'll meet Bob and the others. I wanted a preview." Once again a blush flamed Maddie's cheeks. *She's adorable*, Jack thought. *She blushes every time I say something.* With her porcelain skin, perfectly proportioned features, a mane of curly red-gold hair and the most amazing emerald green eyes, his heart had skipped a beat when he'd shaken her hand. And she was tiny, 5'2" or 5'3" at most and maybe 100 pounds he figured, and as lithe and graceful as a cat. Her photos, while attractive, didn't begin to do her justice. The blushes that kept colouring her cheeks were utterly charming. And she seemed truly pleased to meet him. *Watch yourself, old man,* he told himself. *She's only fifteen.* The attraction he felt to her was not one he should feel for such a young girl. "Keep reminding yourself, she's only fifteen," he muttered under his breath.

True to his word, Jack's car was just outside. The drive to Glasgow passed in a haze for Maddie. She couldn't believe this famous man, this legend, the one man in the world she had been dying to meet, had come to the airport to meet them. To meet her! He hadn't known Joan would be there.

Upon arrival at the hotel, Jack waited while they checked in then escorted Maddie and Joan to their room. "I'll give you some time to settle in," he said.

"It's 10:30 now and we'll be meeting in the Tartan Room at 2:00. You'll meet the others then. If you need anything, my room is just through the connecting door." With that, he let himself out.

"Oh my God, oh my God, oh my God," Maddie repeated. "He met us at the airport. He's drop-dead gorgeous and he's nice too. I thought he might be a snob, but he's not. He's so friendly and handsome too. And I love his accent. I could listen to him talk all day." Maddie babbled on.

"Shall I take it from that, that you like him?" Joan asked, a grin tugging at her lips.

"Oh, yeah," was the breathy answer.

"I'm going to have to keep an eye on you two."

Maddie looked surprised. "What would a man like him want with a snot-nosed kid?"

Joan smiled as she looked at her niece. The girl was strikingly beautiful and totally unaware of it.

Joan had noticed the way Jack looked at Maddie and the way she looked at him. With his blond good looks, strong masculine features, and soft gold brown eyes, it was no wonder the girl was smitten. Not to mention he'd been a major crush of Maddie's since she was old enough to know the difference between boys and girls. Joan made a mental note to keep an even closer watch on Maddie than she had intended.

A knock on the door heralded the arrival of their luggage. The bellman unnecessarily pointed out some of the extra features of the room: large screen television, private bath, coffee/tea tray with electric kettle.

For the first time, Maddie looked around her. Luxurious was the word that came to mind. It was a large room with pale blue walls, two Victorian style canopied beds, and matching dressers. There was a sitting area with a huge TV, a two seater couch and chair and a small writing desk that matched the dressers. The room also had the luxury of a private bath. The view from the window, of cobbled streets and soot covered stone buildings, made it seem like they had stepped back in time to an older Glasgow.

Joan finished unpacking and sat on the edge of her bed. She watched in amazement as Maddie pulled clothes out of her suitcase. "How did you get all of that into one suitcase?"

"I'm good at packing," was the reply. "Besides, if I bring everything with me I don't get homesick."

Exhausted from the trip, the time change, and her emotional reaction to

Jack, Maddie threw herself on her bed. She tried to remember everything he had said and everything she had said. *God*, she thought. *I'm so lame. He must think I'm an idiot*. She tried to remember the feeling that had gone through her when they touched hands. It was unlike anything she had ever experienced. She wanted to touch him again to see if it was just her imagination.

"It's 11:00," Joan said. "Why don't we get cleaned up then have some lunch?"

# *CHAPTER 2*

Jack let himself into his room and sagged against the door. "She's only fifteen," he repeated to himself several times. "I could get arrested just for what I'm thinking. It's going to be a very long six weeks."

Thinking of the way his heart had skipped a beat when he touched her hand, he walked over to the mirror. He gave himself a mental shake and looked at his reflection. "What would she want with an old man? I'm more than twice her age." And yet, there was more to it than a physical attraction. She looked so innocent and vulnerable he wanted to protect her from the world and from lecherous old men like himself. There was something about her that made him want a real relationship with her, not necessarily a physical one, although that would be nice. Maybe he could be a surrogate father to her while she was in Scotland. His daughters were almost the same age as Maddie.

If Maddie didn't want a surrogate father, maybe they could be friends. For the first time in his life, Jack found himself wishing he was younger. If he was twenty, or even fifteen, years younger, she might consider him boyfriend material. He was confused by his reaction to meeting her. She was a beautiful child and she would be a beautiful woman, but he had had beautiful women in his life. Those relationships had been purely physical. In the short time he had spent with Maddie, he found himself wanting something different. He wanted to know her likes and dislikes, her favourite colour, what films she liked – all the things a boyfriend her own age would want to know about a girl he was interested in.

At thirty-four Jack was far from old. He examined himself critically in the mirror. His erect posture had been drilled into him, first by his father then during two years of national service. Broad shouldered and just over 6 feet tall, he was an imposing figure. He studied his face. His gold brown eyes looked back at him. With freshly cut blond hair and cleanly shaven, he decided he didn't look too bad, even if his nose seemed a bit too long. His face had no wrinkles to hint at his age. Not being a vain man, he didn't think of himself as handsome. Most people looking at him thought he was.

Jack smiled at himself, thinking he was being shallow. People you knew didn't judge your looks. They were more interested in your heart. "I'm going to get to know her and she's going to get to know me." He crossed his fingers, then looking at his hand muttered to himself, "As if crossing my fingers would make a difference." He felt like a teenager with his first crush.

Jack wondered if his past history would put Maddie off him. There was nothing terribly sordid, but there was a disastrous marriage which had ended in divorce. The only good thing to come of that marriage was his two daughters who lived with his ex-wife but whom Jack saw regularly when not on tour.

Still confused by his reaction to Maddie, Jack dressed carefully for the get-together in the Tartan Room. He thought if he wasn't young, he could at least appear young at heart. In a golden brown sweater, that was almost the same colour as his eyes, and khaki denim pants, he thought he looked pretty good.

# *CHAPTER 3*

There were several people milling about the Tartan Room when Joan and Maddie walked in at 1:55. A bit intimidated, Maddie was a few paces behind her aunt. Bob and Jack were standing in a corner talking. Jack had changed his clothes and Maddie thought he looked even more handsome than he had before. He had been watching the door and immediately walked over to them, his brother Bob close behind. Introductions were made. Bob, while not the complete opposite of Jack, did not resemble him at all. Shorter and darker than Jack, he had dark brown hair and very deep, dark brown eyes. He was a year older than Jack. Maddie thought one must resemble their father and one their mother.

After a head count, Bob walked to the front of the room. "I think we're all here now. I just have a few words to say then we can introduce ourselves and get to know each other. Welcome. For the show we have highland dancers, pipers, comedian Billie Abbot and, of course, Jack and me. The title of the show is 'A Taste of Scotland'. We're going to wow the tourists with our display of Scottish culture - and maybe even the locals." A chuckle rippled through the room. "As I said, today's get-together is to introduce ourselves to each other. I'll put names to faces then we'd like you to walk around and talk to each other. Take a copy of this tentative program we've worked out. First rehearsal is at 10:00am tomorrow at the theatre. We'll see then if the timing works for costume changes so let's make it a dress rehearsal for our dancers. You ladies are the only ones who have to change," he said, addressing the small group of dancers then turning back to the whole group. "We have a couple hours to get acquainted then the hotel staff will bring in refreshments. That will be about 4:00." After a few more words Bob introduced Jack as the singer and himself as the accordionist of their duo.

"As if they need an introduction," Maddie muttered to herself.

Joan smiled broadly at her niece's comment, feeling a little guilty for eavesdropping on the girl's thoughts. Maddie glanced at Jack then looked away quickly when her eyes met his. He was watching her she thought, a blush colouring her cheeks yet again.

Looking for an excuse to talk to Maddie, Jack walked over. "You'll be wanting to meet the other dancers," he said. "Come on, I'll introduce you." As he took her by the elbow to lead her over to them, the same jolt of electricity she had felt at the airport coursed through Maddie. *My God, she's cute*, he thought. *She must like me; every time I talk to her she blushes*. He groaned to himself, foreseeing a lot of cold showers in the next six weeks. *Give your head a shake, old man. You're going to think of her as a daughter*.

They went over to a woman and a small group of girls standing together. There were four dancers and their teacher. Jack made the introductions, surprising himself by remembering all the girls' names. Four pairs of eyes looked expectantly at Maddie. The fifth pair, belonging to their teacher, looked with admiration.

"It's such a pleasure to meet you," said Mrs. MacDonald, the teacher. "The girls are so excited to be dancing with the youngest ever World Champion. They've been diligently practising to the music you sent."

Maddie blushed again. *Damn*, she thought. *I'm soon going to be permanently red*. She forced a smile and began chatting with the girls. They were shy at first, but warmed up to her quickly. Afraid she would be stuck-up, they were delighted by her friendly open manner and her funny accent.

The other performers gradually made their way over to the small group, introducing themselves as they joined the conversation. The three pipers joined the group first followed by Billie Abbot. Bob and Jack were the last ones to join in.

At precisely 4:00 the door opened and uniformed waiting staff entered with trays of refreshments. It was the living definition of 'High Tea', Maddie thought: tiny sandwiches, scones, tea and little cakes. In all her trips to Scotland, Maddie had never had 'High Tea' and she was delighted.

Jack walked over to Maddie using the piece of paper in his hand as his excuse to talk to her. He handed Maddie the copy of the tentative program, saying, "You ladies are the only ones with costume changes, so read through this and see if you think we've given you enough time."

Maddie took the paper from him. Much as she wanted to, she avoided touching his hand, unsure she could withstand another of the lightning bolts that hit her when she touched him.

As they were heading towards their room, Bob approached Maddie and

Joan, asking if they would like to join him and Jack for supper. The electricity between his brother and Maddie had not escaped his notice. He figured he was going to have to keep a close eye on Jack to keep him out of trouble. The girl was only fifteen. Bob laughed at himself. He knew Jack would never hurt a girl or a woman, but he had never seen his brother thrown so completely off-balance by one. If he believed in love at first sight, he would think Jack was in love.

# *CHAPTER 4*

The dining room was opulent: high ceilings with glittering crystal chandeliers, windows hidden by rich, dark blue velvet drapes against cream coloured walls. The tables, covered with navy blue linen cloths, were formally set with delicate china and heavy silverware and the waiting staff was all uniformed. Maddie felt underdressed in a bright green sundress that matched the green of her eyes, but looking around she realized the other diners were dressed in everything from ball gowns to blue jeans.

During the meal the conversation was mostly between Bob and Joan. Maddie was concentrating hard on controlling her knife and fork under the warm gaze from Jack's gold brown eyes. Every time she looked in his direction he was looking at her. He seemed to be watching her. As well as trying to control her utensils, Maddie was trying not to say anything stupid. The easiest way to avoid that was to say nothing.

The truth was Jack was watching Maddie. He had never seen such a combination of features. She was beautiful: porcelain skin surrounded perfectly proportioned features and rosebud lips, but what really attracted him were her eyes. He was mesmerized by those deep green eyes. He didn't think he'd ever seen eyes that colour before. He could easily lose himself in them. He couldn't help but stare at her. She was so shy every time he talked to her or she caught him looking at her she blushed.

The dinner conversation eventually turned towards a discussion of the show's programme. Joan and Maddie had studied it and were satisfied there was enough time for costume changes. They discussed the rehearsal schedule and on such neutral ground, Jack and Maddie were both able to join the conversation. There were only three full cast rehearsals. Each group was responsible for the content of its own segment and could hold their own rehearsals as required. The full rehearsals would be to check the timing and the stage entrances of the acts.

Bob noticed the ladies were tired and suggested an end to the evening. He and Jack escorted them to their room, agreeing to meet for breakfast at 8:00.

"We'll pick you up," Jack said. "I'm just next door and Bob's across the hall." He gave himself a mental kick, thinking he sounded dumb.

"I'm bagged," Maddie said throwing herself on her bed.

"Dinner did seem a bit stressful for you." Joan smiled as Maddie threw her a dirty look. "Maybe breakfast will be easier."

Surprised there was no response, Joan looked at her niece. The girl was sound asleep. Jet lag and meeting Jack had worn her out. Joan didn't think she needed to wake the girl to get ready for bed. It wasn't a big deal for Maddie to sleep in her clothes. Joan pulled a blanket over the girl and went to get herself ready for bed.

# *CHAPTER 5*

Rehearsal the next day went well and true to her word, Mrs. MacDonald had drilled her girls well. They would be performing a sword dance, a highland fling and a hornpipe, accompanied by the pipers. These dances had been chosen because they could all be done with an odd number of dancers. The sword dance and fling could be done by one dancer as a solo or as a massed dance with any number of dancers all in kilts and velvet jackets. The hornpipe meant the girls had to change costumes into sailor suits. It was not usually a dance for a large group, but could be done with an odd or even number of dancers. With Maddie, there were five dancers. The girls were step perfect and there was plenty of time for costume changes. They had all been practising with taped music and really enjoyed dancing to the pipers' live music.

Maddie spent her time backstage watching Jack. It was safe to do while he was performing. He couldn't look back at her or catch her eye and make her blush.

*He's so elegant*, she thought. *And so enthusiastic performing songs he must have sung hundreds of times*. She admired his interaction with the imaginary audience and the play of emotions on his face, thinking, *He's a true showman,* and wondering if she could ever be half as good. Her time in front of dancing judges didn't seem to be on a par with performing for regular folk. The regular folk would be a much tougher crowd. They would be paying to be there.

"Admiring the scenery?" Joan asked coming up behind her.

Maddie jumped and chose not to reply. They watched the final number then Maddie went out on stage with the rest of the cast for the final bow. Just her luck, the order they went in had her holding Jack's hand for the final bow. When she took his outstretched hand the lightning bolt went through her again. Then when he winked at her she blushed. She hoped this wasn't going to happen every night for the next six weeks. He could electrocute her. Trying not to think about it, she focussed on the imaginary audience.

*Weird,* she thought, *bowing to people who aren't there*. While practicing her dancing, she had often bowed to people who weren't there, but this felt different. For one thing, the theatre was huge.

Following the final bow, they prepared an encore. Years of performing had taught Bob and Jack audiences always wanted more. Because everyone was on stage, they decided they would all sing 'Flower of Scotland' (a song that was often referred to as 'the almost Scottish National Anthem'). Maddie felt very uncomfortable when Jack moved closer to her so they could share his microphone. Her cheeks were flame red for the entire song.

After rehearsal, Bob asked Maddie and Joan if they'd like to join him and Jack for supper again. While really wanting to spend time with Jack, Maddie cringed inside. Yet another awkward meal trying to control her knife and fork and trying not to say something stupid. She was getting seriously tired of blushing every time Jack spoke to her or looked at her. It seemed he was always looking at her.

Jack was trying to think of a way to get Maddie to talk to him. He figured if he could just talk to her he could find out if she actually liked him. Her cute blushes made him think she did, but he wanted to know for sure. She rarely talked directly to him and he couldn't figure out why, although he too was uncharacteristically quiet when she was around.

The show was a big hit. The tourists were delighted by it and even the locals were impressed. The first night, Maddie was also impressed. She had thought they were good at rehearsals, but Bob and Jack seemed to come to life in front of an audience. They picked up every nuance of the audience's reactions and played to them, inviting clapping and singing along to nearly every song. They always wore kilts for their performances and Maddie thought Jack in a kilt was the sexiest thing she had ever seen.

Maddie found Billie Abbot very funny, if a little crude. He was a funny little man who embodied what she thought of as the perfect comedian. He was quite round; not very tall, but very wide. He had a thatch of black hair above a round cheerful face with a perpetual smile and a permanent twinkle in his blue eyes.

Even though she'd been dancing in front of crowds since she was six, Maddie was a bit intimidated by the size of the audience. She was also unsure of dancing with the other girls, although the rehearsals had gone very well. She needn't have worried. The dances were step perfect on everyone's part and they all looked like they were enjoying themselves. Maddie knew she was enjoying herself. She loved dancing to the pipes.

The content of the shows was different each night, with Jack and Bob singing different songs and Billie Abbot telling different stories, but because the format and the timing were the same every night, there were only the three full rehearsals at the beginning of the run. That left Joan and Maddie time to do a little sightseeing and a lot of shopping. They took a bus tour of Glasgow, day trips to Inveraray and Burns' country. They even managed an overnight in Edinburgh one night when the theatre was dark. Another night when the theatre was dark they stayed at a little inn near Loch Ness and went Nessie hunting. The hunt wasn't successful but they had a good time.

At the end of the run, Maddie was sorry to be leaving Glasgow. She had really enjoyed the performances. Yes she was still shy and awkward around Jack, but she was still smitten by him. She hated the thought of not seeing him again. The six weeks seemed to have passed slowly given the discomfort Maddie felt around him, yet at the same time she felt like she and Joan had just landed in Prestwick.

Jack was also thinking the time had passed too quickly. He didn't think he'd had a chance to make a good impression on Maddie. She still blushed when he spoke to her, but she did seem to be a little more willing to talk to him. In all that time, he hadn't been able to get her alone to talk, just talk. Between Joan and Bob, they'd always had a chaperone. He still felt like a teenager with his first crush and he really wanted to get to know her.

The day after the show closed, Maddie and Joan had breakfast with Bob and Jack. Jack thought Maddie seemed a bit sad to be leaving. Maybe he was just projecting his feelings onto her. He had looked forward to seeing her every day, and was going to miss that. He liked spending time with her, even if she was too shy to really talk to him.

Maddie marvelled that Jack would take the time to drive them to the airport. She remembered that day six weeks ago when they had first met. Nothing he had done in the six weeks had tarnished her image of him. Indeed, he had lived up to everything she had imagined about him and more.

Jack escorted them to the boarding gate. Just before he saw them off he plucked up his courage and gave Maddie a hug. Her arms went around him automatically and he gave her a kiss on the cheek. The familiar jolt of electricity ran through her again and his heart skipped a beat. He didn't want to let go, but he did, turning to also give Joan a hug and a kiss. In her surprise and pleasure at the gesture, Maddie didn't notice him hug Joan as well.

As they settled into their seats on the plane, Joan asked, "Well, did he live up to your expectations?"

Maddie looked at her quizzically. "You mean the show?"

"No," said Joan, "I mean Jack." Maddie shifted uncomfortably in her seat. Joan continued, "I know you've had a huge crush on him for years."

Giving up, Maddie answered, "Yes he was everything I hoped for and more, but he must think I'm some kind of idiot. I couldn't even talk to him."

Joan smiled. "I'm pretty sure he likes you too."

Jack left the airport feeling pleased with himself. After six long weeks he had finally kissed her, not on the lips, but he had kissed her. He could still feel her soft skin on his cheek and lips. It was going to be a very long time till next year's show he thought. *Maybe I can phone her. Then she'd have to talk to me. And when we tour Canada in February, I'll see her. I'll send her tickets for her and a few of her friends. That way I'll be sure to see her and I can meet her friends.*

# *CHAPTER 6*

For Maddie the rest of the summer and the fall passed in a whirlwind of dance competitions, all of which she won, and school. Her essay on 'What I Did on My Summer Vacation', with photos and film, was a definite hit with her classmates and secured her an A+ from the teacher. Her girlfriends were very impressed at the sight of Bob and Jack in kilts, although they thought it odd that men should be wearing skirts.

Busy as she was, Maddie had the feeling that something was missing in her life. Thinking about it one afternoon, she realized what the problem was. She was missing Jack. As uncomfortable as she had been in his presence all summer, she still thought about him – a lot – and she missed seeing him every day. She wondered if he ever thought about her then gave her head a shake. She was just a kid. He would have women his own age to spend time with.

As Christmas approached, Maddie was in a quandary. Should she send Jack a Christmas card or was that not cool? She had kept in contact with the other dancers and Mrs. MacDonald, and had no qualms about sending them cards. After a week of vacillating, she decided to send Bob and Jack each a card. She was glad she had when, two days later, she received a card from Jack. She tried hard not to read too much into the signature 'Love Jack'. The next day a card came from Bob.

The day after Christmas the phone rang. Her mother answered and Maddie heard her say, "Merry Christmas to you too. Yes, just a second." She passed the phone to her daughter.

"Happy Christmas," said a voice with a heavy Scottish accent.

"Jack?" Maddie said uncertainly.

"Yes. How are you?"

Despite having sunk heavily to a chair, she managed to reply, "I'm great thanks. How are you?" She realized it was easier to talk to him on the phone than in person. At least he couldn't see her blush!

After they had chatted for about an hour, Maddie realized that it wasn't so hard to talk to Jack.

He eventually came to the real reason for his call. *Real reason*, he thought. *More like real excuse*. "We're running 'A Taste of Scotland' again this summer. Can I count on you to dance for us?" He groaned to himself. He should have said can WE count on you. He hoped she hadn't noticed his slip of the tongue.

"I'd love to," she answered, not then noticing what he had said.

"That's great," he said. "We've already posted the contract."

She laughed. "Good thing I said yes."

Reluctantly, on both sides of the Atlantic, they ended the conversation, but not before Jack virtually asked permission to call her again. She agreed with her standard answer to friends and family, "Any time you like."

As Maddie hung up, she said to herself, "I can't believe I said that. My God, I can't believe we had a real conversation. It's so much easier to talk to him when he's not looking at me. And I don't think I said anything stupid." She was glad her mother and father had gone out. She wanted time alone to savour and relive the conversation. Later, when she mentally reviewed it over and over she thought Jack had asked if 'he' could count on her to dance, not if 'they' could. As much as she wanted to, she tried not to read too much into that.

On his side of the Atlantic Jack's face was wreathed in smiles. She'd actually had a real conversation with him. What's more, she had said he could call her again anytime. And best of all, she wanted to do the show this summer. She had also said she would see him when he and Bob were in Ottawa in February.

Jack was still smiling when he called Bob an hour later to tell him Maddie wanted to work with them again this summer. Bob was pleased but not nearly as pleased as Jack.

# *CHAPTER 7*

When Jack phoned Maddie at the end of January, he was very pleased to hear she had received the tickets he'd sent her for his and Bob's shows in Ottawa. He was even more pleased to hear she intended to use them and had already made arrangements with her friends. He had thought of asking her if she'd like to dance with them but had decided against it. She could just enjoy the shows with her friends. They had two shows and he had sent her four tickets for each one.

Bob and Jack arrived in Ottawa at noon the day of their first performance. They had to set up and rehearse, so Jack didn't have a chance to see Maddie that day. He did call her to say hello and to make sure she would be at the show that night. She told him she wouldn't miss it for anything.

Even before the first show was over, Jack had made Maddie blush. The tickets he had sent her were in the front row. She had brought along her best friends Beckie and Ben and Auntie Joannie. Jack made a point of saying hello to them and waving from the stage. He also told the audience that he was pleased to see a young lady who had danced with them in a show in Scotland. Maddie blushed bright red as the people sitting around them all strained to get a look at her.

Backstage, after the show, Bob and Jack both gave Maddie and Joan a hug and a kiss on the cheek. Trying unsuccessfully not to blush, Maddie introduced Beckie and Ben. They had both really enjoyed the show and said so. Jack was pleased that Maddie's friends seemed to like him. He didn't know it, but Beckie and Ben liked everyone. They were easy going, friendly and enjoyed meeting new people. They were especially happy to be meeting celebrities who were friends of Maddie's.

Maddie had told Beckie about Jack. She had confessed that she found him really attractive and she would like to get to know him better. She had also confessed she was so tongue-tied around him he probably thought she was an idiot. Beckie tried not to be too obvious as she watched Jack to see how he acted around Maddie. She had noticed his face light up when Maddie walked into the room. She also noticed he didn't seem able to take his eyes off her. Fortunately Bob and Joan once again kept the conversation flowing. After not seeing each other for six months, even though they had talked on the phone, Maddie and Jack were both a bit tongue-tied with each other. Beckie thought that was cute. She would tell Maddie later that she was pretty sure Jack liked her and didn't think she was an idiot.

Beckie and Ben were a few years older than Maddie and both had part-time jobs. They were trying to save their money so they could buy a farm and move in together. The next day was Saturday and Ben had to work. Beckie had been able to get the weekend off. Maddie and Beckie were planning to go skating on the Rideau Canal and Beckie invited Bob and Jack to join them. Maddie was horrified, but other than blushing yet again, she managed to keep her expression neutral. Beckie told the boys there were lots of places to rent skates or, if they wanted, they could just walk on the ice. It was Winterlude (the winter carnival) in Ottawa and there were lots of snow and ice sculptures to be seen and beavertails and hot chocolate to be consumed. Jack and Bob both looked uncertain at the idea of eating beavertails. Once Beckie explained they were deep fried pieces of dough in the shape of a beaver's tail with butter, sugar and cinnamon on them, they thought that sounded pretty good.

Neither Bob nor Jack had done much skating while growing up. Despite his athletic build, Jack had not been much of a sports fan and only played what he had to in school. Except for not looking like an athlete, the same was true of Bob. They both agreed to go with the girls, Jack saying he would rent skates. Bob, afraid of breaking an arm and not being able to play the accordion, opted to wear his boots and walk with them. He figured with Jack wearing skates they wouldn't be moving too fast and he would be able to keep up, even on ice.

Auntie Joannie was invited to go too, but she politely declined.

Saturday the sun was shining brightly and it wasn't too cold out; a perfect day for skating. Beckie, proud of her new driver's license, had said she and Maddie would pick Bob and Jack up at their hotel at 11:00. When they arrived at the hotel, Bob and Jack were ready, with coats, boots and gloves on. Maddie had borrowed toques, mittens and scarves from her father and insisted the boys put them on. They parked the car at Dow's Lake (the end of the canal) and went into the *Pavillion*. It was a large modern building in a hexagonal shape and had several restaurants, a skate rental outlet and a skate sharpening facility.

Jack thought it would be nice just to sit in one of the restaurants and watch the skaters through the large picture windows.

Having said he would skate, Jack was hoping there wouldn't be any skates in his size. He was beginning to think it was a bad idea. He was dismayed to find skates in his size and wondered if he should have brought a pillow to tie around his butt. He was pretty sure he was going to fall at least once.

When they got their skates on and went out onto the ice, Beckie took Jack's left arm and told Maddie to take his right. They would hold him up if they could and if he fell they would pick him up. Bob was quite amused at Jack's attempt to skate. Trying not to laugh, Beckie suggested Jack just keep his feet on the ice and she and Maddie would do the skating, pulling him along. That worked out much better. They were able to skate around the lake, looking at the fantastic snow and ice sculptures. Bob and Jack had never seen anything like them.

After about half an hour the girls took pity on Jack and led him and Bob to the beavertail stand. They each ordered a beavertail and a hot chocolate, Maddie's treat, and found a free picnic table. Jack was very relieved to sit down and wondered how he was going to make it back to the *Pavillion* and his boots. He thought skating was over-rated. They enjoyed their snack then Bob and Jack sat at the table while the girls did some 'real' skating. Too soon, to Jack's way of thinking, the girls returned to the table ready to go back. They went back the same way they had gone out, Jack with both feet firmly on the ice and Beckie and Maddie pulling him along. Bob enjoyed his walk on the ice, and he really enjoyed watching Jack's discomfort on skates.

That night at the show, Jack saw Maddie and Beckie in the front row sitting with two people he assumed were Maddie's parents. Once again Jack managed to make Maddie blush. He told the audience he and Bob had been skating and lived to tell the tale. He thanked the two young ladies who had taken them. Once again the audience strained to look in the direction he was looking.

After the show Maddie introduced her mother and father to Bob and Jack. Jack was dismayed when he realized Maddie's parents were not much older than he was. He had enjoyed spending the day with Maddie and Beckie and had managed to forget about the age difference for a while.

# *CHAPTER 8*

Maddie felt a sense of déjà vu as she watched the tarmac of Prestwick International Airport appear to rise to meet the plane. Her Auntie Joannie was once again seated beside her on the aircraft.

This time when they got off the plane and through customs, Maddie was looking for Jack. He didn't disappoint, striding across the concourse towards them with a big smile on his face.

"Well, if it isn't the youngest ever two-time World Champion Highland Dancer. Hi, Joan. Welcome. It seems like we've done this before." He laughed, scarcely containing his pleasure at seeing Maddie again. She was even lovelier than she had been last year. The mane of red-gold curls was longer, her face looked more like that of a woman than a girl; and those brilliant emerald green eyes! He was sure he would get lost in them. Feeling brave, he leaned forward and hugged Maddie, kissing her on the cheek. To keep up appearances he did the same to Joan.

At the hotel, the previous year's scenario was replayed, Jack waiting while Maddie and Joan checked in then escorting them to their room. They had the same room as last year with Jack just through the connecting door.

Once again Maddie relived the feel of Jack's lips on her cheek. Mentally she replayed the conversation in the car, most of which had been between Joan and Jack.

*It really was easier to talk to him on the phone,* she thought.

In his room, Jack was thinking she's almost as distant as she was last year after being so friendly on the phone the four times he'd called her. She'd been a bit shy when he'd seen her in February but now it seemed like they were starting at the beginning again. He studied himself in the mirror. *I don't think I look any different than I did last year. When we talk on the phone she's probably imagining someone her own age, or her father.*

The performers met in the Tartan Room at 2:00 that afternoon. The cast of the show was almost the same as the previous year. There was one different piper and one different dancer. That sense of déjà vu returned as Maddie chatted with the others and watched 'High Tea' being brought in.

Maddie wondered if there would be the same series of awkward meals there had been last year. She and Joan had had breakfast and supper with Bob and Jack most days. She was undecided whether she wanted to spend every meal this year worrying about making a good impression. She couldn't understand why she still felt so shy around Jack. They had had several long conversations on the phone and talking to him had been easy. She guessed it was because she could delude herself into thinking he could think she was the kind of sophisticated, elegant woman he would want. When she had seen him in February, she had had Beckie as a buffer. At least she didn't blush every time he spoke to her this year, only about every second time.

As expected, Bob asked Maddie and Joan to join him and Jack for supper.

The summer was almost a rerun of the previous year. The show was a big hit, with a full house every night, and Jack in a kilt was still the sexiest thing Maddie had ever seen. Again it seemed like every time Jack and Maddie were together either Joan or Bob was with them.

Maddie was not as shy as she had been last year, but she wasn't the same girl Jack had been talking to on the phone. Not for the first time he wondered if his age put her off. Knowing it made her uncomfortable, he tried very hard this year not to stare at her, but it wasn't easy not to. The girl turned heads when she walked down the road. She still blushed when she caught him looking at her, but her reddened cheeks only entranced him. He had fallen hard for a girl less than half his age. Yes, she was beautiful, but it was more than that. She was so innocent he wanted to protect her from the world.

This year, as the show drew to a close, plans were made for next year's show. Because the run had been so successful, with a full house every night, the theatre had asked them to extend it by two weeks next year. At sixteen Maddie was still too young to sign a contract. She took it home with her with a promise to send it right back. Jack was thrilled she wanted to do the show again. He knew she really enjoyed the shows, but she must like him too to spend another summer working with him.

Jack once again took Maddie and Joan to the airport and walked them to the Departure gate.

This time Maddie was expecting a hug and a kiss on the cheek. She wouldn't be caught off guard again. But she was. Instead of a kiss on the cheek, Jack kissed her full on the lips. That all too familiar bolt of lightning ran through her. She floated, rather than walked onto the plane, savouring the feel of his warm, soft lips on hers.

Once the plane was airborne, Maddie eased her seat back and closed her eyes. Much as she loved Auntie Joannie, she didn't feel like talking. She wanted to relive that kiss over and over and dream without sleeping. Jack had promised to phone her and she hoped it would be soon. Despite being together all summer, they really hadn't done much talking to each other and she wanted to know everything about him.

Jack too was reliving the moment. As he left the airport he could still feel the touch of her soft lips on his, and taste the faint cherry flavour of her lip gloss. Jack drove home to his big empty house in Prestwick, thinking how much homelier it would feel with the sound of her laughter and the scent of her perfume. He wondered how long he should wait before he called her. Wanting to call right away, he laughed at himself. She wouldn't even be home yet.

Jack contented himself with consulting his touring schedule and pencilling in the days and times he would call her. When he added them up, there were eight and he wondered if that was too many. He counted off the months on his fingers and decided he could slip in one more call. Surely once a month wasn't too often? Bob and Jack also had a tour of Canada coming up and he expected he would see her when they were in Ottawa. He'd send her tickets again. It was nowhere near as nice as seeing her every day, but he would take every opportunity he got.

Jack was having trouble figuring out his relationship with Maddie. He had never felt like this about a woman. Yes, she was attractive, but it was more than that. He wanted to protect her and he wanted her to like him. When they talked on the phone, there was no trouble talking about any subject, but in person they were still both tongue-tied. That was okay though. He just wanted to spend time with her. He wondered if, for the first time in his life, he was truly in love. He had had relationships with other women, but he'd never felt like this about any of them. He wondered how she felt about him.

# *CHAPTER 9*

This year, at the age of seventeen, Maddie had convinced her parents she was old enough to travel alone. She would be spending the summer in familiar territory with familiar people who had become like an extended family. Reluctantly they had agreed. Joan had thought of saying something about the odd relationship with Jack, but decided her niece's shyness and Bob would keep the girl safe from unwanted attention. If the attention was wanted, and it certainly looked like it was, who was she to stand in the way? Besides, she had gotten to know and like Jack and trusted him not to hurt her niece. He was a gentleman and a gentle man.

Jack met Maddie at the airport, surprised to see that she was alone. He took her in his arms and kissed her full on the lips. When they separated she was blushing.

*Dammit!* she was thinking. *Not again.*

*How cute,* he was thinking. *She does like me.*

As they left the airport, people looked at them curiously. Between his high profile and Maddie's dancing fame (three-time World Champion Highland Dancer) and eye-catching beauty, Jack couldn't decide if it was her or him they were staring at, or the odd couple they appeared to be.

*People probably think I'm her father*, Jack thought.

Once again there was a surreal sense of déjà vu. What had become almost a routine unfolded as it had the previous two years. Conversation on the way into Glasgow was strained between Maddie and Jack. Again he escorted her to her room; the same one she'd had the previous two years, with his on the other side of the connecting door. After seeing her to her room, he consulted his mirror as he had the previous two years. He thought he still looked the same, not any older. He wondered what she saw when she looked at him.

Maddie met the rest of the cast in the Tartan Room at 2:00. This year the cast was all the same as last year, so getting reacquainted was easy. They caught each other up on their lives and had a great chat until tea came.

Surprised Maddie was on her own this year, Bob felt it his duty to act as her big brother. He suggested to Jack that they trade rooms so he was on the other side of the connecting door, but Jack was offended by the suggestion. Bob insisted Maddie join him and Jack for supper and at the same time made plans for breakfast. Throughout the first half of the summer Bob arranged to be with either Jack or Maddie or both, protecting them from each other and themselves. He knew how Jack felt about Maddie and he could see how she looked at Jack, but he wanted any movement towards a romantic relationship to come from Maddie not Jack. Conversation was easier between Jack and Maddie this year, but still a bit stilted. Bob kept it flowing, for which Maddie was grateful.

The show had been such a hit last year that as well as adding two weeks to the run, the theatre had negotiated Saturday matinees. They had a full house every show. Although it was a lot of time on stage, Maddie still managed to find some time for herself. She spent some of that time at the Kelvingrove Museum and the Glasgow Necropolis. She also discovered a museum that was even more suited to her tastes. It was the People's Palace and Winter Garden and it told the story of Glasgow's social history from 1750.

Maddie would be starting university at home in the fall and intended to major in Scottish social history. She studied the exhibits and tombstones, trying to narrow down her field to a specific time period. By the end of summer, she was no further ahead, finding something interesting in every period of Scottish history.

Jack had wondered where Maddie went on her time off but thought it wasn't his place to ask. One day, he was ashamed to admit, he followed her. When she went into the People's Palace he waited a few minutes then went in, hoping she wouldn't feel she was being stalked. He found her in one of the exhibit rooms deep in concentration. He took a deep breath and walked up to her. "So this is where you come when you're not on stage."

Maddie started at the sound of Jack's voice, but did look pleased to see him. She explained her reasons for being there, wondering if she was babbling. He seemed interested and they walked around the exhibits together. He marvelled at the animation in her voice and face when she pointed out different items of interest. They spent a pleasant afternoon together, wandering through the museum. He was astonished at her knowledge of Scottish history. He was also impressed by the way she was speaking to him. It was the same girl he'd been talking to on the phone, not the shy one he'd met at the airport.

The theatre was dark that night so they returned to the hotel for an early supper. Bob met Jack and Maddie in the lobby. *Damn*, thought Jack, *he either has radar or he's following us*. Jack appreciated Bob's brotherly concern for Maddie, but he didn't have to protect her from him. They had had such a lovely afternoon together, talking like old friends, Jack didn't want it to end, but short of being rude, he couldn't think of a way to get rid of his brother.

The following day, Maddie was going to the Glasgow Necropolis. When she invited Jack to go with her, he jumped at the chance. She continued to amaze him with her historical knowledge, pointing out different tombstones and explaining whose they were and what they were known for.

The trips to the museum and Necropolis seemed to be a turning point in Jack and Maddie's relationship. From that afternoon at the museum, Maddie was more open in her conversations with Jack. She realized for the first time, he didn't think of her as a dumb kid. She could actually be, in person, the girl who talked to him on the phone.

Jack had been amazed by Maddie's knowledge and explanations at the museum and the Necropolis. His insecurities surfaced briefly when he thought about how smart she was. He tried to override his insecurity with the comfort of the thought that she was once again the girl who talked to him on the phone. He was delighted to find her in real life. Best of all he finally realized she did like him, something he'd been wondering for three years.

Bob sensed the change between his brother and the girl he'd come to think of as a little sister. Maddie was able to tease both him and Jack and give as good as she got. He gradually backed off and let them have some time alone, realizing she didn't need protecting. After all, he did trust his brother. Jack would never hurt a girl, especially not this one.

On the last night of the show everyone was a bit giddy. It had been a long run and they were all looking forward to a break. Bob and Jack seemed to be playing even more to the audience than usual, picking up on every reaction. When Bob played a solo waltz, Jack walked over to the side of the stage where Maddie was watching from behind the curtain. He motioned for her to come out on stage. She shook her head no. He motioned again nodding. When she didn't respond he took another step towards her. Not wanting him to be embarrassed in front of the audience she stepped out on stage and took his outstretched hand. They waltzed to Bob's playing and the audience went wild. They loved it, and Maddie had to admit, she did too.

The summer had passed all too quickly and Jack once again drove Maddie to the airport. This time, she was expecting it when he kissed her on the lips and responded. They went their separate ways, both reliving the moment. It was going to be a very, very long time till next summer. Jack thought a phone call every two weeks wouldn't be too much. He groaned as he thought of his phone bill, but she was worth every penny. And he would see her when they played two nights in Ottawa in February.

# *CHAPTER 10*

Maddie had seen Jack when he and Bob were touring in Canada, but they were only in Ottawa for two shows. She had introduced him to a couple more of her friends, Katie and her friend Bill. Katie and Maddie had grown up like sisters and each referred to the other's parents as a second set of parents. Jack wondered if other Canadians had second families too. Katie and Maddie didn't look alike but they sounded alike. Their voices had the same pitch, the same inflections and, of course, the same accent. Jack actually had to look at them to tell which one of them was speaking.

Unfortunately, this year the two Ottawa shows were on a Thursday and a Friday. That meant Maddie couldn't spend Jack's day off with him. She had school. She was able to join him and Bob for breakfast on Saturday morning before they left for Montreal. Maddie enjoyed the visit with Bob and Jack, especially with Jack. She really missed seeing him every day, even though they had spoken on the phone every couple of weeks. It just wasn't enough. She was in love and wanted to be with him all the time.

Jack had sent Maddie tickets for his and Bob's Ottawa shows every year. He had met several of her friends. He wondered if it was significant that Maddie never had a boyfriend with her. He'd met her friends and their boyfriends but not one of hers. Were there not any boyfriends or did she consider this a date because he had sent her the tickets?

Maddie was very happy to see spring come. Not only was it the end of winter, which she hated, but it was that much closer to the time she would see Jack. She was determined this year to tell him how she felt about him. It wouldn't be easy for her because she wasn't sure how he felt about her. After all, she was only a little older than his daughters. She knew he liked her, but how well?

# *CHAPTER 11*

*This is turning into something of a routine,* Maddie thought as the plane touched down in Prestwick. Although Jack had said he would meet her at the airport, Maddie had wondered the whole flight if he would. He had for the last three years, why wouldn't he this year now they were such good friends? Although the memory was fading, if she thought really hard about it, she could remember the feel of his kiss when she had left the previous year. He had kissed her when he'd seen her in February, but that had just been a quick kiss in greeting in front of her friends.

Maddie looked anxiously for Jack once she cleared Customs and wasn't disappointed.

"Well," he said, "if it isn't the four-time World Champion Highland Dancer."

He kissed her in welcome and she kissed him back. Then she blushed.

She thought, *Not again.*

He thought, *I hope we're not starting at the beginning again.*

For the first time in four years, for Maddie the ride into Glasgow passed in pleasant conversation. She and Jack caught each other up on what had gone on since their last phone call. Maddie felt a different atmosphere than she had the previous years. For one thing, after their visit to the museum and Necropolis last year and all their phone calls, she was much more comfortable with Jack. Even that damn blushing wasn't as frequent. Maybe it would stop altogether.

At the hotel Jack waited till Maddie checked in. Although following the same pattern as the last three years, it certainly felt different to Maddie when Jack escorted her to her room; the same room she'd had every year. Just being alone with him in a hotel room was exciting, even though he was a perfect gentleman and didn't even try to kiss her.

As had become his pattern, Jack went into his own room, this time through the connecting door, to study himself in the mirror. He was thirty-seven. He was still twice her age, but he was beginning to wonder if it mattered. Not for the first time, he wondered if she cared about the age gap. She clearly liked him. At eighteen, she had changed from the girl he'd first met to a beautiful young woman he had fallen in love with.

# *CHAPTER 12*

This year, there was one huge (for Maddie) difference in the show. When Bob played his solo waltz Maddie and Jack would be dancing to it. She thought she should wear a more suitable costume for dancing with Jack and was very pleased to find a long tartan dress in a local shop. The top was form fitting and it flared to a very full skirt. It fit her slender figure like a second skin. It had long wide sleeves edged in lace and when she put it on, Maddie felt like she lived in another century. Jack nearly swooned when he saw her in it.

A week into the show, it was decided that every time Bob played a solo, Jack and Maddie would dance. The audiences loved the waltz and Jack and Bob had made the decision. Maddie agreed to it immediately. She loved dancing with Jack.

One day when the theatre was going to be dark, Bob, Jack and Maddie took the opportunity to rehearse the changes they had made to the programme and to practice their dances. Maddie and Jack were backstage, practicing the quick-step they would perform for the first time the next evening. Satisfied they had the steps down pat, they stood, both breathing hard from the exertion.

"Dancing with you is like dancing with a feather," Jack said.

"I love the feel of your arm around my waist," she answered. Her deep green eyes looked up into his golden brown ones.

*She's so beautiful,* he thought. Unable to resist, he bent his head and kissed her on the lips, a soft, warm, lingering kiss.

Jack pulled himself away from Maddie saying, "I'm sorry, I shouldn't have done that."

"Why not?"

"You don't want an old man," he answered.

"And you don't want a dumb kid."

They stood close together, looking at each other, still breathing hard. "Oh, my dear, you are neither dumb nor a kid. You're a beautiful young woman. I'm too old for you," he said.

“You’re the only one who thinks so.” Her eyes were locked on his.

With the smallest of hesitations, he leaned forward and kissed her again. As his arms went around her waist hers circled his neck.

There was the promise of passion in the kiss, but the moment was lost as Bob came around the backstage curtain. “Oh my God,” he said. “You two have been mooning over each other for four years. It’s about time you did something about it.” He had seen the change in Maddie and Jack’s relationship and now that Maddie was older he had wondered if something would come of it. At eighteen Maddie was no longer a child. And looking at them, he could see the attraction she and Jack had to each other.

Maddie and Jack managed to look both guilty and surprised at the same time. In the same breath they said, “Was I that obvious?” then looked at each other and laughed.

“You were that obvious to everyone but each other from the day you met. At least now I don’t have to protect you from each other or yourselves.” Using one of Maddie’s expressions Bob said, “We’re going to grab a bite. Are you coming?”

“I’m starving,” Maddie said. “I haven’t eaten since breakfast. Can you wait five while I put on some regular clothes?” In the long, flowing, tartan dress she wore for dancing with Jack she looked like she had just stepped out of an old master’s painting.

“You might want to put on some pants, Jack,” Bob said. “You look very dashing in your kilt but we’re hoping to blend in with the regular folk. You know, try to appear normal.”

Jack laughed and headed to the dressing room he shared with Bob.

# *CHAPTER 13*

Maddie had just come out of the shower and was trying to decide whether to put on her nightdress or day clothes. A tentative knock on the connecting door decided her. Pulling on jeans and a loose shirt, she went to answer the door. Jack stood there with two glasses and a bottle of Drambuie. "I wanted a drink, but I don't like to drink alone," he said.

"You just want to get me drunk and take advantage of me." She grinned at him and stepped aside so he could come into the room.

"Bob and I have revised the programme again and we need to know if you have enough time for costume changes now that you have the extra ones." Setting the glasses and bottle on the coffee table, Jack pulled a piece of paper out of his back pocket and sat down on the small couch.

Sitting beside Jack, their heads close together, Maddie studied the paper. "I'd feel better about it if you could move one of the other numbers to between the waltz and the hornpipe," she said. "That sailor suit is miserable to get into. If you take one from this group and move it in there that will give me lots of time."

"Will it give you enough time for the next change?"

"Sure. Hard as it is to get into, it's easy to get out of."

Jack mentally slapped himself for the image that appeared in his mind.

With their heads so close together Jack found the spicy scent of Maddie's shampoo intoxicating. Trying to distract himself, he poured them each a drink.

She turned towards him. "Slainte," they both said at the same time, clinking glasses then laughing.

Jack suddenly looked serious. "About this afternoon," he started to say.

Deep green eyes sparkled at him. He had lost his soul in them. And those rosebud lips, so perfect for kissing… Once again, unable to resist, he leaned forward and put his lips on hers. She responded warmly. Reluctantly separating, he put both their glasses on the table.

Wanting to kiss her again, Jack studied her. She sat, leaning towards him, lips parted slightly, green eyes glittering in the lamplight. He leaned forward to kiss her. This time as they kissed her arms went around his neck. He leaned back and pulled her towards him. As the kiss deepened, his hands began to explore her body, tentatively at first, gaining confidence as she accepted his caresses. He pulled away from her lips and showered her face and neck with baby kisses. "I want to make love to you," he breathed into her ear.

She said softly, "I've never done this before."

Jack's hand froze in place on her breast and he pulled back slightly. "You mean you're a…" He stopped, seemingly lost for the word.

"Virgin," she supplied. "Yes. Is that a problem?"

"I don't want to take advantage of you," he said repeating her words.

"You're not, Jack. I want you."

"Oh, Maddie, I don't want to hurt you."

Maddie could feel Jack's erection hard against her leg. Her body was responding with feelings she had never before experienced.

"Are you sure?" he asked, fearing the answer.

"I'm sure."

"Absolutely sure?"

"Absolutely sure."

He groaned as his lips met hers again. One hand held her in a close embrace as the other roamed her body, finding its way under her loose shirt. She gasped as his thumb brushed her bare nipple.

He stood, pulling her with him. Once again he asked if she was sure. As she said yes, he scooped her up and carried her to the bed. Lying together on the bed, they began to undress each other. Once she was naked, he studied her perfect body; face flushed and perky breasts with nipples standing erect, skin like satin. She was so tiny, he wondered if he could avoid hurting her. He'd never been with a virgin before.

When Jack finished removing the remaining clothes she hadn't been able to get off him, Maddie studied his body. Her eyes widened at the sight of his erection. "No wonder they call you 'the big yin'," she said teasingly, wondering if they would fit together. He looked so big. The ache and empty feeling between her legs made her want to try.

He kissed her lips, their tongues exploring each other then he trailed kisses down her neck. At the hollow of her throat he stopped, running his tongue around the hollow. As he suckled her breasts, she arched into him, wanting to feel him between her legs. His hand slid up her leg from her knee. She moaned as his fingers brushed against her. He dragged his lips downward across her belly, stopping to tease her belly button with his tongue. He continued kissing the length of her body until his head was between her legs. She gasped and moaned when his tongue touched that part of her that was on fire. He lapped at her, feeling with his tongue, the hard button between her legs that told him she was ready. He concentrated on that spot licking alternately gently and with some pressure. Under this attention she was writhing. Suddenly her back arched and her legs tightened around his head. She thought she was going to explode when the wave of pleasure washed over her.

"Oh, God," she cried. "Oh, God. Oh, Jack." She collapsed back onto the pillows, breathing hard. In all her eighteen years she had never even imagined her body capable of such intense pleasure.

Giving her time to catch her breath Jack kissed the length of her body again, moving in reverse and stopping again to tease her belly button and the hollow of her throat. He moved slowly, savouring the feel of her soft skin, the musky taste of her that lingered on his lips. When he got to her face, her lips met his, her tongue thrusting deep into his mouth.

He left her eager lips and moved down to suckle her breast.

Moaning, she whispered, "I need to feel you inside me, deep inside me." He was more than ready, but held back. When her small hand reached for his erection it was his turn to gasp. He gently removed it, saying it would be over too soon. She placed her hand on his chest, winding her fingers through the curly hair and brushing his nipples.

Seemingly of its own accord, his hand slid slowly down her body, stopping to massage a breast then coming to rest between her legs. He slid his finger into her. Once again her back arched towards him, the wave of pleasure that washed over her leaving her gasping for breath.

Jack rolled them both onto their sides and pulled Maddie's leg up over his hips, opening her up to his throbbing erection. He slowly entered her.

"Am I hurting you?" he gasped.

"Noooo." She was almost crying with pleasure.

Fighting for control of himself, he held her hips still when she tried to move against him. Slowly withdrawing, he elicited a whimper from her and she pressed her body closer to him.

Jack rolled onto his back, pulling Maddie on top of him. He entered her again, letting her take as much of him as she could. When she had taken all of him, he rolled her onto her back, plunging deep inside her. Her muscular legs wrapped around his waist as she seemed to pull him even deeper inside her. With a few short strokes, he felt the irresistible urge for release. He plunged into her one more time feeling the most intense pleasure rush through his body leaving him shaking.

"Oh, sweet Jesus, Maddie, Maddie," he moaned.

Jack lay, still inside Maddie as his erection slowly subsided. He slipped his hand between them once again to feel that velvety spot between her legs. At his touch, another wave of pleasure passed through her. Her muscles contracted rhythmically against him, milking what was left of his erection. Under these ministrations he started to rise again. Thrusting gently this time he surprised himself as he grew hard again. For the first time in his life Jack climaxed twice in a row. Exhausted and gasping for breath they separated, collapsing back on the bed.

"I didn't hurt you did I?" Jack looked worried as he struggled to catch his breath.

"No, my love, you didn't. I've never felt anything like that. I didn't know it was possible."

With an impish grin he asked, "Does that mean you'd like to do it again sometime?"

Maddie chuckled. "You just let me know when you're ready."

They lay together for a few minutes then Jack sat up suddenly. "Oh my God. I forgot the damn condom. What have I done to you?" He looked at her sweet face. The alarm she had felt when he suddenly sat up faded and a small smile tugged at her lips. He rushed on. "It'll be okay. If you get pregnant we'll get married. Hell, I love you. Do you love me? Will you marry me anyway?"

As he lay down again, satisfied with his decision and waiting for an answer, she propped herself on one elbow in the crook of his arm. "There are a lot of good reasons to get married, but a pregnancy is not one of them. You of all people should know that." It was a poorly kept 'secret' that his disastrous first marriage had taken place a mere five months before his elder daughter was born. The only good that had come from that marriage was his two daughters. He winced at her words, but she continued. "We don't need to worry though. I'm on the pill."

"But you are, were…" he corrected himself.

"A virgin, I know. But you ought to know that I had every intention of seducing you."

Jack looked shocked then started to smile. "I love you," he said simply. "For the last four years I've been in love with you. I had to keep telling myself you were too young and you wouldn't want an old man. It was hell not touching you, kissing you. I just wanted to be with you."

"Oh, Jack. I was so sure with all your worldly experience, you wouldn't be interested in a kid. I've been in love with you since that first day we met at the airport. When you touched my hand I felt a bolt of lightning go through me."

"And my heart skipped a beat. I wanted you to like me. You were so quiet around me, I thought you didn't."

She grinned at him. "I was afraid of saying or doing something stupid in front of you."

She settled down with her head on his shoulder, yawning and snuggling closer to him as he smoothed her tangle of red-gold curls.

His hand lingered on her cheek as he kissed her forehead and whispered, "I love you."

They lay together in each other's arms, content and totally comfortable with each other for the first time ever. He felt her body relax as she slipped into a light sleep. Jack lay there watching her, not wanting to move. He wondered what he had done to deserve such happiness.

Maddie stirred, stretched as gracefully as a cat and looked up at Jack. "What are you doing?"

"I'm watching you sleep."

Surprised, she said, "You must have a very high boredom threshold."

He chuckled. "You're so beautiful. You look like a porcelain doll."

"Thank you." Her hand ran through the curly hair on his chest, hinting at moving lower. "Do you want to play with me?"

They made love again, both more confident than they had been the first time. Maddie knew what she was doing this time, and Jack, although still gentle, was less afraid of hurting her. He let her stroke him this time, relishing the feel of her soft curious fingers on his most sensitive skin.

When they awoke, the sun was shining in the window. Jack looked at Maddie, suddenly worried. "Any regrets?"

"No regrets."

He kissed her. "Shite," he said, checking the time. "Bob'll be here in ten minutes to collect you for breakfast." Jack reluctantly got out of bed and began gathering his clothes. Maddie, equally reluctantly, got out of bed. With a quick kiss, he went through the connecting door and she went in to shower.

Maddie was dressed and drying her hair when there was a knock at the door.

She ushered Bob into the room and said, "I'll just be two minutes. Knock on the door and see if Jack's up."

Bob noticed the bottle and two glasses on the coffee table. His eyebrows rose. *What have you been up to, Jack?* Thinking back to the kiss he'd witnessed yesterday, he thought, *You better not have gotten her drunk and taken advantage of her.*

# *CHAPTER 14*

After breakfast the boys had a meeting with their agent and Maddie decided she'd go for a walk.

While they were waiting for their agent to arrive, Bob jumped in with both feet. "You slept with her," he said.

Jack looked surprised. "How did you know?"

"I didn't. I guessed. How could you, Jack? She's so young. She's like a little sister."

"She's eighteen and definitely not sisterly," Jack said defensively, smiling to himself at the memories of a night he would never forget. "Our sister got married when she was eighteen."

Bob's voice mirrored his concern, "But did you have to get her drunk and take advantage of her?"

Jack looked bewildered. "Neither one of us was drunk. Were you watching us?"

"I saw the bottle and glasses on the table in her room." Bob glared at him.

"We were looking at the programme. I don't think she had more than two sips. Did she look like someone with a hangover?"

Bob grudgingly conceded, "She looked happy, really happy. And so do you."

Bob made a mental note to check in with Maddie. He wouldn't be as direct as he had been with Jack, but he felt protective of her, as if she really were his little sister. He wouldn't let anyone hurt her, not even his brother.

The arrival of their agent put an end to the conversation and they got down to work on their contracts.

# *CHAPTER 15*

Maddie had just returned from her walk when there was a knock on the connecting door. When she opened it, Jack rushed in with a sheaf of papers in his hand, his face alight with excitement. She could see Bob and another man sitting at the table in Jack's room.

"Have I got a deal for you," Jack said excitedly. "How would you like to work a cruise with us?"

"Uh, yeah," was the instant reply, "that's a no-brainer."

Slightly nonplused, he looked at her. "I'm serious. We've negotiated a deal for you if you're interested. It's a two week Caribbean cruise leaving Miami December 27$^{th}$."

"I'm in," she said.

Jack showed her the papers he was holding. "This is what they'll pay you, plus bed and board."

Her eyes widened in amazement. "Are you serious?"

"There is one little catch though." Jack looked uncertain. "It would mean sharing a cabin with me."

She looked at him with mischief lighting her eyes. "I don't think that'll be a problem."

"Come and meet John. He's agreed to be your agent too if you want him to be."

With the summer contracts, her mother had acted as her agent. This would require a more formal approach and, at eighteen, Maddie was finally old enough to sign her own contracts. Introductions were made and pleasantries exchanged before they got down to the serious business of contracts. In less than an hour Maddie had an agent and a contract for the cruise. She was bubbling with excitement. They had an hour and a half before rehearsal and Bob suggested they get some lunch. Although Maddie didn't usually eat lunch she would probably have agreed if Bob had suggested they go to the moon.

Over lunch, Bob took the opportunity to check in with Maddie. "My wife is coming on the cruise too. We have a two bedroom suite. If you like, Jack and I can share and you and Betty."

"Thanks, Bob, but Jack and I can share. I promise we won't fight… much."

Bob heaved a mental sigh of relief. Jack had obviously been telling the truth.

Rehearsal went well and after a bite to eat, they returned to the hotel. As Bob went into his room, he saw Jack follow Maddie into hers. He overheard Jack say, "I have something I need to talk to you about."

Jack looked serious as he walked to the couch and sat down. He patted the seat beside him, indicating Maddie should sit. After last night, she was alarmed by the urgency in his voice. "What are you planning to do when the show ends?" he asked.

"I'm not sure," she said. "I could go home and back to school there, but I've been leaning towards the idea of getting a little flat and taking some university courses here. I can transfer the credits I have, and since my major is Scottish social history, it makes sense to go to school here."

"There's another option. I don't want to be apart from you for four months. You could move in with me. I have a big house and you could have your own room, if you want. You don't have to decide right now, just think about it as an option, one that I would really, really like." His words tumbled out in a rush as he braced for a verbal attack.

She looked thoughtful. "I know I won't get a better offer than that."

"Don't answer me now. Think about it. Really think." The decision had been made not to run 'A Taste of Scotland' next year and Jack had been desperately trying to think of a way to keep Maddie in Scotland. He couldn't bear the idea of not seeing her every day.

Relieved that Maddie hadn't said no right away, Jack made a grab for her. Laughing, she threw herself on him and locked her lips on his.

# *CHAPTER 16*

Three days later Maddie returned from the museum in the afternoon. She wanted to talk to Jack about his suggested living arrangements. She'd been thinking about his offer the last few days. In fact, she'd been thinking of little else.

Their love-making had taken on a magical quality, with each of them sensing what would bring the other the most pleasure. Maddie thought there was only one way to find out if she and Jack could live together too, and she was willing (hell no, anxious) to try it. Head over heels in love with him, she could think of nothing she'd rather do.

They had been leaving the connecting door between their rooms open, and as Maddie entered her room she could hear voices in Jack's. They were talking quietly and she couldn't hear what was being said. She glanced into the room and was shocked to see him with his arms tightly wrapped around a very elegant, very attractive woman, who looked to be about his own age. He was stroking her hair and talking softly into her ear.

Maddie stood frozen to the spot. She couldn't believe what she was seeing. Jack was rubbing the woman's back. Utterly devastated, Maddie dropped the things in her hands and ran out of the room. She didn't notice her door slam shut behind her. She ran blindly through the hotel and out the front door, tears filling her eyes to the point she couldn't see. Not knowing where she was going, she rushed into the nearest tube station and down the escalator. Pulling some change out of her pocket, she got a ticket and got on the first train that came along.

Jack heard the door slam and disengaged from the woman who had been crying in his arms. His sister was calmer now and he wanted to introduce her to the love of his life. Giving Jeannie time to collect herself, Jack walked into Maddie's room. Confused, he looked around the empty room. Her purse and some papers were on the floor, but there was no sign of Maddie. The bathroom door was open, so she wasn't in there.

Puzzled, he wondered where she could be. Trying to think of what he'd been doing when he heard the door slam, he brought the heel of his hand to his forehead and gave himself a smack. He'd been holding a crying Jeannie close, stroking her hair and talking softly to her. She'd had a huge fight with her husband and had left him. Jack was trying to comfort her. Maddie must have seen them and come to the wrong conclusion.

"Oh my God, what must she be thinking?" Jeannie was a very attractive woman, almost as tall as Jack, but dark haired like Bob. Jack could understand why Maddie would be upset.

At that point, Bob knocked on Jack's door and walked into the room. Surprised to see his sister, he greeted her warmly. Despite being siblings, the three of them had always been close friends and Bob was happy to see her.

Greetings over, Bob asked Jack, "What's going on with Maddie? She just ran past me without saying anything. She looked like all the demons in hell were on her tail." Jack groaned inwardly and told Bob what had happened. "Oh my God, Jack. We have to find her. Where would she have gone?"

Jack was worried. He knew Maddie was tougher and much stronger than she looked, but alone and upset in Glasgow was the last place he wanted his love to be. It could be a dangerous city for a vulnerable girl. His thoughts raced. Where would she go? The first place he thought of was the museum, but which one? The three of them went out to look for her. Along the way, they looked in doorways, shops and down alleys. Jeannie had seen pictures of the lovely young lady and knew who they were looking for.

They went to the Kelvingrove museum first, it being the closest. Once there, they went from one exhibit room to the next, searching in vain. There was no sign of her. Jack showed her photo to the guard at the door, asking if he'd seen her. She was memorable and the guard recalled seeing her earlier.

"But I'm pretty sure she left."

They went on to the People's Palace and met with the same result. She had been there but had left hours earlier.

Jack's heart sank. Where else would she go? She wouldn't be able to get into the Necropolis. It would be closed for the night. They returned to the hotel, hoping she'd returned, but there was no sign of her. Bob noticed her purse on the floor of her room. "She can't have gone far," he said. "She didn't take her purse."

"It just gets worse and worse," Jack said, desperately. "She's alone in a strange city, with no money, thinking I betrayed her. Do you think it's too early to get the police to look for her?" He was grasping at straws.

Bob looked thoughtful. "If we tell them we think she might hurt herself, they'd have to look for her."

Jack hadn't thought his heart could drop any further, but at these words he sagged against the couch. The thought that Maddie might hurt herself hadn't occurred to him. He recalled a conversation he'd had with her about her cousin who had killed himself last year. Deeply sympathetic to him, she had said life just got too hard for him. He thought he'd been worried before, but now panic overtook Jack. Surely he hadn't just made life that hard for Maddie? Surely she wouldn't... He wasn't so sure. As an only child, her cousin had been the closest thing she'd had to a big brother and she had loved and admired him. Jack knew she loved him and was afraid of what she might do to herself. He couldn't imagine the sense of betrayal she must be feeling.

Tears in his eyes, Jack reached for the phone. After getting an outside line, he dialed 999. He tried to explain to the officer who answered the phone what the situation was, but gave up and handed the phone to Bob. Jack cringed as he listened to Bob explain the situation, emphasizing Maddie was a tourist and had no money or identification with her. The last thing Jack heard Bob say before he rang off was, "We're afraid she might hurt herself – or worse."

It hurt Jack physically to listen to Bob stressing the point. He was pacing the room. "We have to go out and look for her."

"No, Jack. We have to wait for the police. They're better able to look for her."

While waiting for the police to arrive, Jack told Bob and Jeannie the story of Maddie's cousin.

# *CHAPTER 17*

While this was unfolding, Maddie was sitting on a train. She didn't know where she was going, she didn't care. She didn't notice the tears that were streaming down her face or the people who looked at her curiously. She rode the train to the end of the line, then got off and got on another. She had changed trains four times. Her tears had temporarily stopped and her emotions had turned to anger. The temper that went with her red hair began to surface.

"The bastard. How could he? How could I have been so stupid, so naïve?" She was as angry with herself as she was with Jack.

It was getting late and Maddie was exhausted. She had no idea where she was. She checked the subway map and tried to work out how to get back to the hotel. She noticed the clock on the wall. It was 4:20. She had left the museum at 3:00 and thought it should be later than that.

Unable to sort out the map, Maddie went to leave the tube station. She thought it would be easier to orient herself above ground or just take a taxi. As she went to put her ticket in the turnstile, she realized she had lost it. She didn't have her purse and she'd used the last of her pocket change to buy the ticket. She went and sat on the platform bench, wondering abstractly how she would get out of the station then deciding she didn't care. She would just ride the trains. She looked around the deserted platform. Shouldn't people be coming home from work now? Shouldn't the platform be crowded? It was almost 5:00.

Maddie thought about that for a moment. It couldn't be 5:00am could it? She hadn't been riding the trains all night? She thought about that. She had been riding the trains all night. Miserably, she boarded the first train that came along. She took a seat and leaned her head against the window. The tears started again. Angrily she wiped them away with her sleeve. If he could do that to her, why was she wasting her tears on him?

*Because I love him,* she thought miserably. A fresh round of tears ran down her cheeks.

A grubby looking man who appeared to be about twenty sat down beside

Maddie. His hair was greasy, his shirt was dirty and his jeans were ripped. He tried first to make conversation with her. When she didn't respond he put his arm around her shoulders. Aware enough of her surroundings to realize what was going on, Maddie asked him to remove it.

"Aw, c'mon, baby, we can have some fun," he said. "It'll cheer you up."

She jabbed a sharp elbow into his ribs, knocking the wind out of him.

An elderly lady on the train had been watching the girl since she'd gotten on. The woman was touched by the girl's tears and wondered what could have made her so unhappy. It had to be a boy. And it wasn't that sleazy one who had just sat down beside her. She moved to the seat opposite Maddie, handing her a tissue to wipe her eyes. "I've been looking all over for ye, lass. I thought I'd lost ye." The young man, seeing the ease of his target disappear, moved further down the carriage, looking for another target. "Are ye a'right, lass?" the woman asked.

Pulling herself together, Maddie gratefully took the tissue and dabbed at her eyes. She probably had mascara all over her face, but she didn't care. In a shaky voice, she said, "I'm fine, thank you."

The woman didn't believe her. She moved to the seat beside Maddie and sat with her, talking quietly to the girl. Maddie didn't answer, but she was comforted by the woman's kindness and her tears stopped flowing.

At the next station, two police officers boarded the train carriage. They seemed to be looking for something, or someone. Maddie paid them no attention until they stopped and stood directly in front of her. "Maddie Campbell?" the taller one said uncertainly. She looked at him and acknowledged her name. "Would you come with us please?" It wasn't an invitation.

Maddie looked trapped. Her new friend sprang to her defence. "What do you want with her?" she demanded. "She's not bothering anyone."

Not sure it was any of her business the officer responded, "She's been reported missing and at risk. We have some extremely worried people looking for her."

Maddie thanked her new friend and rose meekly to follow the officers. Not satisfied with this arrangement, one led her and one followed. After looking all night while on patrol, they had finally found her and she was not going to disappear again on their watch.

The two policemen had, coincidentally, met up with several other policemen outside the tube station and decided to blitz the subway looking for the girl before heading out on patrol again. Their guess had paid off with a minimum of effort.

Maddie absently noticed a few officers get off some of the other cars of the train. *Jeez*, she thought. *Did he have the whole police force looking for me? Why did he bother? He has that other woman, one his own age.* She mentally kicked herself for being so stupid as to think he would really love her. She had thought he had been sincere, but she was young and naïve. What did she know of the world and of men?

The officers assisted her into the police car and the taller one radioed control. "We have her. She's fine. We'll take her to the hotel."

At least she wasn't being arrested, but the last place she wanted to go was back to the hotel. She hoped Jack would be out looking for her (although why would he bother?) and she could get her things and get to the airport without seeing him.

# *CHAPTER 18*

When the phone rang, Jack nearly jumped out of his skin. He made a dive for it and picked it up before it rang a second time. "Yes," he said, "yes, Officer." His voice and his hands were shaking. Two worried looking faces were watching him.

Bob thought he might have to take the phone from his brother again. He'd never seen Jack in such bad shape, pale as a ghost and exhausted from worry and pacing all night. He understood Jack's despair that he was sure Maddie thought he had betrayed her and his worry that she might hurt herself or worse.

"You found her? Is she okay? Where is she? Can I come and get her?" The questions tumbled out of Jack's mouth in a rush. His knees buckled and he sat down hard on the bed. "She is? You will?" Jack rang off and wiped his hand across his eyes, trying to fend off the tears he felt gathering.

Bob and Jeannie were alarmed. "Jack, what is it? Is she okay?"

"She's okay. They're bringing her back here, but they may have to hospitalize her if they think she might hurt herself. Oh, Bob, I really fucked up. She'll never forgive me if I get her locked up." Jack didn't often swear, but he was worried sick.

Jeannie was feeling very guilty. This whole thing was her fault. If she hadn't come running to her brother when she'd had a fight with her husband this whole mess would never have happened.

A firm knock on the door heralded the arrival of the two police officers with Maddie in tow. Her beautiful hair was tangled, her green eyes red rimmed and dulled by tears, and traces of mascara had made dark streaks on her pale cheeks.

*She looks miserable,* Jack thought. *How could I do this to her?*

She ignored Jack and ran to Bob. He folded her in a big bear hug and said, "Are ye a'right? We've been so worried."

"I'm fine," she said, bursting into tears.

Bob didn't look convinced and continued to hold her while she cried against his shoulder.

Jack felt like there was a knife in his heart. She'd run to Bob, not him. She hadn't even looked at him. She wanted nothing to do with him and even though he was innocent, he couldn't blame her. He realized how bad it must have appeared. Jack sat miserably on the side of the bed. Bob took Maddie over to the little couch and sat down with her. She was still crying, trying but unable to stop. He rocked her gently.

The officers, satisfied by Bob's solicitous manner and Maddie's reaction to him, agreed that Maddie was in good hands. They couldn't work out the relationships in the room, but there was genuine relief on everyone's face except Maddie's, although she appeared comfortable enough with Bob and he was taking care of her. They left without any word of committing her.

*Thank God for small mercies*, thought Jack.

After what seemed an eternity Maddie's sobs turned to hiccups. Bob was still rocking her and Jeannie had been handing her tissues. The wastebasket was half full of soggy *Kleenex.* Jack was still miserable, sitting on the bed on the other side of the room.

Jack went into the bathroom and ran cold water on a facecloth. He handed it to Maddie. She took it without saying anything, without looking at him. He felt the knife in his heart make a quarter turn.

Maddie held the cloth to her face. The cold water felt good on her burning cheeks and eyes. The hiccups finally stopped. Much calmer, she took the cloth from her face, unsure where to look.

Bob made the decision for her. "Maddie, I'd like you to meet our sister Jeannie."

Maddie's jaw dropped. "Yyyour sssister?" she stammered. "But I thought…" For the first time she actually looked at Jack. He looked as miserable as she felt.

Bob and Jeannie went into Jack's room closing the connecting door quietly. Those two needed time to talk to each other.

# *CHAPTER 19*

Jack and Maddie talked for nearly two hours, him trying to reassure her that she could trust him and her apologizing for not trusting him. They told one another the story of their previous night, crying for each other. When Maddie saw Jack's tears, she was overwhelmed. How could she have doubted him, put him through hell because of her own insecurities? She had trusted him blindly and really couldn't believe he'd betrayed that trust. Would he ever forgive her for doubting him?

On his part, Jack was wondering what he'd done to make Maddie think such a betrayal was even possible. He tried to think of anything he might have said or done that would lead her to believe him capable of such a thing. He literally hadn't looked at another woman since that first day he'd met her four years ago. He wondered if he should be angry she could think so little of him, although he had to admit, it must have looked pretty bad. Far from being angry, he was so relieved she was safe and back with him, he just wanted to hold her.

Both lost in their own thoughts, Jack put his arms around Maddie. She melted into his embrace and they sat together for a long time, not saying anything. Eventually Maddie said, "I'm so sorry, Jack. I should have known you would never hurt me. Can you ever forgive me for doubting you? It looked bad, but I should have known there was a good explanation. I was just so excited. I was going to tell you I'd move in with you then I saw you with another woman in your arms. It broke my heart. I didn't give you a chance. I just ran, thinking the worst."

Jack looked at her, absorbing her words. "I know it looked bad, luv, but you have to believe I'd never hurt you. There hasn't been another woman for me since the day we met. You took my breath away and I've loved you ever since. Wait," he said, realizing what she'd said. "You said you'd move in with me?" He was almost afraid of the answer.

"If you still want me to."

"I spent last night in hell. I don't ever want to let you out of my sight again." He hugged her tighter then leaned down to kiss her. He loved her so much and she was going to move in with him. The world would know she was his. That is, the world except her family. They hadn't kept up with the new era of 'free love' that had started after Woodstock and were unlikely to approve of the living arrangements. *That's okay*, he thought. *They're far enough away they don't have to know.*

While Jack was thinking, Maddie's stomach let out a demanding growl. "Oh my God," he said. "Have you eaten anything since breakfast yesterday?" She admitted she hadn't. When he suggested breakfast with Bob and Jeannie she readily agreed. She was starving, and she wanted to get to know his sister. Asking for ten minutes to clean herself up, she headed for the bathroom. It had been a very emotional night for her and for him too.

Jack went into his own room to give her some space, but left the connecting door open so Maddie could join them when she was ready. Bob and Jeannie were sitting at the small table in Jack's room. Jeannie's eyes were red, but she looked composed and smiled at him. His big brother really was good at comforting the ladies.

Jack told them he and Maddie were going for breakfast and they would like Bob and Jeannie to join them. Jeannie was delighted. "I really want to get to know someone who is so important to you."

Jack gathered some clean clothes and went into the bathroom to change out of his rumpled ones.

Ten minutes later Maddie walked into Jack's room, showered and in clean jeans and an embroidered shirt, damp hair curling around her face.

*Wow!* thought Jeannie. *She's a knockout. If she's half as nice on the inside as she is on the outside it's no wonder Jack is so in love with her.* She realized how silly that was. Jack was not the kind of shallow man that judged a person by their looks. Maddie must be that special.

At first breakfast was a bit strained between Jeannie and Maddie. Each felt responsible for the miserable night the other had had. After they had apologized to each other several times, Jack stepped in and changed the subject. "Can I tell them our news?" he asked Maddie. Dark green eyes sparkling, she nodded. The other two leaned forward in anticipation. "Maddie has agreed to move in with me." He looked at Bob, grinning like the Cheshire cat. "That way we'll have a chance to get used to each other before the cruise."

Bob and Jeannie congratulated them, Jeannie thrilled that her baby brother had found love. Feeling slightly guilty, she excused herself to go and ring her husband to apologize. She seemed to be doing a lot of apologizing. With the events of the previous night, she thought their fight had been stupid and insignificant. She hoped he would think the same. Indeed he did and when she went back to the table she told them he was going to join her in Glasgow for a few days.

Deciding they had had enough to eat and enough tea and coffee to float the Royal Navy they left the dining room. They were all exhausted and everyone was going to lie down. Jack asked Maddie if she wanted him in her bed or if he should use his own. What she said touched his heart. “Would you just lie with me and hold me?”

They had a show that night, so Jack set the alarm for 5:00pm. Maddie thought back to the previous 5:00 and shuddered. It was like a nightmare that had finally ended.

Jack climbed into bed and put his arms around Maddie. She kissed him good night or good morning and was asleep almost before her head hit the pillow. Jack lay awake, watching her sleep, eventually drifting off himself. When the alarm went off they were both reluctant to get up. Refreshed by a good day’s sleep, they wanted each other. It was 5:00 and the show was at 8:00. Jack figured under the circumstances he could skip a meal. Maddie didn’t eat before a show anyway.

Maddie was sitting up and was just swinging her feet to the floor when Jack touched her arm. The old, familiar lightning bolt ran through her. This time she could do something about it. She let him pull her towards him and settled back into his arms. He kissed her gently, starting to undo the buttons of her satin nightshirt.

# *CHAPTER 20*

On August 17$^{th}$, the day after the show ended, Maddie moved into Jack's house.

Wanting to make Maddie comfortable but also wanting her to say no, Jack again offered her a room of her own. He was crushed when she said yes, but she continued, saying she could use an office of her own. She had made arrangements to take off campus courses from the University of Glasgow and needed a place to work. His heart soared. She did want to share his bed. They'd been sharing her bed all summer, but this was different. This was his home. And she wanted to be a part of it!

They had two weeks together before Bob and Jack went on tour and Maddie went back to school, and they made the most of their time together. They took long walks on the beach and played bad golf. Considerate of Maddie's love of history, Jack took her to explore several castles, both ruins and residences, staying in charming country inns.

The one thing Jack had to do during their time off that Maddie didn't join him for was to speak to his daughters. He had spoken to them on several occasions about his 'friend' Maddie. They had been happy he had found someone to keep him company. After the divorce, Jack's ex-wife had found someone to share their lives and the girls always felt bad that their dad was still alone. They were always interested when he told them about his friends, especially the women. They were happy for him when he told them Maddie was going to move into his house. He didn't say she already had. What he hadn't told them about her was her age. He had told them Maddie was quite a bit younger than him, but he hadn't said she was almost the same age as them.

Jack's daughters were anxious to meet Maddie, but Jack wanted to talk to them a bit more about her before they met. He thought it would be better to let them get over the shock of Maddie's age before they met her. He was a bit nervous the day he was going to tell them. He arranged to take them to a film then out to eat afterwards. That was when he would tell them.

When Jack pulled the car up in front of his ex-wife's home to pick up the girls, his hands were sweating on the steering wheel. It was funny he thought, he didn't care about the age gap between him and Maddie except when it came to telling his daughters. He wondered again if they would care.

The three of them were just about finished eating when the girls started asking Jack about Maddie. The previous year the girls had been to see 'A Taste of Scotland'. When Jack told them his lady friend was the dancer from the show, they were impressed. They hadn't been close enough to her to notice how young she was and they had been more interested in showing people they were Jack's daughters than in any of the rest of the cast. Siobhan, the elder daughter, asked him what Maddie was like. He started off by saying she was nice and had a great sense of humour and he loved her and she loved him. He figured there was no longer any point in trying to conceal the truth.

"She's quite a bit younger than me," he said.

"You already told us that, Dad," said Charlie the younger girl. "Just how old is she?"

Jack took a deep breath. "She's eighteen."

Both girls looked at him in horror and at the same time said, "Eeeewwww."

"Jeez, Dad," said Siobhan. "Is this one of those 'May December' romances? You're old enough to be her father. She's our age."

Jack was a bit insulted. "She's very mature for her age."

"Well yeah, Dad," said Charlie. "We always see older men with younger women."

"But," added Siobhan, "We didn't expect it to happen in our family. I can understand you liking a much younger woman, but what's it like for her being with you? Is she after your money?"

Now Jack was really insulted. "I don't expect you girls to understand, but I'm not an old man. She doesn't need my money. She's making her own. She's also made her own choice." He repeated, "I'm in love with her and she's in love with me. Now can we forget about her age? I know you're going to like her when you meet her."

The conversation was a bit strained for the rest of the evening. Jack was normally reluctant to end an outing with the girls, but tonight he was actually relieved. When he got home, Maddie was waiting anxiously for him.

"How did it go?"

"We've had better evenings."

"Do you want to talk about it?"

"They thought that I struck gold and they were sorry for you. They couldn't imagine why someone their age would want to be with an old man."

"Ouch. What did you tell them?"

"I told them you weren't after my money, you'd made your own choice and I'm not that old. I also told them you're wise and mature beyond your years and that we love each other. They can't wait to meet you. They think you're a freak. I'm expecting a call from their outraged mother."

As expected, the following morning the phone rang early. Maddie answered and a frosty female voice asked to speak to Jack. She shrugged her shoulders and handed him the phone. The diatribe started immediately.

"Jesus Christ, Jack. What the hell do you think you're doing? That girl is the same age as our kids. What kind of pervert are you, sleeping with children? And what about her? At her age the only reason she'd be interested in you is for your money – the inheritance that our daughters should get."

Jack cringed at his ex-wife's words and tried hard to hold his temper. "I didn't expect you to understand."

He was about to say more, but she started again. "Where did you find the little gold digger, nursery school? I can't believe you would expose the girls to this. It's sick. You're disgusting."

No longer trying to keep his temper, Jack interrupted her. "I'm not listening to any more of this crap. When you're ready to be civil we can talk, but as usual you are running your mouth off about things you don't understand." He rang off, slamming the receiver down.

The remainder of their two week break passed peacefully with no more contact from Jack's ex-wife, Edith. Maddie drove Jack to Prestwick International Airport, both of them dreading the parting. For the first time in his life, Jack didn't want to go on tour. Their brief holiday had reinforced their love for each other and he didn't think he could stand to be away from her for three weeks.

As they walked to the Departure lounge Maddie said sadly, "The tables are turned now. It's you who's flying to Canada and I'm staying here."

As they were consoling each other with lies of the time passing quickly, Bob arrived, looking very cheerful. His wife Betty was with him and the ladies were introduced to each other. Betty was an attractive woman, about the same age as Bob. She had short blonde hair, a twinkle in her blue eyes and a friendly smile. She expressed surprise that she and Maddie hadn't met sooner, suggesting they get to know each other while the boys were away.

Bob and Jack's flight was announced and they reluctantly made their way to the Departure gate. With a quick hug and kiss for both Betty and Maddie, Bob was through the gate and onto the plane. Jack lingered, not wanting to leave Maddie. Tears welled in her eyes and in his. To prevent embarrassing either one of them he leaned down and kissed her. Then he kissed her again, and again, and again. They were on the final boarding call before he let her go and walked onto the plane.

Maddie and Betty went into the café for what turned out to be a very pleasant chat. Maddie liked Betty immediately. Betty had a good sense of humour and loved to tell stories. For an hour she regaled Maddie with stories of Bob and Jack on tour. She had been with them on a few tours and was happy to share her funniest memories of those tours. Maddie and Betty found they had several other interests in common too, including a love of crafts and cats. They agreed to meet at Betty's for a 'craft day' the day after tomorrow. Maddie was anxious to meet Betty's two cats. Driving home to Prestwick, Maddie marvelled at the thought of the phrase 'home to Prestwick'. In two short weeks it really had become home.

Maddie walked into the house, immediately feeling Jack's absence. It was the first time she had been alone in his house and it felt very lonely. Not sure what to do, she made herself a cup of coffee and took it into her office. She looked at the pile of brand new textbooks on her desk. School started tomorrow and she figured she might as well get started on her studies. She wanted to do as much of her work as she could while Jack was away so they could spend time together when he was home. That was the joy of taking off campus courses; as long as she had assignments in on time and showed up for exams she could work to her own timetable.

Sitting down heavily in her chair, Maddie reached for the top book on the pile and opened it. Not thinking she could concentrate, she was surprised when she looked at the clock and saw it was almost 8:30. She'd been reading for three hours.

Jack called her every day but the house still seemed empty and Maddie missed him more than she had thought possible. Even with the excitement of school starting and her new-found friendship with Betty, the three weeks of the tour crawled by. Eventually it was time to go to the airport to get Jack. Maddie dressed even more carefully than usual in skin tight black jeans, long black boots and a green embroidered shirt that matched her eyes. She wanted to look good for Jack. She did look good.

Unable to sit around the house, Maddie arrived at the airport two hours before the flight was due. She went into the café, where she'd agreed to meet Betty, in, oh, an hour and a half. She wasn't hungry, but she got a sandwich and a cup of tea and sat down. She would have preferred coffee, but in the airport café the coffee didn't really look like coffee. It was the wrong colour.

With nothing else to do, Maddie started people watching. It was something she usually enjoyed, but today was different. She was impatient for the time to pass. Finally Betty arrived. The plane would be landing in half an hour. Betty wanted a cup of tea, so Maddie had what was her fourth cup since she had arrived.

They left the café and went to check the arrivals board. Maddie was delighted to see the plane from Toronto had already landed ahead of schedule. She was so anxious to see Jack again, the fifteen minutes the plane was early seemed like a gift.

Maddie and Betty stood just outside the Customs hall waiting for the boys to clear it. When Jack emerged from the room, Maddie launched herself at him. Laughing in delight, he picked her up and swung her around.

Once home, Jack suggested going to bed. He was jet-lagged and Maddie had been up most of the night before, too excited to sleep. She was pretty sure he didn't have sleep in mind.

# *CHAPTER 21*

The following morning, after breakfast, Jack asked Maddie to come into the sitting room. "We need to talk," he said. Curious, she went in and sat down on the settee. Jack sat down beside her. "I missed you so much," he said for the hundredth time.

"Not nearly as much as I missed you."

"We have two weeks off, then another three week tour. I hate the thought of being without you for that long again. Would you consider coming with us? You wouldn't be expected to work, but you could if you want to," he asked hesitantly, almost afraid of her answer.

Maddie's jaw dropped. She hadn't expected this. Stunned, she didn't say anything and Jack's heart sank. He'd been so sure this was the solution.

"You want me to go on tour with you?"

"Very much."

She looked at him, her whole face lighting up. "That would be so cool!" she exclaimed. "Is it okay with Bob?"

"I wanted to ask you first, but I can't see him objecting."

Later that day Jack rang Bob. "That's a great idea. Maybe then you won't be moping around the hotel the whole time we're not on stage. Do you think she'd dance for us? And sing that song with you?"

"I can certainly ask her." 'That song' was 'The Way Old Friends Do'. Jack had heard Maddie singing along to one of their tapes. With Bob's help, he had convinced her to sing it as a duet with him. It had been added to the programme midway through the summer and the audiences had loved it.

Jack found Maddie in her study. "I've just talked to Bob." She looked at him in trepidation. "He wants to know if you'll dance and sing."

Her perfect features clouded in disbelief. "Are you serious?"

"Quite. I'm not sure what kind of contract we can negotiate for you at this late date, but you'll at least get expenses."

"Oh my God. I've never been to Australia or New Zealand. And it'll be spring there. What kind of clothes do I take? I know Australia's hot but New Zealand has a climate like Canada. And I won't have to rattle around in this big house alone, we'll be together. I'll have to get all my assignments done before we go."

As she paused for breath Jack laughed. "Shall I take that as a yes?"

She threw herself at him and hugged him as hard as she could.

"I'll call Bob and let him know. Then I'll call John and see what he can negotiate for you. And I'll make your travel arrangements. Hotels are no problem, but we have a lot of flights to organize." Jack headed into his office, Maddie trailing behind him. The first call was to Bob. "She'd love to come and she'll sing and dance."

"Let me talk to her." Bob's voice held a hint of humour as he teased her. "Do you know what you're in for?"

"No," she said then quickly added, "but there's only one way to find out."

Betty wanted to talk to Maddie too and after a short chat, they agreed to meet for lunch the next day. They were becoming very good friends.

Jack's next call was to his agent, John, who also happened to be Maddie's agent. He explained what they wanted to do and left it in John's hands. The third and final call was to the travel agent, to try and get them all on the same flights. Jack turned to Maddie. "That was easy. Everyone else is doing the work."

"I'll have to set up some rehearsal times with Bob. There's no piper so I guess I'll be dancing to the accordion… or to the little voices in my head."

"Let's make it the accordion," Jack chuckled.

To celebrate their day's accomplishments, they went out for supper and a walk along the beach. The moon was almost full and the beach was as bright as daylight. Maddie's eyes glittered with moonlight and excitement.

The next day, Maddie got down to work. She had a lot to do if she was going on tour in two weeks. 'Going on tour'. She rolled the phrase around in her head a couple times and decided she liked it. She made a list of the things she had to do – her schoolwork, rehearsals with Bob, get her costumes ready, get her travelling clothes ready, pack. She was on the third page of her 'to do' list when Jack walked in.

"You've only got two weeks you know," he said dryly.

"Oh some of these things are as simple and quick as sewing on buttons. I just have to remember to do everything. I've broken it down into small bits so I can feel like I'm scratching a lot off the list every day." When she finally got done writing her list, Maddie counted fifty-three items on it. The most intimidating thing on the list was meeting Jack's daughters. She knew she would like them, but she was afraid they wouldn't like her.

# *CHAPTER 22*

Maddie was nervous. This was the day she was going to meet Jack's daughters. She dressed carefully then dressed again. She wanted to make a good impression, but she wasn't sure if she should try and look older. His elder daughter was fourteen and at only four years older than Siobhan, Maddie felt a strange dynamic. Would the two girls think she was too young for their father or would they even care? Would they like her? What would happen if they didn't? Jack had a good relationship with his girls and a great relationship with Maddie. She didn't want either relationship to suffer. Jack wasn't much help. He just kept saying, "Be yourself. They'll love you."

Maddie gave up. She figured she might as well be herself. It wasn't like she was trying out for the role of stepmother. She was their father's friend. The fact they were living together didn't enter into the equation. That was what Jack kept telling Maddie. Knowing his girls and knowing Maddie, he was sure they would all like each other.

Maddie waited in the car while Jack went to the door of their home to get Siobhan and Charlie (Charlotte). Still nervous, Maddie was relieved she didn't have to meet Jack's ex-wife. He had told her some horror stories of the woman and Maddie wasn't ready to face her yet. She appeared at the door of the house before Jack had walked up the path. Maddie thought she looked normal, but even through the closed windows of the car she could hear the woman yelling at Jack.

"What do you think you're doing exposing our girls to this sick relationship?"

Determined to keep his cool, Jack ignored her words and asked if the girls were ready. The two girls pushed past their mother and went out to hug their father.

Jack and the two girls got into the car. He made the introductions. It might have been an awkward moment, but Maddie got off on the right foot right away.

"Oh, Siobhan," she said, "I love your sweater. Where did you get it?"

Jack felt like the odd man out when his girls and his woman started talking about the latest fashions and where the best places were to shop. He was pleased they were all getting along, but it was his turn to feel the strange dynamic.

Not being sure of how the evening would go, Siobhan and Charlie had decided they would like to go to their favourite pizza restaurant. In case they felt awkward with their dad's 'friend', they would at least be comfortable in their surroundings. Maddie and Charlie discovered they had something in common. They were both picky eaters. Jack thought it was going to be hard to order a pizza that everyone liked, but it turned out to be easy. Charlie and Maddie both hated vegetables. Siobhan and Jack both liked everything. They ordered two pizzas and everyone was happy.

Jack had told his daughters that Maddie travelled on tour with him and Bob and they wanted to know what it was like. Jack objected, saying he had told them many times what it was like going on tour. They wanted to know what it was like from Maddie's point of view. Tall, blonde and willowy, Siobhan wanted to be a model. Charlie, shorter and dark haired, wanted to be an actress. They both wanted to know what it was like for Maddie to be in the spotlight. They sat talking long after the pizza was done.

On the way back to the car, Charlie said she wanted to go for ice cream. Siobhan said it would be bad for her figure, but when Maddie thought it sounded like a good idea she changed her mind. Maddie had a really good figure, and some really nice tight black leather pants. If she could eat ice cream and not worry about it maybe Siobhan could too.

Jack was very pleased with the way the evening had gone. The girls and Maddie had gotten along really well together. There hadn't been any awkward moments and the conversation had flowed. His hope that they would get along had been realized. The girls no longer thought Maddie was a freak. Jack and Maddie were both thrilled when, two days later, Siobhan phoned to see if Maddie would like to go shopping Saturday with her and Charlie. They wanted to show Maddie the best places in town to shop.

By the time they left for Australia, Maddie had completed all fifty-three things on her list. The one difficult item on the list, meeting Jack's daughters, had turned out to be the easiest. Maddie liked the girls, the girls liked her and they didn't seem to care that she was living with their father.

# *CHAPTER 23*

Maddie marvelled at the turquoise waters and white sand beaches that passed under the plane as it descended into Sydney airport. He and Bob had been to Australia many times but Jack didn't remember ever being as excited about it as Maddie was. Looking at the country through her eyes, he enjoyed a new appreciation of his surroundings.

Their first show was in Sydney. They'd had two days to get used to the time change and to rehearse. When he sang the opening number 'Let's Have a Ceilidh' Jack watched Maddie dance the highland fling and he didn't think he'd ever seen her feet so high off the floor. Her toes were almost on point like a ballet dancer's. Mentally he patted himself on the back for coming up with the idea of bringing her along. The audience's enthusiastic applause reinforced the wisdom of his decision. Throughout the show Maddie continued to display the same high level of energy. She always smiled when she was dancing and Jack knew she was enjoying herself. The audience's reaction to her was heartwarming. They loved her.

Two shows in Sydney meant they had some free time during the days. Jack good-naturedly went along with Maddie's wish to go sightseeing. They went on a bus tour of the city which went to all the usual tourist spots, including the Sydney Opera House, the Harbour and Bondi Beach. Jack had already seen most of the sights, but once again he was looking through Maddie's eyes and found he was enjoying himself more than he had expected. Always considerate of Maddie's interests he also took her to Sydney Wildlife World and the Royal Botanical Gardens. She was a real animal lover and she loved seeing the indigenous animals. She was amazed by the size of the tropical plants.

Maddie had really wanted to see Ayer's Rock, but it was too far to go. All their concerts were in coastal cities and the Rock was far inland. She figured there'd be other trips and she would see it another time. This was her first tour with the boys and she was enjoying it so much she was going to do her best to ensure it wasn't the last one.

They had ten shows in Australia; then it was on to New Zealand for six more. It was a brutal schedule, but Jack knew he and Bob could do it and he was sure Maddie could keep up. Her dancing seemed to increase her energy. They had two shows in both Melbourne and Brisbane, and with a free day between, took the opportunity to do some sightseeing there as well.

As much as she had enjoyed Australia, New Zealand was the place Maddie was really looking forward to seeing. For as long as she could remember, she had loved looking at the pictures of the long fingers of water that reached into the cliffs on the South Island. She really wanted to visit Milford Sound. It looked like one of the sea lochs in Scotland. She was also fascinated by the history of the Mauri people and wanted to visit some of their sacred sites and the bubbling pools at Rotorua. She managed to convince Jack that they should stay a couple of extra days and do some sightseeing. When Bob saw the list of places they were going, he changed his plane ticket so he could go with them. He too had been enjoying looking at things from Maddie's perspective, but he also thought it would be nice to see some places other than just the cities and theatres where they performed.

# *CHAPTER 24*

Despite several dinner invitations Maddie and Jack had chosen to spend their first Christmas together alone.

Jack had never done much decorating, but Maddie loved Christmas, so they bought some decorations and put up a Christmas tree. Jack couldn't believe how much it changed the atmosphere in the house. Maddie spent three days baking Christmas goodies so as well as looking Christmasy, the house smelled like Christmas. What had been just a house was becoming a cozy home.

Jack's ex-wife, Edith had Siobhan and Charlie for Christmas, but against her better judgment and with a lot of pressure from the girls she had agreed the girls could have a pre-Christmas dinner and overnight with their father and Maddie. She hadn't yet met Maddie, but the girls clearly liked her so she couldn't be all bad. She couldn't blame the girl for being half Jack's age. The girls didn't care about that, nor did they care it was Christmas; they were excited about having a sleep-over at their dad's with their friend Maddie.

December 22$^{nd}$ Jack and Maddie picked up the girls. Maddie could see their mother trying, from behind the curtain, to get a look in the car at her. For dinner the girls wanted to go to their pizza restaurant. Jack thought it wasn't very Christmasy, but allowed himself to be convinced. As they had before, Charlie and Maddie shared one pizza and Siobhan and Jack another. When they got back to the house they exchanged Christmas gifts. The girls were very pleased that Maddie had helped Jack with his shopping this year. Instead of just giving them a card with money in it, he had actually bought gifts that Maddie had picked out. They loved the new clothes and jewellery and Jack still gave them each a card with money in it.

Edith had been concerned about the sleeping arrangements, not wanting her girls to be in a house where their father was sleeping with a teenager. It turned out not to be an issue. The girls and Maddie made beds of blankets and cushions in the sitting room. After opening gifts, they all watched Christmas films on telly and gorged on Maddie's Christmas goodies. Feeling left out, Jack went upstairs to bed while the three girls had a pj party. When the girls told Edith about their overnight, she began to think maybe Maddie was more mature than she thought.

Because they were leaving on the cruise Christmas night, Maddie and Jack celebrated their Christmas on the 24th. Maddie cooked a small turkey with all the trimmings and Jack once again marvelled at the diversity of talents this woman, HIS woman, had. They exchanged their gifts. Jack had gotten Maddie a beautiful gold bracelet with set in emeralds. She loved emeralds. She had gotten him the golf clubs he had been admiring. He wanted to cancel the tour and try them out right away, but the club was closed for the season.

That night Maddie and Jack went to the Christmas Eve carol service at the Auld Kirk of Ayr. Jack had been a member of the congregation there for many years. When they were home they usually went to Sunday services there and Maddie had made friends with some of the women. Jack and Maddie had accepted an invitation to a Christmas Eve get-together at the home of Gemma, one of Maddie`s friends. On the way home, it was late and the roads were deserted. They passed gaily decorated houses, some with lights still on and people celebrating. It started snowing; big, fat, fluffy flakes landing gently on everything. Maddie hated snow, but she did have to agree it looked pretty and it added to the Christmas feeling.

Even though her family was far away and she was missing them, Maddie didn't feel like she was missing out on Christmas. She had family and friends here now too. She, Bob and Jack would be touring Canada in February and she and Jack would be spending a few days in Ottawa after the tour. She could have Christmas with her family a bit late.

Christmas morning Maddie and Jack slept late, made love and lounged about until it was time to go to the airport. They agreed; their first Christmas together had been perfect.

# *CHAPTER 25*

Maddie was so excited about the cruise, she had spent three days packing and unpacking then repacking, unable to decide what to take. As she stuffed her suitcase yet again she thought of that day four and half years ago when Auntie Joannie had gotten such a kick out of how much she managed to get into one suitcase. A lot had happened in the intervening time, all of it good. She couldn't believe how different her life was now.

Maddie loved cruises. The only ones she had been on before were with her parents. This one would be totally different. Not only was she working on the ship, she was being paid an outrageous amount of money to do something she loved doing. Even better than that, it would be romantic. She would be with the man she adored.

They had one show to do on the first night of the cruise and two each night after. The captain had agreed to let them on board to rehearse and set up the day before departure, so they went right from the airport to the ship. They were well prepared for the first show.

Maddie was delighted with the enthusiasm of the audience at the first show. They sang and clapped along anytime Jack suggested it and sometimes when he didn't. At the end of the show the audience demanded an encore then tried to convince them to do a second one. As the curtain came down, the audience was still applauding.

Betty had come with them for a bit of a holiday and the four of them went out on deck after the show. They stood at the stern of the ship, watching the lights of Miami in the distance. Jack was once again looking at things through Maddie's eyes. Although he enjoyed touring anyway, the tour of Australia and New Zealand had been incredible with Maddie's fresh perspective. The cruise would be a fresh perspective for all of them. Bob and Jack hadn't worked a cruise before.

Maddie never ate before a show and was hungry. They decided to try out the midnight buffet. It turned out to be so good they thought they might do it every night. It suited Maddie's eating habits of a large breakfast and another large meal after the shows. The others were impressed by the variety of foods.

Once back in their cabin Jack took Maddie in his arms. "I'm going to rock you in my arms and the ship is going to rock you in bed."

She smiled impishly at him. "I'm pretty sure you're going to rock me in bed too."

December 29th, the night before Maddie's 19th birthday, when the curtain came down Jack said to her, "Let's go out on deck and get some air."

She thought it odd that he asked. It was what they'd done the last two nights. But then he'd been acting oddly all day.

Still in costume, they walked hand in hand. Concerned about him, Maddie asked, "Are you alright?"

"What do you mean?"

"You've been twitchy all day."

"Twitchy?" She often used 'Canadianisms' he hadn't heard.

"Nervous, jumpy."

They stopped walking and leaned against the rail at the stern of the ship. The moon was full. It cast shadows on the ship's wake and made Maddie's green eyes shine. She looked so beautiful in the moonlight. In her long, full, tartan dress, Jack thought she could have been the lady of an old Scots laird.

Maddie looked at him anxiously. Jack knew he didn't have much time before Bob and Betty came looking for them and he wanted to do this before they came. Not sure how to start, he kissed her. Her response gave him courage.

"There's something we need to talk about," he said hesitantly. "We've been in love with each other for four years and we've basically been living together now for the last seven months. I'd like to do something about that. You know I love you more than life itself."

"Yes and I love you at least that much," she said uncertainly, worried by the direction of the conversation and waiting for a 'but…'

Taking both her small hands in his large ones, Jack dropped to one knee. "Will you marry me, Maddie Campbell?" Her eyes opened wide in surprise and one small hand flew to her mouth. "Will you?"

"Yes… yes, yes, yes."

He stood and took her in his arms. His lips were soft and warm against hers.

Ending the kiss, she asked, "Why were you nervous about asking me?"

"I was afraid you would say it was too soon, or you were too young and it would ruin our relationship."

"Oh, baby. How many times do I have to tell you I love you more than life itself before you believe me?"

"I can never hear it or say it enough. I have something for you." Jack rummaged in his sporran, pulling out a small box. When he opened it, Maddie gasped. It was the most beautiful ring she had ever seen – a gold claddagh with a heart shaped emerald between the two hands. Diamond chips made the crown sparkle in the moonlight. Tears welled up in her eyes as he slipped it on her finger. It was a perfect fit.

"Are you crying?" he asked. She nodded as the tears ran down her cheeks. He reached into his sporran again and handed her his handkerchief. As she dabbed at her eyes, he put his hands on her shoulders. "Do ye nae like it? I can get ye a regular engagement ring, ye ken, a diamond."

"No," she shook her head. "It's perfect. I love it and I love you."

"Are you sure?"

She smiled through her tears, nodding her head. "Yup. I'm pretty sure I love you."

"Seriously though if you'd rather have a diamond ring…"

"No I love this one. It's perfect." She dabbed at her eyes again.

Bob and Betty had come out on deck looking for them. It was becoming a routine that after the second show they would go for a stroll and then all four of them would meet up and go to the midnight buffet. Too far away to hear the conversation, Bob and Betty were alarmed by what they saw. Jack had his hands on Maddie's shoulders and she was crying and shaking her head.

Rushing up to them Bob said, "For Christ's sake, Jack. What did ye do to her?"

Jack looked sheepish. "I asked her to marry me, she said yes and she's been greetin' ever since."

Betty squealed. "You're getting married?" She threw her arms around Maddie. "I'm so happy for you." Betty admired Maddie's ring. When Jack asked Betty if she thought he should trade it for a diamond she said if it was hers she wouldn't trade it for the world.

As Betty relinquished Maddie and went to hug Jack, Bob moved in to hug Maddie. "I've always thought of you as a little sister. If he makes you cry again tell me and I'll beat him up for you."

Maddie laughed through her tears. "I've never been so happy."

"I hope I never see you sad," Jack observed.

Bob handed Betty his handkerchief so she too could wipe her eyes. He looked at Jack, perplexed and said, "Women are like the Irish – happy things make them cry."

Betty suddenly looked at Maddie. "Have you eaten since breakfast? It's nearly midnight."

"No, I don't eat till after the last show. Dancing isn't conducive to digestion."

"We need to get some food into you," said Betty.

"Kiss and make up and we'll get a drink to celebrate," said Bob.

# *CHAPTER 26*

Alone in their cabin later, Jack wished Maddie a happy birthday. "I've never had such a happy birthday."

"I have a wee birthday present for you," he said, reaching into his sporran and pulling out another small box, slightly larger than the ring box, and handing it to her. This one was wrapped in shiny green foil.

As Maddie opened the package, she said, "You've already given me the best birthday present ever, a ring that tells the world I'm yours."

Maddie gasped when she saw what was in the box. A pair of earrings that exactly matched her ring sparkled at her from a green velvet background. "They're absolutely beautiful."

"Are you going to cry again?" Jack asked uncertainly.

Tears welled up in her eyes, making them shine in the dim light. "No I'm not," she said and kissed him. "You know me so well," she said.

Looking in the mirror, Maddie put the earrings on then turned to Jack. "How do they look?" she asked. Still in her long, tartan dress with the wide sleeves edged in lace, she truly looked like she had stepped out of an 18th century painting.

"You are so beautiful," he said, "inside and out. How did I get so lucky?" He kissed her softly still marvelling at his good fortune.

"Let's get ready for bed," she said with a hint of promise in her voice.

Maddie took what she thought was her sexiest nightdress and went into the bathroom to change. What he saw when she came out took Jack's breath away. The red silk gown clung to her body like a second skin, hinting at what was underneath. The lovelight shining in her eyes was for him. He took her in his arms and kissed her. The kiss was gentle at first then deepened into a very passionate one.

Maddie could feel Jack's erection through the thin fabrics of her gown and his pj bottoms. He could feel the hardness of her nipples against his bare chest through the soft, slippery fabric of her gown. His hand slid up to cup a breast.

He pulled away from her lips and trailed small kisses down her throat till he reached her breast. He licked and suckled her nipple through the thin fabric. She moaned in pleasure as he eased her onto the bed. As he slipped off his pj pants she grasped his erection. He gasped and stretched out beside her, pulling her body closer to him. He slid into her, rolling on his back with her on top. His hands cupped the globes of her butt massaging the soft velvety skin and moving under the scrap of red silk that still clung to her body. She exhaled sharply as his hands grazed her bare nipples. She returned the favour, teasing his nipples with her hands then her tongue. Groaning in pleasure, he rolled them both over. Teasing her with long, slow strokes he withdrew each time and rubbed against her entrance. She was writhing, repeating his name. When the wave of pleasure washed over her he increased his tempo, riding his own wave of pleasure before hers was over.

Afterwards as they lay in each other's arms, Maddie was admiring her ring. Jack, still not sure he had chosen right, offered once again to get her a regular diamond ring. She refused, laughing as she said, "No. This one has just been christened."

# *CHAPTER 27*

The next morning Jack woke with a headache. "Too much celebrating last night," he muttered to himself. Maddie was not in the room. Alarmed, he went out into the sitting room. She sat on the couch with a calendar in her hands. "Happy birthday, luv," he said giving her a kiss. "What are you doing?"

"I'm trying to find us a wedding date before you change your mind," she said with a smile.

"Not happening. We could have the captain marry us today," he suggested.

She looked dismayed. "No. I want a real wedding; a church wedding, with our friends and family, with flowers and music and bridesmaids and groomsmen in kilts and a big party with lots of dancing."

He smiled at the urgency in her voice. "Then that is what you shall have. Have you picked a date yet?" he asked, sitting down beside her.

"I'm looking for a window when we have two solid weeks off: one to get ready and one for a honeymoon. We're off for all of March but that won't give us time to plan a wedding. Nor does it give my family time to make travel arrangements. The next time I see is in September."

"That far away? You could change your mind," he moaned.

"Not a chance, you're stuck with me now." He looked like a cat with a canary.

She handed him the calendar. "See if you can find anything sooner."

It was an exceptionally busy schedule this year and Jack was disappointed that he couldn't find anything sooner either. He tried to talk her into a March wedding, but she had her heart set on a big wedding and he didn't want to disappoint her. They could spend their time in March planning it.

Although they had the second half of October and most of November free at this point, they agreed on September 23$^{rd}$. They had nothing booked between September 16$^{th}$ and October 3$^{rd}$. It gave them just over two weeks, the soonest they had a complete break longer than a week.

"There is something we could do though. We could handfast."

Maddie's face lit up at Jack's suggestion. Handfasting was something their highland ancestors had done when there wasn't a clergyman available to marry them. The two people involved made a contract to be faithful to each other for a year and a day. The contract was renewable if they both wished. In Scottish tradition it was considered a valid marriage until a preacher could be found or until the contract expired.

Bob and Betty came out of their cabin dressed for the day. Bob looked a little the worse for wear, having helped Jack with the celebrations the previous night. "Happy birthday, Maddie. Put some clothes on, Jack and we'll get some breakfast."

"We have some more news," Jack said to him. "We're going to handfast. You and Betty can be witnesses and maybe the captain."

Betty looked excited but Bob groaned, "More celebrating. Mimosas all around."

On their way to breakfast, they met one of the ship's officers and asked if they could have a word with the captain. While they were eating, the captain came to join them for coffee. Jack explained to him what they wanted.

The captain looked delighted. "I'd be honoured to be a part of it. When would you like to do it? I could legally marry you in a regular civil ceremony you know."

While Jack recounted Maddie's reasons for not wanting a 'real' wedding on the ship, the captain ordered more mimosas. They agreed to have the handfasting on the following day, New Year's Eve.

After a birthday lunch for Maddie, the rest of the day was spent relaxing in the sun, chatting with the other passengers and napping before the shows. Two shows a night took a lot of energy, but they all enjoyed them.

# *CHAPTER 28*

That night, when the curtain went up for the first show, Bob took the microphone from Jack. Looking at the audience, he said, "Tonight's show is going to be a bit different. We're celebrating. It's Maddie's birthday and Jack and I think as a birthday present from her to you, she should spend the whole show on stage and sing and dance with Jack. What do you think?"

Cheers and yesses came from the audience, many of whom had seen a show the previous night. Maddie took the mike from Bob. "You're going to make me work harder on my birthday?" she said in mock horror. "You should be giving me the night off."

Another series of cheers interspersed with, "No night off," came from the audience. They started singing 'happy birthday', Bob joining in on the accordion.

Bob took the mike again. "We're celebrating something else too. Last night my brother asked Maddie to marry him and she said 'yes'." Even louder cheers came from the audience. "There's not so much of an age difference between them as you might think," he said. "Maddie is older than she looks, (in costume for the sword dance, she looked about fifteen) and Jack is a lot younger than he looks."

The audience exploded in laughter. One voice shouted from the front row, "Gie her a kiss, mate." Jack leaned forward and kissed Maddie. "Nae like that," came the voice again, "a real yin."

Jack took Maddie in his arms and tipped her back and to the side, covering her lips with his. They held the kiss for a full minute, his tongue seeking hers.

When he let her up, she took the mike again. Shaking her mane of red-gold curls, she said, "Oooohhh, I enjoyed that, thank you." The audience applauded enthusiastically. "Just before we get started," she said, "I want to remind you all that I'm a dancer not a singer." They all laughed.

The show went off without a hitch, Maddie harmonizing beautifully with Jack. When the second show started, Bob said, "Some of you will have already heard this, but some of you haven't." He told the same story that he had for the first show.

The same voice as before yelled, "Gie her a kiss, mate, a real yin."

Jack was happy to comply.

As the curtain came down, Jack said to Maddie, "Let's go out on deck. I can't repeat the drama of last night but it's a beautiful night."

As they strolled the deck, other passengers they encountered offered 'happy birthdays' and 'congratulations'. They found a deserted spot at the stern rail and stood looking out at the moon over the water. Jack slipped his arm around her.

"Are you sure about tomorrow?" he asked.

"Yes, I am. Are you?"

"Aye," he said. "I've never been so sure of anything."

# *CHAPTER 29*

In the captain's office the next morning, Jack and Maddie held hands while Betty tied a ribbon around their wrists, binding them to each other. A traditional handfasting required a contract of a year and a day. Knowing their wedding day was well within that time, they pledged themselves to love, honour and be true to each other for the length of their contract.

The captain had arranged for the ship's photographer to take pictures. Dressed in costume, the ladies in long, flowing tartan dresses and the men in kilts and formal jackets, the group was very photogenic. The captain, in full dress whites, joined them for a few of the photos. After a toast to the happy couple, Jack and Maddie retired to their cabin to seal their contract.

That night, being Hogmanay, everyone, including the performers had a few drinks before the show to toast the New Year. Even Maddie who rarely drank had a couple. After all, she was celebrating. At the beginning of the first show, the captain presented Maddie and Jack with several framed photos of the handfasting and told the audience about it, including an explanation of what it was.

The show passed quickly in a whirl of good spirits. Their energy level was high. Bob and Jack, in even better spirits than usual, spent the entire show trying to make each other laugh. The audience participated even without prompting from Jack.

At the beginning of the second show, the captain repeated his speech, giving Maddie and Jack even more framed photos. The audiences loved the unfolding of the love story on their cruise, many of them wishing they had witnessed the ceremony.

As was becoming a routine, Jack and Maddie went out on deck in full costume after the second show. Once again they were offered 'congratulations' by all they encountered. They stood at the rail, watching the moonlight play on the waves waiting for Bob and Betty to join them.

"This is so romantic," they both said at the same time, then laughed. Jack kissed her sweet face. They looked at each other, and once again both spoke at the same time, "I love you."

Bob and Betty arrived as they were chuckling over that.

When they walked into the dining room everyone there stood up and applauded. Still in costume they were easily recognized. Even those who hadn't been at the shows had heard the news. As well as toasting the New Year, they toasted the happy couple. Someone yelled, "How does it feel to be an old married lady?"

Looking all of her nineteen years, Maddie laughed. "Wonderful. I have the man I've always wanted." She and Jack were both grinning from ear to ear.

The voice they had heard the previous night once again shouted, "Gie her a kiss, mate, a real yin."

After they had complied, Jack whispered in Maddie's ear, "Wait till later, I'll show you a real kiss."

After another round of applause, the other diners left them alone. In anticipation of the New Year's imminent arrival, Bob had gotten a round of drinks for the toast. As they toasted the New Year, Jack and Maddie were looking at each other, both thinking the old year had been unbelievably good. They anticipated the new one being even better.

As usual the buffet was loaded with wonderful dishes. As Maddie ate, she felt the buzz from alcohol on an empty stomach slowly fade. She looked at Jack seriously, thinking, *I could not love this man more,* and remembering the crush she had had on him as a young teenager. He had lived up to everything she had imagined about him. At the same time, he was looking at her thinking how lucky he was to love a woman like her who loved him back. When they caught each other's eye, he winked at her and she blushed.

*Dammit*, she thought, *we're not going to start that again.*

# *CHAPTER 30*

Two days before the end of the cruise, the captain asked to see Bob, Jack and Maddie in his office. "I feel like I've been called into the principal's office," Maddie said. "I wonder what he wants."

The captain wasted no time in coming right to the point. "You've had a very successful run on this cruise. The audiences love you. I'm wondering if you would be interested in working another cruise. Before you answer, head office has already been in contact with your agent and you are available for the dates we want you in March. Your agent will be calling you later today, but I wanted a chance to soften you up before you talked to him." They all laughed. "Seriously though, the audiences love you and we'd really like to have you back. I think this is the first cruise I've ever watched a show more than once. Our communications officer has arranged a ship-to-shore call for you with your agent at 14:00hrs. That will give you some time to discuss it."

They left the captain's office each deep in thought. They had been looking forward to the break, but they had also all really enjoyed the cruise. They went back to their cabin to discuss the offer. Jack weighed in first.

"I like the idea. Yes we have two shows a night, but we've got a lot of time to ourselves. It's almost like a holiday. Besides, March in Scotland is miserable." They all agreed on that.

Bob was less sure, although it had been suggested he bring Betty along again. "We have a brutal schedule this year. I'm already going to have to wear a nametag when I see my kids. I need to think about this for a bit."

Although she didn't feel her vote carried the same weight as Bob's and Jack's, Maddie offered her opinion. "I know this cruise has been really exciting for Jack and me and we couldn't hope for another one that would equal this one, but I'd like to do it. I agree with Jack, Scotland in March is pretty miserable. The idea of warm sunny days is very appealing."

Bob's objection had been half-hearted and it didn't take much to convince him it was a good idea. Betty, who had been listening, was all for it. For her it was a holiday. By 14:00hrs they had agreed they would do it. It was basically the same as this cruise: two weeks, one show the first night and two the others.

John did have one surprise though. He asked Maddie if she would be interested in teaching some highland dancing to the children on the cruise. There were a lot of children on March cruises and the ship line was always looking for different activities for them. Maddie was intrigued. While the boys talked with John, she thought hard. It would mean less time to relax and enjoy herself, but she really enjoyed teaching dance too. And it was only two hours a day. Although not the deciding factor, the increase in her paycheck would be significant too. She told John she would do it.

"You must be psychic," Jack said to Maddie later. "You knew we couldn't get married in March. You do realize the next cruise won't be as eventful as this one was? The only thing that I could think would make it this exciting is if I knock you up!"

"Don't even think about it," was the reply. "When you knock me up I'll be out of a job. Anyway, not before the wedding."

Jack was pleased that she had said 'when' not 'if'. They hadn't yet discussed having children.

# *CHAPTER 31*

Christmas in February in Ottawa. There were so many things wrong with that statement. Maddie hated Ottawa winters. It was either snowing or the temperature was minus something obscene. This time she was so happy to see her family she almost didn't care about the weather - almost. A week earlier they had played two shows in Ottawa, but there hadn't been time to see everyone.

Maddie's best friend, Beckie, had called her on her birthday. Unable to contain herself, Maddie had told her she and Jack were getting married. Beckie had been sworn to secrecy. She was allowed to tell her man Ben, but only after she swore him to secrecy too. Although Beckie and Ben had both grown up in the city, they had saved up their money, bought a hobby farm and moved to the country. Maddie thought they embodied the idea of a perfect farm couple. They were what Maddie thought of as country people: down to earth, grounded in reality, friendly and welcoming. They delighted in having visitors and were ideal hosts. Maddie and Jack were staying with them.

Maddie had also phoned Auntie Joannie to tell her, and she too had been sworn to secrecy. The big announcement would be made at a family 'Christmas' dinner. Difficult as she found it, Auntie Joannie managed to keep the secret.

When the announcement was made, there was loud cheering. Jack had charmed all of Maddie's relatives. Although he had met most of them backstage after their shows, the only one who really knew him was Auntie Joannie. She had told them about him and they welcomed him into the family. He smiled to himself when he heard the ladies in the family 'oohing and aahing' over Maddie's ring. He guessed he had chosen well after all.

Jack and Maddie had brought the wedding invitations with them. They hadn't wanted to post them earlier as it would have spoiled the surprise, but they hadn't wanted to delay their delivery either. The wedding was to be in Scotland in September and they wanted to give those who would come enough time to make travel plans.

Even though they liked Jack, Maddie's parents were not sure about their daughter marrying a man so much older than her. They didn't know how much older he actually was. They asked her several times if she wanted a man so much older than herself. She gave them the same answer each time. "We love each other and age is only a number. It doesn't define a person. Anyway, he's young at heart."

Maddie's parents had been wondering why Maddie was staying on the farm with Beckie and Ben instead of with them. It became apparent after the big announcement. Maddie hadn't wanted them to know Jack was with her. Anyway, the sleeping arrangements would have been awkward. Her parents were old fashioned. They would not have let Jack and Maddie share a room.

Jack and Maddie spent three of their four days in Ottawa visiting Maddie's friends and relatives and sightseeing. Jack wanted another tour given by a local. With Beckie and Ben, they went to the Parliament Buildings, the Mint and the Natural History Museum, reminding Jack of his first trips through the Kelvingrove and the People's Palace with Maddie. They also went skating on the Rideau Canal. It was Winterlude in Ottawa and they again saw some amazing snow and ice sculptures at Dow's Lake. Jack was no better at skating than he had been the first time they had gone and once again Maddie and Beckie pulled him along. Bob didn't even try. He walked in his boots, even though Ben offered to keep him on his feet in skates.

Beckie and Ben had been working under the radar to make some plans themselves. Between them they had planned both a surprise wedding shower and a stag for the last day of the visit. The invitations had been sent out in January, but the reasons for the parties were not disclosed until after the big announcement. Maddie and Jack were touched by their thoughtfulness.

All too soon, the visit was over. Beckie and Ben drove Jack and Maddie to the airport. Maddie tried to convince them to get on the airplane with her and Jack and come 'home to Prestwick'. They parted, with Beckie and Ben promising to come soon for a visit. At the very least they would be coming to the wedding.

# *CHAPTER 32*

As predicted, the second cruise wasn't as dramatic as the first one. For Maddie and Jack it was still very romantic. Each night after the second show they went out on deck. For some reason no one else used what they had come to consider 'their spot' at the stern rail of the ship. They would go there in costume right after the show to wait for Bob and Betty. It had become a routine. Maddie and Jack would stand watching the moon, arms around each other, occasionally kissing while Bob and Betty strolled the deck. After their stroll, they would join Jack and Maddie and would all go to the midnight buffet. It was a routine Maddie loved. By the time the second show was over she was usually starving.

Jack had gotten used to her habit of an enormous breakfast and no food again till another enormous meal after the shows.

Betty was still amazed at the quantity of food Maddie could consume and not add an ounce to her weight. She was a little envious. On the last cruise Betty had gained eight pounds. It had taken her all the time between cruises to lose it. She was hoping she didn't do the same thing this time. For her, Bob and Jack there were four meals a day; breakfast, lunch, dinner and midnight buffet. Betty wondered if she should sign up for Maddie's dance class to burn off some of the calories. Unfortunately she was a little past the age limit.

Maddie had decided she would teach children from age six to ten; six and seven year olds the first hour and eight to ten year olds the second hour. Her lessons were for both boys and girls. They were geared to beginners, but those with some experience were also welcome.

The classes turned out to be a big hit, with more and more children showing up each day. Maddie had gone 'way back' in her memory to try and remember the first things she had learned when she started dancing. She had a good way with children and knew how to talk to them. She also had a good understanding of how their minds and memories worked. As well as studying history in university she was taking psychology courses.

At her first class Maddie told the children they would be doing a lot of things during each class. She asked the group of six and seven year olds who had signed up, "How many new things do you think you can remember every day?" Although the answers ranged from one to twenty-five, most of them looked relieved when she told them they only had to remember two.

At the end of the first class Maddie asked the children, "Who can guess what the two most important things we learned today are?" She was pleased by the answers: point your toes, count, make 'stags' with your fingers. The children were surprised at how simple the first day's task was. "Remember to stand up straight and smile." Maddie repeated this with the older group of children and got the same reactions.

Although they didn't have dancing costumes, Maddie had decided each class would perform an abbreviated version of a highland fling for their parents on the last day of the cruise. It meant that they would have to work very hard, but they were all enthusiastic. There was only one child who didn't want to but she only came to the first class and didn't come back.

Maddie was thrilled with how eager to learn the children were and how quickly they picked up the simple steps. Although she was on the cruise for two weeks, most of the passengers were only taking one week cruises. Most got off in San Juan and new ones took their places. For her this meant she had to teach the children a short version of the highland fling in six days so they could perform it for their parents.

The day of their performance the children had an hour to practice before their parents came to watch. Maddie was impressed at how well the little ones did. Their dance wasn't perfect, but they all looked like they were having fun. Everyone stood up straight and they all smiled. The parents were thrilled. Many of them spoke to Maddie about signing their children up for dance lessons. Most of them were from the US so Maddie couldn't recommend specific schools, but she did tell the parents what to look for in a teacher.

Curious, the captain had come to observe the little show. Very impressed with how the children performed, he was even more impressed by their enthusiasm and how much they appeared to be enjoying themselves. Between the adults' shows in the evenings and the children's show, the Buchanans were a big hit. He was determined to press the ship line's head office to book these people as often as they could get them. He admitted to himself that it wasn't just for the passengers; he too really enjoyed the shows. And it wasn't just the shows. Occasionally the group went ashore but most days they spent out on deck. They were easily recognizable, personable and most importantly they were willing to chat with everyone. Most of the ship's entertainers spent their free time either disguised or hiding in their cabins.

# *CHAPTER 33*

Between tours, the wedding plans were being made. Maddie wanted a big wedding and Jack went along with her plans. He couldn't say 'no' to her about anything. Together they booked the church, the pastor and the reception hall. Bob had a friend who was a photographer and when Jack and Maddie saw samples of his work, they booked him right away.

Jack wanted to make the honeymoon plans and organize he music for the reception. Maddie agreed. She was busy worrying about flowers, dresses and bridesmaids. She was delighted when Beckie and Katie both said they were coming to the wedding and would be thrilled to be bridesmaids. She couldn't imagine getting married without the two friends who had been so important to her growing up. Siobhan and Charlie were over the moon when Maddie asked them to be bridesmaids. She also asked Betty and Jeannie who were very pleased to accept. Maddie would have liked to ask her friend Gemma, and Judy and Lynn, a couple of other friends from the church, but she had to stop somewhere. It was to be a big wedding, not a circus.

Edith was outraged when she heard Jack was going to marry 'the little gold digger'. When the girls told her they were going to be bridesmaids she was furious. Jack was prepared for another round of verbal abuse from her. After the outing when Maddie asked Siobhan and Charlie to be bridesmaids, Jack went home and waited by the phone. He didn't have to wait long. He let it ring three times, then braced himself and picked it up.

"For Christ's sake, Jack. What the hell do you think you're doing? It's bad enough that you live with a child, now you want to marry her? It's not just your business you know. What kind of example are you setting for the girls? And when are you going to realize she wants your money, not you? That's money the girls should be getting, not her."

Jack kept a lid on his temper and let Edith rant on. When she finally stopped for a breath, he interjected. "Can I say something now? For all your talk you seem more concerned about the money than anyone's feelings. Maddie doesn't want or need my money, she's making almost as much as I am. I haven't forgotten the girls. Although I'm not planning on dying in the immediate future, I've taken care of them in my new will. You have nothing to complain about. I've never even been late with a child support payment. I'm getting more than a little tired of you referring to my future wife as a child and a gold digger. She is neither. She loves me for me and I love her. We're getting married because we want to, not because we have to. (This was a dig at Edith's marriage to him.) End of argument."

"There's no argument, Jack. If you want to make a fool of yourself go ahead. Just don't involve my girls. They won't be bridesmaids when you marry a child."

Jack was trying very hard to control his temper, but Edith had had many years practice provoking him.

Maddie was sitting across the room from Jack. Although she couldn't hear the words, she could certainly hear Edith yelling into the phone. She could tell Jack had had enough. He took a deep breath and in a low voice said, "You spiteful bitch. This wedding is happening and the girls want to be part of it. Maddie and I want them to be part of it. All you accomplish by saying no is hurting them. Maybe you should meet Maddie then you wouldn't be so quick to judge her." Maddie's eyes opened wide in alarm. So far she had been spared contact with the girls' mother and she had hoped to continue that. Without taking a breath Jack continued, "Think about that and when you're ready to be civil call me back. I've had enough of this."

For the next two days there was silence from Edith. Charlie and Siobhan both called several times in tears. They thought their mother was being unreasonable not letting them be bridesmaids. Jack and Maddie both agreed, but were careful not to let the girls know they thought Edith was a shrew. The situation reached a crisis point when Charlie phoned in tears and asked if she and Siobhan could come and live with Maddie and Jack.

Although he had wanted to wait till Edith called him, Jack couldn't bear to see his girls being used as pawns. He phoned Edith and invited her to lunch with him to meet Maddie. He figured she wouldn't make a scene in a restaurant. As a parting shot he suggested Edith bring 'that lazy sod' she lived with.

The following day Maddie and Jack were the first to arrive at the restaurant. Maddie was so nervous she didn't think she'd be able to eat. She had dressed carefully, trying to make herself look older. When Edith and her man Jim arrived, Maddie was sipping a gin and bitter lemon. Maddie studied Edith. She thought Edith looked normal enough – average height, a few extra pounds but not fat, brown hair. Her face would have been pretty if it hadn't been for the sour expression on it. Jim was an average looking guy, not as tall as Jack but broader through the shoulders. Were it not for the paunch he looked like he could be a football player.

After the introductions, Edith's first words were directed at Maddie. "Are you old enough to drink?"

Maddie gritted her teeth and said nothing. She didn't trust herself to speak. Jack immediately jumped to her defence. "For God's sake, Edith, give it a rest. The reason we're here is to talk about the girls, not pick on Maddie. We're getting married. The issue is whether or not you're going to let the girls take part in our day."

"I will not have my girls be a part of this sick charade. You two can do what you want, but you're not corrupting my girls."

In a low voice Jack said, "They're OUR girls. This is their father's wedding and they want to be a part of it. You're just alienating them by being so spiteful. Did you know Charlie phoned me yesterday and asked if she and Siobhan could come and live with us?" Edith had been about to say something, but Jack's words shocked her. Jack continued, "She says you are being unreasonable and I have to agree. We love the girls and it's obvious they love Maddie. They are welcome to move in with us."

Edith choked on her drink. "Jim are you going to let him talk to me like that?"

Jim said nothing and continued sipping on his beer. He agreed with Jack, but knew better than to say anything.

Jack started on a new tack. "You know the girls are at an age where the courts would listen to them and consider their request to live with their father. Do you really want to go that route?"

Edith was almost speechless. "You wouldn't... They wouldn't dare," she started to say. In the years they'd been together she had always been able to browbeat Jack and get her own way. She wasn't used to him taking such a firm stand. He used to just walk away from her and she would do what she pleased. Unsure what to do, she turned her focus to Maddie. "And what do you think about this? You may think you want Jack but do you want an instant family of teenagers? They're the same age as you. What kind of authority do you think you would have dealing with them?"

Maddie was seething inside but managed to maintain a neutral expression and voice. “I love the girls and if they think they would be happier with us they are more than welcome to move in. By telling them they can’t take part in our wedding you’re only hurting yourself. They think you are the evil one and not their father.”

“You’re just repeating what Jack said. Don’t you have anything else to say?”

Maddie smiled. “I only speak when I have something worth saying.”

Edith was not used to being spoken to like this. She had been goading the girl trying to produce a hysterical reaction and prove her immaturity, but the little gold digger was still calm and not taking the bait. Her intention to show Jack how childish the girl was wasn’t working. She sat silently for a few minutes, picking at her food. Used to pushing people around and getting her own way, she was at a loss as to what to do next. She started repeating herself. “If you want to marry a little girl, Jack that’s your business, but keep my daughters out of it.”

“Edith, you need to think about what we’ve said. Maddie and I are getting married. We will be very disappointed if the girls can’t take part in our wedding, but the girls will be shattered. This is a no-win situation for you. You either let them do something you don’t want them to do or you risk alienating them for good. Your choice. We’re leaving now. Think about what we’ve said. I’ll call you tomorrow for your answer.” With that, he threw some money on the table and he and Maddie left.

“Nice to meet you,” said Maddie as she passed Edith.

The following day Jack phoned Edith. When he said ‘hello’ she said, “The girls can be bridesmaids,” and rang off.

Jack turned to Maddie. “One nothing for the good guys. You were awesome yesterday. She was trying to get a childish reaction from you and it didn’t work.”

Maddie replied, “You catch more flies with honey than with vinegar.”

Jack smiled. “I should take lessons from you.”

# *CHAPTER 34*

Edith spent the next two days with her best friend Barbara. Barbara was a bitter woman with a sharp tongue. She knew everything or at least thought she did. Edith wanted her help to try and stop the wedding.

The first plan Barbara suggested was simple. Edith should go to the wedding. When the pastor asked if anyone had any objections she could object. Edith wasn't so sure.

"What grounds do I object on?"

Barbara thought for a minute then said, "On the grounds that it's an unnatural relationship. She's too young and he was probably after her before she was legal."

Edith hesitated. She liked the idea of objecting but said, "I don't like those grounds. No matter what I think, I don't want the girls thinking their father is a paedophile. Anyway, how would we prove that? It would have to be something else."

Not giving up on what she thought was a brilliant idea, Barbara answered, "We don't have to prove it. All we have to do is plant a seed and let people think what they will. Everyone loves a scandal." She ignored Edith's worry about the girls' feelings.

Edith wasn't convinced. "No," she said. "We need something before it gets to the wedding day."

Barbara was thinking as fast as her malicious brain would let her. "We could set Jack up with a whore, take a picture and show it to the girl. She'd dump him immediately."

"And just how could we set that up? He's completely blotto over her. He'd never let himself be set up."

Barbara was getting frustrated. Her two best ideas had been rejected. She wasn't used to people saying no to her but she knew Edith was stubborn. Barbara wracked her brain. "If we can't set up Jack, we could set up the gold digger."

"That has even less chance of happening," Edith said. "She wouldn't trust anything I suggested."

While Barbara was frustrated, Edith was getting depressed. "There isn't any way we can do this."

Not one to give up a dirty fight, Barbara disagreed. "There has to be something. I know," she exclaimed. "It's perfect. We can send an explicit love letter to Maddie and have Jack think she's having an affair with a younger man."

Satisfied that this was indeed the way to go, she was annoyed when Edith said, "And how could we be sure Jack would see it?"

Barbara was annoyed. "Edith, you ask for my help and you say no to everything I suggest. You're going to have to work it out on your own. There's no pleasing you."

"Don't get shirty, Barbara. Have another cup of tea and we'll work on it some more. We could just push her under a bus."

After two days of what became more and more ridiculous schemes, they were no further ahead. Edith was becoming resigned to the fact that Jack's wedding was actually going to take place, and her girls would take part. Not only could she not find a way to stop the wedding, she couldn't even find a way to make her girls not want to be a part of it. She had to be careful not to drive the girls away from her, although, despite what she said, Edith was sure Maddie wouldn't want two teenagers moving in with her and her new husband, even if they were friends.

Edith finally agreed they should send the little slut a love letter signed John. Barbara wrote the letter so Jack wouldn't recognize the hand writing. Edith had no way of knowing Maddie would show it to Jack and both of them would have a good laugh, guessing who it had come from.

With her only real attempt to stop the wedding a failure, Edith resigned herself to the fact that Jack was going to marry his child bride. Although her only experience of Maddie had left a bad taste in her mouth, the girls continued to sing Maddie's praises. For the sake of the girls, Edith decided she would at least try and be civil to Maddie and Jack. She wouldn't go out of her way to contact them but she would stop calling the girl names.

Nonetheless, Edith was enraged when Siobhan and Charlie started planning a bridal shower. She refused to let them use her house, so the shower was held at Jack and Maddie's. The girls wanted it to be a surprise for Maddie so they enlisted Jack's help to keep her out of the house while they set it up.

# *CHAPTER 35*

Maddie and Jack's wedding day dawned bright and sunny. Maddie couldn't believe their luck. September days in Scotland were often cloudy and grey. Being very superstitious, Maddie believed the sun to be a good omen. Following the superstitious tradition of the groom not seeing the bride before the wedding she had asked Jack to spend the night before the wedding at Bob's. Unable to say 'no' to her, Jack had good-naturedly gone along with her request. The men would get ready for the wedding at Bob's and the ladies at Maddie's.

In their time together, Maddie had not slept alone except for the one tour Jack had gone on without her. It felt strange to wake up without him there. "Oh, well," she said to herself, "that changes for good today."

The day was spent with her bridesmaids, getting ready for the wedding at 3:00. The ladies had gathered at Maddie's at 9:00. A procession of groomers paraded in and out of the house, ending with the hairdresser and make-up artist. These last two were friends from backstage and would be at the wedding. The two flower girls were thrilled at being included in the activities with the ladies. They had never before had manicures or pedicures and considered themselves very grown up.

Maddie's floor-length dress was exquisite. It was white lace over white satin. The long sleeved bodice was body hugging and fit her slim figure like a second skin. The skirt was long and full and the lace over the satin made it look like she was surrounded by a cloud. Small pearls worked into the lace gave it an added dimension. It was slightly longer at the back so although it didn't have a train, it did trail slightly. The bridesmaids and flower girls were in dark green satin. Their dresses had form fitting bodices, long sleeves and long full skirts. They each wore the string of pearls Maddie had given them as wedding gifts.

By 2:00 they were all ready. Maddie took a mental inventory – something old, something new, something borrowed, something blue. The combs that tamed her mane of red-gold curls and held her veil in place had been found in an antique shop – definitely old. Jack had given her a gold locket as a wedding present, something new. She touched it and smiled. Beckie had loaned her a lace handkerchief that had belonged to her aunt and Maddie had on a blue garter, ready for Jack to remove at the reception. Satisfied she was ready, she sat down.

"We did it," she said to her bridesmaids, "with half an hour to spare."

The eight girls looked at her with big smiles. Beckie her best friend, Katie her oldest friend, Betty Bob's wife, Jeannie, Bob and Jack's sister and Jack's two daughters, Siobhan and Charlie. How lucky she was that they had all been able to come. Bob's and Jeannie's daughters were the flower girls and were very excited to have such important roles. Bob's son and Jeannie's younger son were page boys and were getting ready with the men. Jeannie's older son was a groomsman. It was a large wedding party, but Maddie had wanted a big wedding. She was only getting married once.

Beckie and Ben and Katie and Bill had flown in from Ottawa with Maddie's parents three days earlier. With all of them staying there, the house had been crowded, but everyone had been in great spirits, ready to celebrate. Auntie Joannie and several other of Maddie's relatives had arrived the following day and her aunts, uncles, cousins and grandmother been settled into a nearby hotel.

Maddie's parents had gone ahead to the church and Maddie and the bridesmaids and flower girls waited for the limos that would take them to the Auld Kirk of Ayr, and the man Maddie loved more than anything or anyone. As she walked out the door of the house, Maddie's jaw dropped. The two limos she had been expecting were, instead, two carriages each pulled by two white horses. Jack had changed the transportation arrangements without telling her. She was moved by his thoughtfulness, once again thinking how well he knew her. She was so lucky. He knew her that well and loved her anyway.

At the church, Maddie had a sudden attack of nerves and started to shake, a worried look on her face. She was sure of what she was doing, but was afraid something would go wrong with the day. She thought Edith might do something to try and spoil it. The door opened and she saw Jack, standing at the front of the church with his six groomsmen and two page boys all dressed in kilts and formal jackets. His expectant smile was all she needed. The shaking and the worried look were replaced by a huge smile. Nothing could spoil this day.

As the organ music soared in 'The Wedding March', the flower girls and bridesmaids started sedately down the aisle. Maddie wanted to push them out of the way and run to the front of the church. She managed to restrain herself, using her father's arm as an anchor. At the front of the church, Maddie's father handed her to Jack. This was it, a dream that she'd had for a lifetime was about to become a reality.

Jack could not believe how breathtakingly beautiful Maddie looked. He had seen her looking like she had stepped out of a painting, but today she looked like an angel coming for him. He thought his heart would burst. Electricity crackled between them when he took her small hand in his.

The traditional ceremony was beautiful. Maddie's parents 'gave' her to Jack. Not really expecting an answer, Maddie still held her breath when the pastor asked if anyone objected to the marriage. She half expected Edith to have snuck into the church to disrupt the wedding. Maddie heaved a sigh of relief when there was no reply. The pastor continued on to the part of the ceremony where she and Jack repeated their vows and pledged themselves to love, honour and be true to each other for the rest of their lives, and both said 'I do'. The bridesmaids, Maddie's mother, aunts, grandmother and Jack's mother, all had to dab the tears from their eyes. Maddie's eyes were bright with unshed tears of joy. Jack wondered if she was going to cry. Then he wondered if he was going to cry. Disaster was averted when the pastor pronounced them husband and wife and asked Jack to kiss his bride.

The pastor introduced them as Mr. and Mrs. Buchanan. There were broad smiles and an enthusiastic round of applause from the wedding guests. Mr. and Mrs. Buchanan walked down the aisle to the organist playing 'We've Only Just Begun'.

The next two hours were spent in a flurry of photographic activity. Maddie thought her favourite photo would be the one of her and Jack in the old cemetery – the end of life and the beginning of life. Her mother thought it was ghoulish.

The reception line and the meal passed in a blur for Jack and Maddie. They lost count of the number of times their guests clinked spoons to glasses, demanding they kiss. Everyone laughed when Jack kissed Beckie, the maid of honour and Maddie kissed Bob, the best man. They laughed even harder when Jack kissed the flower girls and Maddie kissed the pages. Following the meal, Maddie couldn't believe how many toasts, roasts and speeches there were. It felt as if everyone who knew them wanted to say something. Several Scottish entertainment friends of Jack's were there wanting to roast him. Among them was Billie Abbot, the comedian from 'A Taste of Scotland'. He regaled the guests with stories of the early days of Jack and Maddie's relationship and had them almost rolling on the floor laughing. They were all amazed that such a rocky beginning had such a happy ending.

Jack had chosen the music for the party. Although there was a live band, when they got up for the first dance, Maddie was touched to hear a tape of him singing 'Could I Have This Dance For The Rest Of My Life`. As they danced, he sang along in her ear. She joined him on the last chorus.

Before Maddie went to change out of her wedding dress, she threw her bouquet. It was caught by Jack's younger daughter, Charlie, who was all of fourteen. There was loud clapping and cheering when Jack removed Maddie's garter and threw it. Beckie was alarmed when Ben caught the garter, afraid it would upset their status quo.

When she went to change, Maddie was sorry the party was over. But then, she reasoned, an even bigger party was just beginning for her. She reappeared looking stunning in a bright green dress that exactly matched her eyes and a short hand-tailored jacket in the Buchanan tartan. Jack could hardly contain his delight. Jeannie smirked, remembering their trips to the tailor in Glasgow to have the jacket made. Maddie had had a very definite idea of what she wanted.

Jack announced their departure, but urged their guests to continue partying. The guests saw the newly-weds into the car and resumed partying as requested. Anticipating having a few drinks at the wedding, Jack had hired a car and driver and had made the arrangements for the honeymoon.

The car took the newly-weds to Glasgow for a two night stay in the bridal suite at the Glasgow Central Hotel. Maddie was surprised to see her parents had arranged for champagne in their room. Not being drinkers themselves, it surprised her they had thought of it. Following their stay in Glasgow Maddie and Jack spent two nights at the Balmoral Hotel in Edinburgh. Maddie thought she was really being spoiled. These were her two favourite hotels in the country. The highlight of the honeymoon for her was the trip on the Jacobite steam train across the Glenfinnan Viaduct. This was something she had wanted to do for a very long time and she was again moved by Jack's thoughtfulness.

Maddie and Jack had decided since they travelled so much they would like to spend some time at home. When they returned home, their houseguests had all moved into hotels. They had five days and four nights to themselves before heading out on the road again - this time to ten cities in the U.S. Two of those days they spent sightseeing with their visitors. Maddie's grandmother had been born in Scotland and wanted to see again her old home near Oban so one day they drove up the coast to Oban, checking out the tourist town of Largs as well. The other day they spent in Glasgow. The rest of the time Maddie and Jack spent alone with each other.

# *CHAPTER 36*

When she and Jack returned after a very pleasant and successful tour of the US, Maddie applied for UK citizenship. She wasn't keen to give up her Canadian citizenship, but they had all agreed travelling would be easier, especially in the Commonwealth countries, if they all had the same passports. She was also living, working and going to school in Scotland so it would eliminate the need to keep extending visas and the fear that they might not be extended.

Because she was applying for citizenship as the newly-wed wife of a citizen, there were a number of hoops Maddie had to jump through, one of which was three visits over six months from inspectors to assess the validity of the marriage. Too many couples had married just for citizenship rights and immigration was trying to plug the holes in the system. The visits were surprise visits and could be as early as tomorrow or as late as six months from now. The third visit would definitely be near the end of the six months, just to ensure the marriage was lasting. Maddie made a mental note to keep the house tidy. She elected to take the written test first, and surprised herself with a perfect score. Jack was not surprised.

Saturday was the St. Andrew's Ball and for once they weren't working and could enjoy the party as guests. With Bob and Betty and two other couples, Maddie and Jack made up a jolly table. As the evening progressed, the drinks flowed freely and although not rowdy, their table grew loud. Jack and Maddie spent most of the evening on the dance floor. Some of the guests watched their expert steps, but it was different than being on stage and they could snuggle and hold each other tight for the slow dances. As they came off the dance floor, at one point, Maddie noticed a woman that seemed to be watching them. Thinking it was just their high profiles, she thought nothing of it. A lot of women had crushes on Jack.

The woman was watching them closely, particularly Maddie and her interactions with the others. She was charmed by the affectionate gestures Maddie and Jack made on the dance floor: the kisses after each dance, the way they looked at each other, how they held each other, especially for the slow dances. She wasn't sure, but she thought Jack was singing some of the love songs in Maddie's ear.

In the powder room Betty and Maddie were trying to tame their hair. Betty's straight, blonde hair was short and easier to manage than Maddie's long red-gold curls. The woman who had been watching them walked into the powder room. Seeing her opportunity she walked over to Maddie.

"Aren't you, Mrs. Buchanan?" Maddie replied in the affirmative and the woman continued. "I've been watching you and your husband dance. You make a lovely couple and you dance beautifully together." Slightly embarrassed, Maddie thanked the woman; then she and Betty went back to their table.

"That was odd," Maddie said as they took their seats. Overhearing, Jack asked her what was odd. She explained what had just happened. His reply was to tell her they should give the woman something more to watch and he led her onto the dance floor.

The woman from the powder room smiled to herself. She had a job to do and this was going to be so easy.

Knowing none of them would be in any condition to drive home that night, Bob and Jack had booked rooms at the hotel where the party was. Watching Maddie and Jack board the lift, arms around each other, as she left, the woman smiled to herself again. This job was going to be a pleasure.

# *CHAPTER 37*

Three days later, Jack woke to the sound of Maddie moaning in her sleep. He woke her gently to find the cause of the problem. She squinted at him through pain filled eyes.

"My head. I think it's going to explode."

"I'll call 999." He reached for the phone.

"No. Please just get me some painkillers. I think I still have some of those ones with codeine left… and my wintergreen oil." Her voice sounded weak and faraway.

Jack hesitated. He really did want to call 999, but went instead to get the tablets and the oil. He returned with a glass of water in one hand and the bottles in the other. Maddie struggled to sit up, pain whitening her already pale features. She looked like a ghost. She took two of the pain tablets and rubbed oil on her forehead, her temples and behind her ears. She sank back onto the pillows exhausted. Jack wondered about the oil, but Maddie had great faith in the natural healing powers of oils, and he was all for anything that would ease her pain.

Jack returned to bed and took her in his arms. She was almost asleep, or unconscious, he couldn't tell which. "You tell me if it gets any worse."

She grunted acquiescence. Jack looked at the clock – 5:03. Unable to sleep, he watched Maddie as she slept; an uneasy sleep punctuated by moans. She woke again about 7:00. The pain had eased somewhat and her voice was stronger. She rubbed on more wintergreen oil and lay back again.

"I'm supposed to get my hair cut at 9:30," Jack said. "I'll call and change it to tomorrow."

"Don't be silly. I'll be fine. It's not as bad now and I'm just going back to sleep." She managed a weak smile. He looked uncertain. "Please," she said. "I really am just going back to sleep."

Her voice sounded stronger, so he reluctantly agreed. He couldn't seem to say 'no' to her for anything.

Downstairs making his breakfast, Jack debated taking Maddie a cup of tea or coffee. Like the other Canadians he knew, her day couldn't start without coffee. She loved it when he brought her coffee in bed but if she wasn't feeling well maybe she'd rather have tea. Finally deciding not to disturb her, he sat and flipped through the newspaper as he ate.

At 9:00 Jack quietly let himself out the front door. Quiet as he was, Maddie heard the door close. She sat up in bed. *My head is almost back to normal*, she thought as she rubbed on more wintergreen. She got up slowly, feeling a little off balance. *Must be the codeine,* she thought. She straightened the bed and pulled on jeans and a loose shirt.

By the time she got downstairs, she felt almost human again. She made herself coffee and went into the sitting room, turning on the record player. The sound of Bach's 'Sheep May Safely Graze' played just on strings filled the room. It was her favourite piece of music ever written. Sitting on the settee, she pulled out a bag that was beside it. Taking the contents out of the bag and spreading them on the coffee table, she sorted then surveyed her handiwork. The church was having a 'bring and buy' on Saturday and she had made several doll outfits, towels with crocheted tops and miniature needlepoint houses. There were a couple of things that needed finishing. She glanced at the sewing machine she had borrowed from Betty. It was sitting on the table with a couple of completed doll outfits and several more partly done ones. Overall she was satisfied with her work. She would finish as many as she could, but she already had a sizable donation ready so if she didn't get any more done, she would finish them for the next sale. The church ladies would be pleasantly surprised.

Maddie was seriously considering working on finishing one of the doll outfits when the phone rang. Saved by the bell, she answered on the second ring. Jack's concerned voice said, "I didn't wake you did I?"

"No, luv. I'm up, dressed and downstairs."

"Is the heid any better?"

"Almost back to what passes for normal."

He chuckled sounding relieved. "I'll be home in half an hour," he said.

Maddie had no sooner rung off than the doorbell sounded. She opened the door to a woman and a man in business suits and overcoats.

"Good morning," she said.

The woman spoke. "Good morning, Mrs. Buchanan."

Maddie looked at the woman. She was wrapping her still foggy mind around trying to remember where she had met the woman. "We've met haven't we? You look awfully familiar." When the woman answered with the explanation of meeting her at the St. Andrew's Ball, Maddie remembered the woman who had been watching them. "Of course. You look very different in business clothes."

"I'm Siobhan Bourke, this is John Sutherland. We're with the Immigration Review Board. I believe the Citizenship Office told you we'd be calling?"

"Yes they did. Please come in. My husband is out right now but he should be home in about half an hour."

"That's fine," said Ms. Bourke. "With these surprise visits we really have to take our chances."

Maddie took their coats and ushered them into the sitting room, forgetting she had left a mess on the table. *Oh, well,* she thought, *surprise me and you get what you see.* Noticing the small clothes on the table Mr. Sutherland asked Maddie if they were expecting a child. Nonplussed Maddie said, "No. Oh the clothes. Those are doll clothes I made for the church 'bring and buy' on Saturday."

Ms. Bourke had thought they looked too small for a baby. Sitting down, they both pulled files out of their briefcases. Mr. Sutherland opened his and made a note. 'Participation in community groups and events'.

A little uncomfortable with the note taking, Maddie offered them a tour of the house. "That would be great. We have a list of standard topics we have to deal with and that is on our list." Ms. Bourke seemed to be the spokesperson.

The ground floor consisted of the sitting room, kitchen, dining room and parlour. There was a small powder room and a laundry room off the kitchen. Upstairs the doors were all open but one.

"Our bedroom, Jack's office, my office, bathroom." Maddie took a deep breath as they approached the closed door. "Please excuse the mess in the spare room. We're off on tour Monday and we're trying to get our costumes organized." She opened the door. There were two suitcases open and partially packed on the bed, several garment bags hanging up and a sea of different tartans in every available space. Ms. Bourke made a mental note to herself. *They obviously do things together and there is only one useable bedroom.*

Once they had settled back in the sitting room, Maddie offered tea or coffee. Ms. Bourke smiled. "I understand Canadians make very good coffee."

"No pressure," Maddie said good-naturedly, going into the kitchen.

While Maddie was in the kitchen Ms. Bourke said in a low voice to Mr. Sutherland, "Their home is beautiful. It's cozy, well decorated and smells like wintergreen." Mr. Sutherland agreed – bonus points for the Buchanans. The office was always suspicious when there was a big age difference between husband and wife.

When Maddie returned from the kitchen, Mr. Sutherland was studying the framed photos that covered the walls. "It'll be coffee in five. Those are Jack's trophy walls. I'm in a few of the later ones." There was a framed wedding picture sitting on the piano. Mr. Sutherland thought it odd that the picture had been taken in a cemetery. "I see you're looking at the wedding picture," Maddie said. "To us it represents the end of one life and the beginning of another." Maddie pointed out a picture of the handfasting, also framed, sitting on a small table near the piano. "And you see this photo? We handfasted on a cruise last December." Ms. Bourke and Mr. Sutherland both looked confused. Maddie explained handfasting was a traditional form of marriage generations ago when there wasn't always a pastor available to perform a wedding. Ms. Bourke made notes in her file. In the minds of the Buchanans they had already been married for nearly a year.

"You don't sound like a Canadian," Ms. Bourke said.

Laughing, Maddie replied, "Jack has corrupted my lack of accent."

Maddie's face lit up when she heard the front door open. Jack's voice filtered down the hall. "Want to run your fingers through my short straight hair, or my long curly ones?" Maddie blushed and laughed as she headed towards the door.

"Feeling better? I brought something to cheer you up."

"Mind your manners," she said as he hung up his coat. "We have guests."

"Did I embarrass myself?"

"I'd say."

"This help?" he asked as he handed her a bouquet of her favourite red and white carnations and a single red rose.

"Aw, thank you, sweetheart. They're beautiful." She kissed him then led him into the sitting room and introduced him to their guests. He mentally kicked himself for the comment about the hair.

"I'll just put these in some water and get the coffee."

"I'll do it," Jack said.

Maddie hesitated. "You can help. You suck at flower arranging."

"You are feeling better."

She grinned at him. Coffee and biscuits served, they settled down for a chat.

"Are you not well?" Ms. Bourke asked Maddie.

"I woke up with a vicious headache."

Jack chimed in, "But then I went out."

Maddie looked at him, bantering back, "I've called you a lot of things, luv, but never a vicious headache."

They all laughed. By the end of the interview they were on a first name basis.

Just before Siobhan and John left, Maddie asked if they had ever seen the show. "We're doing dinner theatre tonight and I have a couple of promo tickets if you'd like to come?"

Jack looked alarmed. "You're not dancing tonight."

"I'm fine and I am."

"I've already told Bob we were on our own tonight."

"You'll just have to untell him."

"Only if you promise to lie down all afternoon."

"Deal."

Siobhan and John left with tickets in hand. As they walked down the path Siobhan said, "What a nice couple. That's a real marriage if I've ever seen one. Did you see how her face lit up when he came home? And he brought her flowers. It's too bad we have to bother them with two more interviews."

John agreed. "I hope the office doesn't consider these tickets a bribe."

"All part of the job," Siobhan said. "We see them at home, we see them at work and I saw them at play. We have to assess their interaction." She had told him about the St. Andrew's Ball and he agreed it was too bad they had to pester them, but he had really enjoyed the interview and was looking forward to the next one. They rarely had such a pleasant time working. Most of the people they visited were openly hostile.

Siobhan and John loved the show. Afterwards they went backstage to talk to Jack and Maddie. "You looked like you were having so much fun," John said.

"We were. If you do what you love you'll never work. It'll always be playtime," Maddie told him.

Bob came over and introductions were made.

After they left, Jack told Bob who Siobhan and John were. "Are ye's off yer heids?" he asked. "Fraternizing with the enemy."

"They're not the enemy. They just have a job to do and we have nothing to hide. Besides, we just scored major brownie points."

Bob still had a little trouble with some of Maddie's expressions. He thought about that one then had to agree.

# *CHAPTER 38*

Jack and Maddie had been home from Australia for two days, when the doorbell rang. Siobhan and John were standing on the doorstep. Opening the door, Maddie said, "Oh dear, we have a mess in the spare room again."

"That's not a problem," Siobhan said laughing. "We know what to expect."

Jack had been playing the piano in the sitting room and hadn't heard the doorbell. At the sound of voices he stopped. He was expecting Bob. They were working on a new song and he was anxious to get at it.

Maddie escorted Siobhan and John into the sitting room. Disappointed it wasn't Bob, Jack was nonetheless pleased to see them. The sooner they got these interviews over with, the sooner Maddie would get her citizenship and new passport. Openly affectionate with each other, he had no doubt she would pass all the tests. The previous interview had gone well and she had already aced the written test.

This time it was Jack who took Siobhan and John on the house tour. It was a bit more chaotic than the last time they had been there. Siobhan noted the washing machine was going full speed and there were piles of sorted laundry lined up on the floor – a perfectly normal day in anyone's life. All the better for their report. There was no question in her mind that as soon as the last interview was done, Maddie would be a UK citizen.

The second interview consisted of a few more personal questions. "Do you plan on having children?" asked John.

Maddie answered, "Yes, but we're going to wait a few years. As soon as we get pregnant I'm out of a job."

John noted the use of 'we' rather than 'I'.

Jack added, "But if it happens sooner that's good too."

John wished they could do the third interview later this week just to speed up the process, but the rules said the third interview was near the end of the six months. He really liked this couple and they were obviously in love with each other. He hated intruding in their lives this way.

At that point the doorbell rang and Bob walked in, accordion in hand. After a quick peck on Maddie's cheek, he asked if he was interrupting. Assured by Siobhan and John that he was welcome, he sat down with them. Siobhan had noticed Maddie's closeness with Jack's family at the St. Andrew's Ball, and nothing she saw now made her change her mind. Everything she was seeing made her as reluctant as John to have to do a third interview, although she did enjoy the company.

This time, at the conclusion of the interview, Bob offered Siobhan and John promo tickets. They were happy to accept. Betty was at the show that night and Siobhan and John were once again impressed by Maddie's interaction with Jack's family.

# *CHAPTER 39*

On Friday morning Maddie sagged against the bathroom sink trying not to throw up. Concerned at her quick departure from the bed, Jack had followed her into the en-suite bathroom. "Are you okay?" he asked the green face looking at him. She hadn't had anything to drink the previous night, so it wasn't a hangover. She swallowed hard several times. He rubbed her back saying, "Just let it out. You'll feel better."

"I hate throwing up," Maddie said, swallowing hard. The green was starting to fade from her face. This was the fourth morning in a row. Jack hadn't been aware of the other three mornings but she didn't think she could continue to hide it from him. She leaned her back against the wall and slid down till she was sitting on the floor. Jack got her a glass of water and sat down beside her.

"We need to talk," she said to him. Jack did a double take. That was usually his line and heralded a life-changing event. She continued, "This isn't how I planned to tell you, but I think I'm pregnant," was her unexpected statement.

"Are you sure?"

"No, but I think it's a pretty safe bet." She swallowed hard again. "I have one of those home pregnancy tests. I was going to use it this morning."

"Break it out," Jack said barely able to contain his excitement.

Maddie swallowed hard once more and pointed to the medicine cabinet.

Jack whooped for joy when the test showed positive. Maddie was grinning from ear to ear. "I don't believe it. We're going to have a baby." Jack thought his heart would burst. This woman he loved more than anything was going to have his child – and she was happy about it. He hoped it would be a girl who looked just like her mother.

Scooping her up in his arms, Jack took Maddie back to bed. "You need to rest."

"I'm fine," she said, kissing him. "You can't keep me in a cocoon for nine months."

Jack got back into bed and took Maddie in his arms. They lay together grinning at each other for a long time then Jack said, "You stay here. I'm going to bring you breakfast in bed. Do you want coffee or tea?"

Later that morning, Jack rang Bob. "We're going to have to change the programme," he said without any preamble.

Bob, just barely awake, asked, "What are ye on aboot?"

"We're going to have a baby. Maddie's pregnant. We're going to have a baby." Jack repeated himself, hardly able to contain his glee. She had told him and now he had told someone else. That made it real. He thought life couldn't get any better.

Bob wanted to talk to Maddie and overhearing the conversation, Betty wanted to talk to her too. By the end of the conversation they had made plans for dinner and a celebration that night at Bob and Betty's.

At Bob and Betty's they discussed the upcoming tour, Maddie insistent that she could still work, Jack equally insistent she shouldn't. Bob weighed in on Jack's side and Betty on Maddie's. Eventually it was agreed that Maddie's doctor would make the final decision.

# *CHAPTER 40*

Cleared by her doctor to go on tour Maddie was determined to make the most of this trip to Canada, thinking it might be the last in a series she had come to love. Jack was keeping a close eye on her. He was still trying to talk her out of the tour, despite her doctor's approval. It seemed to him Dr. Carson didn't understand the nature of Maddie's dancing and just how much energy it took. Add to that, Maddie was sick every morning. Admittedly, by breakfast time she was herself again and able to eat a hearty breakfast, but he still didn't like the idea of her dancing. He had no issue with her going on the tour; in fact he wanted her to. He just thought the highland dancing was too much.

Maddie was looking forward to the tour. It was a tour of Canada and after the last show, she and Jack were going to spend a few days in Ottawa with Beckie and Ben at the farm. Maddie had already told Beckie she was pregnant, but was looking forward to surprising everyone else with their news. With both her mother's and father's sides of the family, the group was too big for anyone's house so to accommodate the whole group they rented the party room at Maddie's favourite restaurant. Jack made the announcement. Maddie's family, happy to see her anyway, was thrilled with the grand announcement.

Jack insisted on another tour of Ottawa given by the locals. This time they went to the experimental farm green houses, the Natural History Museum and walked through the Byward Market. They also took a drive through Gatineau Park, but, it being winter, Maddie thought the park looked pretty bleak. She told Jack they would come back sometime in the summer or fall and he could see the real beauty of the park. He was still impressed with the park's deep snow covering and the odd shaped icicles hanging from everything.

They had had twelve shows in three weeks and with time changes, jet lag, sightseeing and visiting, by the time Maddie and Jack got home Maddie was exhausted. She spent two days in bed and another two relaxing on the settee. They had two weeks off, then an eight day tour of Ireland and three mini tours in Scotland. With Dr. Carson's help, Maddie had convinced Jack she was able to dance her full programme on all of these tours. As a compromise, she had promised after the last one there would be no more highland dancing. She would continue to sing and dance with Jack until she felt too awkward to dance gracefully.

# *CHAPTER 41*

On a Sunday morning six weeks later, Maddie woke Jack. Her beautiful face was etched with pain. “Something’s wrong,” she said.

Jack jumped out of bed and pulled on some clothes. He scooped her up and carried her to the car, with her protesting she could walk. It was 4:00am and there was no traffic. They made it to the hospital in less than six minutes. Despite wanting to carry her in, Jack let her walk but slipped her into the first empty wheelchair he saw. She didn’t argue. Her beautiful face was contorted by pain and misery.

When Jack explained what was happening, the triage nurse sent them into an exam room right away. Maddie had just lain down on the bed when a doctor came in. He examined her, his face serious, then regretful.

“There are very few options we have. You’re in premature labour, something we don’t normally see until six or seven months. At just five months I’m not optimistic about the success of our intervention. All we can hope to do is stop the contractions. The baby isn’t viable at this stage.”

Jack looked at Maddie’s face. The pain he saw there was not physical. “We’ll try whatever we can,” he said.

After saying, “The nurse will be in with an antispasmodic injection,” the doctor left the room.

Following the shot, Jack sat holding Maddie’s hand while she dozed. About 11:00 she woke up crying. “Oh God, Jack. It hurts so much.”

He was alarmed to see the blanket covering her turning red as it soaked up her blood. She was haemorrhaging.

“I’m sorry,” the doctor said. “There isn’t anything more we can do. The baby isn’t going to make it.”

Tears leaked out of Maddie’s eyes. Jack’s heart broke for her and for himself too. They had so been looking forward to this baby they had already started throwing names at each other.

The decision was made to let the baby expel itself naturally, supposedly that being the least invasive option and the most likely way to avoid further haemorrhaging. As Jack held Maddie's hand, he questioned the wisdom of that decision. She had already lost so much blood they'd had to give her three units and she was so tired.

It was finally over. Maddie wanted to hold the baby. It was a boy and he was so tiny. He took his last breath lying on Maddie's chest, with Jack's hand cradling his back.

Through tears Maddie said, "We have to have a funeral for him."

Jack knew it would be hard on both of them, but he did agree with her. This baby had already become a part of their lives. While the nurses cleaned Maddie up and made her comfortable, Jack sat in the waiting room trying not to cry.

Eventually the doctor came in to tell Jack they were going to keep Maddie overnight. She had lost so much blood and her blood pressure was very low. They had settled her in a private room. When he walked in quietly she appeared to be asleep. Even in her sleep he thought her tired face was beautiful and his heart ached for her. By the time he reached the bed her eyes were open and tear filled. She reached for him and he sat on the side of the bed, holding her tight, stroking her hair while she cried. He cried too, but didn't let her see that. She cried for what seemed a long time, then started apologizing to him as if it were her fault. He repeatedly reassured her it wasn't and they would get through their loss together.

Jack stayed at the hospital with Maddie that night till the nurses kicked him out. He didn't want to leave her but they insisted. He found the house empty without her. He realized it was the first time since they'd been together that he had slept alone in the house. He didn't get much sleep.

The next morning Jack was at the hospital early. If Maddie was okay, she would be discharged today. He didn't want her to have to wait for him. He also couldn't bear the thought they'd have to keep her another night. She was very teary that morning, but they were both relieved the doctor said she could go home as long as she rested. If she started to haemorrhage again she was to come right back to the hospital.

Maddie's idea of resting was planning the funeral for the little boy who never had a chance at life. They named him James Edward in honour of both grandfathers. Tuesday morning Maddie and Jack met with the funeral director. He was very sympathetic and helpful, but picking out a tiny casket was almost more than they could bear. The director left them alone for a few minutes to comfort each other and regain their composure. They chose a tiny white coffin with blue satin lining then returned to the director's office.

The plan for the actual funeral was simple. It would be on Thursday at the Auld Kirk of Ayr. There would be a short visitation before the service and a reception after. Their own pastor would officiate. He would say a few words of comfort, but there would be no eulogy. The hymns chosen were children's hymns, ones Maddie and Jack remembered from Sunday school. 'Jesus Loves Me' Maddie thought was particularly appropriate.

The service was short and somber, followed by interment in the kirkyard. Maddie thought the weather was appropriate for a funeral. It was a cold, damp, windy day that matched her mood. As the tiny casket was lowered into the ground, Maddie sagged against Jack. The heavens opened and the rain came down.

At the reception afterwards, Maddie and Jack both had difficulty accepting the condolences that were offered. The pain was still too fresh for them to talk about. Bob, Betty, Siobhan and Charlie all did their best to keep the conversations neutral, but by the time Jack and Maddie got home, they were completely drained of energy and emotion. They sat together on the settee, not speaking, both lost in their own thoughts. They had both been surprised by the large number of people who attended the funeral and felt blessed to have so many good friends.

# *CHAPTER 42*

The following morning Jack felt Maddie slip out of bed and heard her go into the bathroom. A few minutes later she called to him, "Jack can you help me please." He went into the bathroom, to find her sitting on the floor. She was very pale. "My legs don't seem to want to support me. Can you help me back to bed?"

Jack scooped her up and carried her back. As he deposited her on the bed he said, "You're awfully pale. Is there something wrong?"

Maddie hesitated. "There's a lot of blood," she said.

"We're going straight to the hospital," he said pulling on his clothes.

At the hospital they saw the same doctor they had seen before. The doctor confirmed Maddie had been hemorrhaging again. She felt threatened when he said they might have to keep her in hospital for a couple of days. "Please don't make me stay," Maddie pleaded. Jack explained the exceptional circumstances and stresses of the previous three days. Maddie swore up and down she would stay in bed if the doctor let her go home. He agreed, but said if she had to return they would have to keep her. If they couldn't stop the hemorrhaging they would have to do a hysterectomy.

When they returned home, Jack put Maddie to bed. As he pulled the duvet up and tucked it around her, he asked if there was anything he could get or do for her.

"Are you really busy right now?" she asked him.

"No, luv. What can I do for you?"

"Would you just lie with me and hold me for a few minutes?"

Jack lay on the bed and folded Maddie in his arms. "We'll get through this together," he said.

"It's just so hard. Life is so unfair. The poor little man never had a chance." She wiped a tear from her eye.

Jack hugged her a little tighter. "We've got each other and together we'll get through it. There was a reason this was meant to happen." Maddie shifted in his arms and Jack asked, "Are you in pain?"

"No, I'm just so tired."

"Close your eyes. I'll stay with you till you're asleep." He kissed her forehead and they lay together not saying anything. He felt Maddie's body relax gradually as she fell asleep. He lay there thinking for a few minutes, then carefully disengaged from her and got up without waking her.

The doctor's threat to keep Maddie in the hospital and the fear of a hysterectomy were enough to keep her in bed for the weekend. Jack was concerned that he and Bob had dinner theatre gigs Friday and Saturday nights and wanted to cancel them. Maddie had to work hard to convince him she would be fine and she would stay in bed. Each night he called her before the show, during intermission and after the show. Because she was in bed all the time, Maddie was sleeping at odd hours and when Jack came home from the shows he brought take away, so they had dinner at midnight. Jack was looking after Maddie and bringing her meals, but he was the first to admit he wasn't a great cook. He did, however, excel at take away. He knew all the best places.

Monday morning dawned cold and grey. Maddie, tired of spending her days in bed, had joined Jack in the sitting room. She lay on the settee. With a fire burning in the grate, the room was cozy and warm, but Maddie had a blanket over her anyway. Jack had just finished reading the newspaper and was wondering whether Maddie would be comforted or disturbed by him playing the piano. He had made her favourite breakfast, cinnamon waffles and bacon, and although she had tried, she hadn't been able to do much more than pick at it. For the last week all she had done was pick at her food. His heart was aching for her and he didn't know how to help. He too felt the sorrow of their loss, but it seemed to hit her harder.

Jack knew Maddie wasn't reading the book she had in front of her; she hadn't turned a page in the whole time he'd been reading the news. Unsure whether it would make her feel better, worse or indifferent, he decided he would play the piano for a bit. If he played what she called 'happy music' it might cheer her up.

This decided, Jack had just sat down at the piano when the doorbell rang. Siobhan and John were standing on the doorstep.

*Great*, he thought. *This is just what we need today.* Nonetheless he put on his charming smile and invited them in.

"I'm sorry we have to bother you again," said Siobhan, "but this is the last interview then your wife becomes a citizen. She's met all the other requirements."

Jack wondered if Maddie would be pleased enough about that to smile. She hadn't smiled since the previous Sunday, no make that the Saturday night. It had been a hard week. When he had tried to be strong for her, she had thought he didn't care about Jamie. He'd wrapped her in his arms and said, "I am sad about him, but I'm sadder to see you hurting so badly." After that they had both cried for the child that might have been. There had been a lot of tears this week. Maybe visitors were what they both needed.

At the sound of voices, Maddie had put her book down. As they entered the sitting room she was folding the blanket she had been huddling under. Jack was always amazed at the way she could compartmentalize her emotions and put on a happy face. He knew it cost her a lot of energy and he was thankful she didn't feel she had to do that around him. He loved the way she was so open with him about her real feelings even when she was sad, although he hated to see her sad.

The interview began as the previous two had, with a tour of the house. This time the spare room door was open and the room was tidy. After the short tour they sat down to talk. As the questions turned to those of family and children, Maddie excused herself and ran to the kitchen. Jack excused himself and went after her. She was holding tight to the edge of the sink, tears coursing down her cheeks. He put his arms around her from behind and rested his chin on her shoulder.

"Why don't you go upstairs and lie down? I can finish the interview."

She looked at him with pain filled eyes. "Thank you, luv, but I'm okay. Just give me a minute to pull myself together. I'll make some coffee."

"You don't have to you know."

"I know, but it's time I put on my big girl panties and get back to life." Sometimes she still came out with expressions he had to think about. He looked doubtful but she continued. "Seriously I'm okay. Just give me a few minutes. But you could tell them what happened."

Taking Maddie at her word, Jack returned to their guests. He told them the sad story and they expressed their regret at having poked such a raw wound, offering to finish the interview another day. By the time they had offered, Maddie had returned from the kitchen, a tray of coffee and biscuits in hand. Although her eyes were red, she was composed. When John started to express condolences, she shook her head indicating that part of the conversation was over.

The rest of the interview went well. They had tonight and tomorrow night off, so Maddie offered them promo tickets for Wednesday's show. Jack looked alarmed when she said that and when she left the room to get the tickets he followed her.

"You won't be there," he stated.

"Yes I will."

"You're supposed to be resting."

"I need to do this, Jack. I've been moping around the house for three days. I need to get out."

"I can take you out."

"No. I need to work. I need to know there is something I can actually do right."

Jack looked pained by her words. "Maybe just one number. We'll see."

Although not meaning to eavesdrop Siobhan and John heard this exchange. When Maddie and Jack came back into the room, Siobhan said to Maddie, "I don't know if this will make you feel any better, but congratulations, you've exceeded expectations for all our interviews. We'll do the paperwork this afternoon and tomorrow you can apply for a UK passport."

Walking down the path a little later Siobhan said quietly to John, "Big as he is and small as she is, she's obviously not afraid to stand up to him."

John added, "And she has him wrapped around her little finger. She always gets her way."

Before the show Wednesday night, Bob too expressed concern about Maddie dancing. They finally all agreed she would limit her part in the show to waltzing with Jack and singing their duet. After the show, for the first time since Maddie had started working with the boys, she was too tired to join them for supper, suggesting she go home and Jack go out. He refused and took her home. He helped her get ready for bed and she was asleep before her head hit the pillow.

The rest of the week, Maddie spent her days in bed so she could work the shows. By Saturday, she was able to both dance all but the highland dances and go for supper afterwards.

# *CHAPTER 43*

Two weeks later they left on a tour of Australia and New Zealand. Jack had been reluctant about Maddie's going, but as he had discovered over the time they'd been together, she could be very persuasive/stubborn. Neither of them wanted to be apart for three weeks, but he thought Maddie was pushing herself too hard. He would have been happy if she had just come for the trip and maybe danced with him, but he was worried about the highland dancing. She still wasn't herself.

Walking on the beach one afternoon in Darwin, they encountered a woman with a baby in a pushchair. Maddie admired the baby and stopped to chat with the woman. After they walked away, Maddie dissolved in tears. She should still have been pregnant. Jack's heart ached for her. Leading her to some beach chairs, they sat down.

Jack said, "We need to talk."

Maddie just looked at him through teary eyes. "Oh no," she said. "Every time you say that we have a life changing event."

"But they've all been good ones," he said, thinking back. "I asked to you sing and dance with us and that worked out well. I asked you to move in with me and that was good. I asked you to come on tour with us and that worked. I asked you to marry me, and that was the best. I'm batting 1000," he said using one of her expressions.

She smiled. "Okay, what is the grand idea this time?"

"I think we should try again for a baby."

A look of panic, followed by pain, washed across her perfect face. "Jack, I can't."

"I don't mean right away. Your body is still recovering, but maybe in a couple of months or so."

She liked the idea, but fear gripped her. She questioned her ability to carry a child to term and couldn't face the alternative. She didn't think she could survive another miscarriage. Her body was still recovering, and she wasn't sure she could ride the emotional roller coaster again without losing her mind. "I really don't know."

Understanding her perfectly, he said, "Just think about it. We planned on having children in a few years. This is just advancing the schedule. Together we can do it."

Maddie was quiet on the way back to the hotel. She was thinking hard about what Jack had said. She was thinking about another life changing event. The pregnancy and loss of Jamie had been a life changing event, and not a good one. She wavered between fear and hope. Jack's faith in her ability to have his child touched her. Maybe they should try again. As had become the pattern, he didn't want an answer right away. She had some soul-searching to do.

For the rest of the tour, Maddie rode the emotional roller coaster. Her hormones hadn't yet returned to normal and now she had Jack's proposition to consider. She wavered from fear to hope, longing to doubt. One day it would seem like the best idea she had ever heard. The next day even the thought of it reduced her to a blubbering mess. Jack was thinking he shouldn't have said anything so soon.

Maddie tried to remember if she had ever said no to one of Jack's 'we need to talk' speeches. She couldn't remember turning down any of his ideas, and they had all worked out well. She just didn't know what to do. She knew Jack wanted a child and she wanted to give him one, but questioned her ability.

On the plane on the way home from Sydney, Jack turned to Maddie and said, "There's something we need to talk about." Maddie looked trapped. "No," he said. "Not that. Not yet. I'm thinking we should take a little holiday, just the two of us. We haven't ever had a real holiday other than our honeymoon. Think of it. You, me and a romantic little inn in the country. We just need to decide when and where."

She loved the idea and they spent most of the flight trying to decide where to go.

When they got home, Maddie and Jack found John had booked several 'mini tours' for them in Scotland and northern England. He had also firmed up their tentative plans to revive 'A Taste of Scotland', in conjunction with STV.

Their holiday plans were shelved for later.

# *CHAPTER 44*

With her current paying job, Maddie was no longer eligible for the amateur dancing competitions that had meant so much to her. At the age of eighteen, she had retired from the competitions while she was still on top, but she was happy to coach young aspiring dancers. Due to her touring schedule, she wasn't able to teach highland dancing regularly, but when home she often helped out Mrs. Williams with her local dance school. The girls were delighted to be taught by the only ever four-time World Champion Highland Dancer.

With the revival of 'A Taste of Scotland', Maddie was looking for four, or maybe five young dancers. The TV film was going to be taped in front of a live audience, so they needed to be step perfect. She had a large pool to select her dancers from and it wasn't easy to choose. She elected to go with five dancers this time, wanting as many of the girls as possible to have that experience. She was in a quandary over how to eliminate some of the candidates. They were all good dancers and working so hard. Discussing her dilemma with Jack, he suggested having each girl do one dance. With three dances, instead of just having five dancers, she could use five different ones for each dance, meaning fifteen of the girls would have the chance to participate. Maddie loved the idea. By doing this she would be able to use all of the older girls and there would be no hurt feelings.

Despite the show being taped in Glasgow, Maddie was using her local girls from Prestwick. She knew their strengths and weaknesses, making it easy for her to slot them into the dance they would be best at. They could work out transportation later.

The girls were thrilled to be dancing on TV. While Maddie was away on tour, Mrs. Williams worked them hard. Back from the tour, Maddie was impressed with their progress. She wanted them to perform well, not just for the show, but for their own self confidence. Some of them were going to competitions and she wanted them to have all the advantages available to them. The competitions were stressful but the show would help them learn to manage their stress levels. After performing on TV and in front of a live audience, a few judges would be nothing.

On the day of the taping the girls were all nervous. Maddie had arranged for the pipers to come in early to put the girls through their paces. The first attempt was less than successful, but by the time they had all done their dances twice more the girls were more comfortable and performing at their best.

Maddie herself was a bit nervous. This was the first time she had been responsible for a whole segment of a programme and she wanted it to go well. She needn't have worried. Step-perfect, the girls even looked like they were enjoying themselves. Maddie relaxed and enjoyed dancing with them. The taping went well. Billie Abbot was again the comedian working with them. Maddie still found him funny but crude. And of course Bob and Jack were their usual energetic selves, interacting with the audience and having them sing and clap along. The show was almost identical to the ones they had done before. Maddie still thought Jack in a kilt was the sexiest thing she had ever seen.

The show was taped in the afternoon and they had arranged a cast party for suppertime. The young dancers were a bit intimidated by the legendary Bob and Jack, but got on well with the pipers. It made Maddie think back to all those years ago when she too had been intimidated by Jack. She marvelled at how much things had changed.

# *CHAPTER 45*

Finally, after the taping the group had some time off. Maddie and Jack dusted off their holiday plan and checked into a romantic little inn in the Highlands. The White Stag Inn was just perfect. It stood by itself in a small glen and was decorated as a hunting lodge. Maddie was not impressed by the antlers on the walls of all the common rooms, but they didn't spend much time in those rooms. They spent their days exploring, hill walking and fishing. One day they even caught fish that the kitchen staff at the inn cooked for their supper. They spent their nights making love.

On the last night of their holiday Maddie said to Jack, "We need to talk." Both of them were nervous when the other used that expression, especially Jack. That was usually his statement.

Before she could change her mind, Maddie continued. "I've been thinking and you're right." Really confused, Jack waited for her to elaborate. "We should try again to have a baby."

Caught totally off-guard, Jack just sat there for a minute then his whole face lit up. "Are you sure?"

"I'm sure."

"Absolutely sure?"

"Absolutely sure."

They realized at the same time that this was the very same interchange they'd had the first time they had made love. They both smiled at the memory.

Jack took her in his arms and kissed her. "How did I get so lucky? I must have been really good in a previous life."

Their lovemaking that night was sweet and tender. He paused before entering her, rubbing against her entrance and making her gasp in pleasure. Then he entered her slowly, maddeningly slowly. With each long, slow stroke he withdrew driving her rapidly to the edge. She was moaning and repeating his name over and over. When the wave of pleasure hit her it rippled through her, each ripple gaining strength until a final wave shook her to the core. Her rhythmically clamping muscles milked Jack until the wave took him too and he collapsed beside her, both of them fighting for breath.

The following morning, they were both reluctant to leave but their agent, John, had been working hard and they had a full schedule ahead of them.

# *CHAPTER 46*

Hitting the road again, Jack was concerned for Maddie. They had been working hard on getting her pregnant and once it happened he didn't want her to exert herself. Knowing this and agreeing, Maddie put her whole being into every performance, not knowing which one would be her last. She really enjoyed performing and would hate giving it up, but the alternative was even better. Doubts of her ability to have a child still washed over her periodically, but she had made a promise to Jack and she was going to do her very best to keep it.

Although not saying anything to each other, Jack and Maddie were both beginning to worry. The first pregnancy had happened accidentally. This time, despite trying nearly every night, it wasn't happening. Not for the first time each of them wondered to themselves if it was going to be possible. As the months went by with no sign of a baby, they each began to question their own abilities, blaming themselves and not each other for their lack of success. For Maddie, it was a double-edged sword. She desperately wanted Jack's child, but she also wanted to continue performing. She wondered if her attitude was partly responsible for their lack of success.

Jack had asked John for a bit of a break, without saying why. They still had mini tours and dinner theatre, but the international tours were on hold. During this time, Jack and Maddie took the opportunity to return to the White Stag Inn for another short holiday.

On tour once again, the group headed for New Zealand. Their popularity was such now that they toured one country at a time. Gone were the days when they could accommodate two countries in one trip. They liked to restrict their tours to a maximum of three weeks, and with the number of venues in each country requesting their appearances, despite the long plane trips they divided their tours between New Zealand and Australia, and Canada and the US. They considered UK gigs to be almost local and made them into localized mini tours. They had been doing a lot of TV work and guest appearances for other entertainers as well. They had all really enjoyed working on 'Hogmanay at the Castle', a variety show celebrating the New Year.

Following the tour of New Zealand, they had two weeks off then headed to Ireland for a short tour. In Dublin on a day off, Maddie and Jack were in their hotel room. Maddie had been acting strangely all day and Jack couldn't figure out what was going on with her. Deciding to spoil themselves with room service, they had a very pleasant dinner in their room.

Afterwards, bundled up, they went out on the balcony of their room together to watch the sunset. Maddie had wanted to wait till the full moon rose, but she could contain herself no longer. With a huge smile on her angelic face, she handed Jack a stick. Caught off-guard, it took him several minutes to work out what it was. He looked at her questioningly, then he realized what it was; a home pregnancy test stick and it showed a plus sign. He didn't know whether to laugh or cry.

"Is this ours?" he asked. Maddie's broad smile was all the answer he needed. He kissed her, wrapping his arms around her. A million questions ran through his mind and started spilling out his mouth. "Are you sure? How are you feeling? When did you find out? How are you feeling? When are we due? How are you feeling? Why didn't you say something sooner? How are you feeling? You haven't been sick every morning or have you?"

When he paused for breath Maddie leaned in and kissed him.

"I'll answer all your questions last one first. I have not been sick at all. I am feeling fantastic. I wanted to be absolutely sure before I said anything. We're due in September. I found out for sure three days ago. We can thank our lovely holiday at the White Stag."

Jack was so happy that for probably the first time in his life, he was speechless. He guided Maddie inside to the small love seat at the window and sat down beside her. He wrapped his arms around her and they sat for a long time, each lost in their own thoughts. They watched as the sun fell below the horizon lighting the wispy clouds in an amazing show of reds, pinks, purples and golds. Maddie thought this was the best time of day and there was nowhere she'd rather be than wrapped in Jack's arms watching the full moon rise.

Jack couldn't take his eyes off Maddie. "You're watching me," she said.

"I can't believe my luck. I have the most beautiful woman in the world in my arms and she has my child growing inside her." He kissed her. Then he kissed her again. Heart overflowing, he made passionate love to her.

Lying in bed afterwards she said, "Am I to assume you are pleased?"

He looked at her in disbelief then started to laugh. "I am as pleased as you are."

They were both wreathed in smiles, emerald green eyes and gold brown eyes glowing with love for each other. They fell asleep smiling, wrapped in each other's arms.

Morning dawned sunny and bright. Lying in bed and looking out the window, Maddie was sure this was a good omen. Just to reinforce their good luck, she had waited for a sunny day to take the pregnancy test and a sunny day to tell Jack.

*I'm getting more and more superstitious,* she thought. *Must be spending too much time with the fairies and little folk.*

Jack woke with a warm Maddie in his arms. His face immediately concerned, he asked her if she needed to go and throw up.

"I haven't had to at all this time," she said. Without saying anything, they were both remembering the previous pregnancy when Maddie had been sick every morning. Maybe this was a good sign and they would have a better conclusion to this one. Maddie's superstitions were rubbing off on Jack.

They met Bob for breakfast and told him their news, making it feel real. He rushed off to phone Betty and tell her.

After breakfast they discussed the logistics of the differences this would make in their performances. After much discussion, they eventually agreed that they would finish out this tour of Ireland with no changes to the programme, but after that Maddie would be restricted to singing and dancing with Jack. No more of the high energy, bone rattling highland dancing. They deferred till later the decision on whether or not to get another highland dancer.

# *CHAPTER 47*

Jack was so proud of Maddie. Despite all that had been going on in their lives and all the distractions she had had (the touring, the TV show and the loss of Jamie), it was her university graduation day. She had worked hard on her studies and had earned her baccalaureate in History. She not only passed her courses, she got high honours in all of them. Jack had never been to a university graduation before and he was surprised by the large number of graduates. What didn't surprise him was that Maddie made the Honours List. Bursting with pride, Jack was pleased to see there were only seven other names on that list. From those days so long ago when they had walked through the People's Palace and the Glasgow Necropolis together, he had known she was smarter than most people.

Maddie was pleased to graduate, but she was not nearly as excited about it as Jack was. When they got home from the afternoon graduation ceremony, she was surprised to see the house full of people and banners up all over saying 'Congratulations Maddie'. She was amazed that Jack had put together a surprise party for her, and managed to keep it a surprise.

Jack had invited some of the ladies from the church that Maddie had made friends with and their families. His sister, Jeannie and her family had also come and, of course, Bob and his family, and Siobhan and Charlie, but most of the guests were Jack's showbiz friends. There were more people there than Maddie thought the house would hold but fortunately it was a beautiful summer day and the party spilled over into the back yard. Maddie knew Jack was showing her off and she was delighted he was so proud of her.

Jack made a little speech explaining to his friends why they were there and how smart Maddie was, how proud of her he was, listing just a few of the things, good and bad, they had been through during which she had still managed to keep up and excel at her studies. For the first time in years Maddie blushed at something Jack said. As had happened two years earlier at their wedding, Jack's friends all had something to say. This time it was Maddie being roasted rather than Jack. Because she was pregnant, Maddie was the only one of the adults not drinking. By the end of the night no one was sober but her. Some of the roasts were a little personal and a little off colour. Maddie spent most of the following day fielding calls from their friends who were calling to apologize to Maddie for things they had said or didn't remember but might have said. Each time Maddie assured them she wasn't offended. And she really wasn't. She was actually pleased that she had been accepted by this group to the point where they would tease her. Jack's friends were now her friends too.

# *CHAPTER 48*

It never failed to astonish Maddie how quickly the press could get hold of a story and what they considered newsworthy. Walking down the street in Prestwick's city centre while doing some shopping, she saw a sandwich board advertising the daily newspaper. Splashed across the front page was 'Jack and Maddie Prepare to Welcome First Child'. She didn't know whether to feel honoured or violated. She bought a copy of the paper and took it home with her. When she got home, Jack was reading a different paper with an identical headline.

"Who would have thought we were so famous?" he asked with a grin. "You'd think they have someone watching us."

"Well, you wanted the world to know you knocked me up. I guess they do now."

They were both hurt to think that Jamie had been forgotten by the press. In their minds, this would be their second child.

Once they passed the point at which they had lost Jamie, Maddie and Jack started preparing for this baby's arrival. Jack had wanted to start right away, but respected Maddie's superstitions. She didn't want to jinx this baby.

Maddie's office was moved into Jack's office. They had decided before they could share the space and turn her office into the nursery. They had friends and family all over the world and they wanted to keep the spare room available for the numerous houseguests they had.

The baby was due around September 7$^{th}$. Maddie danced with Jack on stage until the beginning of July. She still travelled with the boys, singing with Jack, till the middle of August but she felt she was too awkward to dance gracefully. They had all agreed that once they returned from their US tour August 12, she wouldn't travel with them anymore. The boys only had one short tour in Ireland at the end of August then John had arranged a month off for them. Unused to being home alone, Maddie missed Jack terribly when he was in Ireland. He missed her so much he called her at least twice a day. He hated being away from her and being so close to the baby's arrival made it even worse.

Maddie had been unsettled for three days, lumbering from one thing to another trying to get everything done before the baby arrived. Right on schedule, on Thursday the 7th of September, Maddie woke Jack at 01:17. "It's time, Jack. It's really happening."

At the hospital, Maddie was taken into a labour room. By the time Jack had the paperwork done, the nurses had settled her in a bed. Now all they had to do was wait. Jack was a bit squeamish but he wanted to be there for Maddie and to see his baby being born. He just hoped he wouldn't pass out or throw up. From what he'd heard, birth was a messy business. When his two older girls had been born it was not the fashion for fathers to be in the delivery room. He had sat in a smoke filled room with the other fathers, contributing to the blue haze and waiting.

They wanted to have the child naturally, but as the time dragged on Jack questioned the wisdom of their decision. Maddie was tiring and in a lot of pain. When they reached the fifteen hour mark, Jack tried to convince her to have them give her drugs. She glared at him, the first time ever, saying, "I haven't come this far to have it all spoiled by drugs now." Another contraction sent pain shooting through her and she questioned herself.

As the eighteen hour mark approached, the baby was finally ready. The doctor came into the room all smiles. "Are you ready to do this?"

Jack looked a little green but Maddie was more than ready to have the torture end. The doctor watched as two contractions rippled through Maddie's body then said, "Push."

Three strong pushes and their baby was out. Jack took inventory: two arms, two legs, ten fingers, ten toes. She was perfect. Laughing gleefully Jack kissed Maddie. All thoughts of passing out or throwing up had left him as he watched the miracle of his daughter's arrival. When they put the baby on Maddie's chest, he put his head on the pillow beside hers. Together they looked at this tiny human being they had created.

While Maddie and the baby were being cleaned up and settled in her room, Jack went out to the waiting room. Bob and Betty were there with flowers and Siobhan and Charlie with balloons. Jack handed Bob a cigar with a pink ribbon on it. He handed the ladies each a chocolate cigar with a pink ribbon. "Good thing the ultrasound was right."

Siobhan and Charlie had been very excited when they were told they were going to have a new sister. They had been thrilled when Jack and Maddie had told them they were going to have a sibling and both had been hoping for a girl. They wanted to make her a real girly girl, dressing her in little pink dresses and teaching her about boys and make-up. Maddie had been wary of accepting their offers to babysit, afraid she would come home to find the baby wearing lipstick and mascara.

When they all went into her room Maddie was sitting up in bed holding the baby. Although she didn't want to give her up, she handed her to Jack. "It's your turn. She's not heavy – 7lbs 2oz."

Looking into the face of the little girl he could see the beauty and fine features of her mother. With his brown eyes and Maddie's green eyes, Jack was surprised to see the baby's were blue, but the nurse told him most babies were born with blue eyes that changed colour as they got older. The baby had fine blonde fuzz all over her head. Maybe there would be some of him in her after all, at least the blonde hair, but he was glad she had her mother's looks. He and Maddie had four names they were considering for her and the moment he looked at her he said, "Emma."

Maddie agreed. That's what she had been thinking too. Emma was going to be another heartbreaker. Jack thought maybe he should get a shotgun, but reasoned he had plenty of time before the boys started chasing her.

Unbeknownst to Maddie, Jack had arranged for her friends and relatives to visit and help with the baby in a steady stream for the first four months. Beckie was the first one to come and she was there for a month. Nanny and Granddad had the next three weeks, followed by Katie and Bill for three weeks, then Auntie Joannie for three weeks.

Jack had been refusing to go out on tour again, not wanting to leave Maddie alone with the baby. When he'd worked out the schedule with her family, although no longer worried, he was still reluctant. He would be home for the first month, while Beckie was there, but would be gone for two of the three weeks his in-laws would be there. That wasn't necessarily a bad thing but he hated the idea of leaving his two girls.

Beckie was waiting at the house when Jack brought Maddie and Emma home. She hadn't gone to the hospital as she wanted to surprise Maddie. Jack hadn't said anything to Maddie about people coming. She was surprised and delighted to see Beckie. Although baby Emma was too young to go out much, Maddie convinced Jack to take Beckie sightseeing a few times with Siobhan and Charlie. She really appreciated Beckie's help, but didn't want her to work the whole time she was there. Beckie had been to Scotland a few times, but she hadn't spent much time in Prestwick or Glasgow. Maddie also wanted her to get to know Jack and his older daughters better. They were all sorry when it was time for Beckie to leave, but she would be back for Christmas with her Ben.

Maddie's parents had been there for three days when Jack went out on tour for two weeks. He found it ironic that while his Canadian in-laws were in Scotland, he was touring in Canada. He felt bad about leaving Maddie, wondering how she would get along with her mother for that long. They were both strong personalities and wanted things done their own way. He hoped her father would referee. Betty, Siobhan and Charlie were all frequent visitors and Jack arranged for them to take turns taking Maddie's parents out a few times. With either Betty or the girls staying with Maddie and Emma, Maddie's mother felt more comfortable going out. She wasn't leaving Maddie alone with the baby. Jack called Maddie twice a day to check on how things were going and because he missed her. She looked forward to those calls. Despite the visitors, the house felt empty without him.

Back from his tour, Jack was delighted to see Maddie and baby Emma at the airport to meet him. Looking around, he realized that other than Betty there to meet Bob, it was just the two of them.

"We escaped," said Maddie. "Actually we've been getting along surprisingly well. My house, my rules. And it really is nice to have them there." She had convinced her parents to do some sightseeing with Betty and the girls and had bought some alone time for herself and Emma. She loved her parents, but having them around all the time was stressful. Jack wanted to spend a couple of days with Maddie and Emma but offered to take her parents out the day before they went home. "I knew there was a reason I love you."

The next houseguests were Katie and Bill. Katie and Maddie had grown up like sisters and were surprisingly alike. They didn't look alike, Katie had long blond hair and blue eyes, but they had the same build and the same laugh. On the telephone Jack couldn't tell their voices apart.

Now that Emma was old enough to go out in public, the five of them were able to do some sightseeing together. Jack's birthday also fell during the time Katie and Bill were there. A few of his friends arranged a little get-together at Jack's local pub. Not willing to risk Jack trying to drive after an evening at the pub, Maddie, Emma and Katie dropped him and Bill off at the pub. While Emma slept in her car seat beside them, Maddie and Katie had a nice dinner at

Maddie's favourite restaurant. When it was time to pick up the men, Maddie gave Katie the choice of babysitting Emma or babysitting two intoxicated men. Katie chose Emma.

The following day was spent quietly. Jack and Bill were both suffering the effects of their fun the night before. By dinner time they were feeling better and the five of them went out to eat. Once again Emma slept in her car seat while the adults ate. Jack and Bill got along very well and Jack was again sorry he had to go on tour. It was only a short one week tour of the north of Scotland so he got to spend two weeks with these visitors. Two nights before they left, Jack and Bill had another night out at the pub with a few of Jack's friends. Once again they spent the next day feeling sorry for themselves. Not at all sympathetic for the self-inflicted suffering, Katie and Maddie went out on a haunted walking tour that evening leaving Emma with the men. When they returned, all were asleep in front of the telly. Bill was folded up on the settee, Jack was sprawled in the big chair and little Emma was snuggled in Daddy's arms. Jack had enjoyed Bill's company and he was as sorry to see Katie and him leave as Maddie was.

Auntie Joannie was their next visitor. Jack had been looking forward to seeing her again. He really liked her and other than backstage at a couple of shows, it had been a long time since he'd seen her. He associated her with meeting Maddie and changing his life forever. He had no more tours before Christmas so they were able to enjoy their time together. Although it wasn't tourist season, a lot of the local landmarks were decorated for Christmas and they did a lot of sightseeing and driving around at night to see the lights and decorations. Auntie Joannie even babysat a couple of times so Jack and Maddie could have a 'date night'.

After Auntie Joannie left, Maddie and Jack had a week to themselves before Beckie and Ben came for Christmas. The house seemed empty after having so many people there for the last thirteen weeks. They enjoyed the quiet and enjoyed their daughter.

When Beckie and Ben arrived Maddie was excited. Jack too was happy. He really liked them and it made Maddie so happy to have them there, he would have put up with them even if he didn't like them. Wanting them to have a good time, Maddie had made some plans for when they were there. One of those plans was a three night stay at the White Stag. It had become a favourite of Maddie's and Jack's, even more so because that was where Emma had been conceived.

When they told Beckie and Ben that, Beckie looked alarmed. "Don't get any ideas, Ben."

Christmas was a jolly affair. They went to the Auld Kirk of Ayr for the carol service Christmas Eve. This was becoming a tradition for Maddie and Jack and Maddie had wanted to share it with Beckie and Ben, knowing they would enjoy it. It was also becoming a tradition that they go to Maddie's friend Gemma's Christmas Eve get-together after church. Gemma was delighted to have the Canadian visitors as well this year. She was also delighted to have Emma join them. Emma was a good baby and seemed to enjoy the party. She loved having people around her. The other guests, especially the other children, all made a fuss over her.

Emma's first Christmas Day was chaotic. She didn't know what was going on, but she was excited by all the people in her house. Her cousins were fascinated by her and took turns holding her and playing with her. They didn't understand why she wouldn't play with their toys; she just sat and laughed.

For dinner there were fifteen. As well as the five of them, there were Bob and Betty and their two kids, Jack's sister Jeannie with her husband and three kids and Jack's mother. Emma was the only one too small to eat at the table but she sat with the others while they ate. Dinner was a feast. Beckie, Ben and Maddie had spent a week baking all kinds of Christmas goodies. Baking wasn't Jack's forte. He had played Christmas carols on the piano and acted as the official taster. Christmas Day Maddie cooked a huge turkey with all the trimmings. The guests also all brought contributions for the dinner.

After dinner and the clean-up Jack went looking for Maddie. He found her in Emma's room with the baby latched onto her breast sucking greedily. Maddie hadn't noticed him come in and when he softly said, "Madonna and child," she looked up and smiled. She really did look like the Madonna he thought, her angelic face was not marred or lined by the time they'd been together. She was amazing. She still looked fifteen. He silently thanked God for this incredible woman. He believed only God could have made her love him as she did.

With Emma fed and settled in bed, after a lullaby sung by Daddy, Maddie and Jack went back to their guests. Bob had all the kids playing a game. Maddie wasn't sure what it was, but it involved a lot of laughing and she was glad to see them having fun. The other adults were sitting talking in small groups. No one was terribly hungry for tea or supper, but Beckie and Maddie made turkey sandwiches and got out more of the Christmas treats they'd made.

Ben had made his amazing cream puffs, and full as they were, no one could resist them. Stuffed full of good food and bags bulging with Christmas gifts the company left about eight.

Boxing Day, as was becoming another tradition, Jack and Maddie hosted a brunch for some of their showbiz friends. Another first for Emma, she was again excited by the activity around her. She didn't even mind being passed from person to person as the women all wanted a chance to hold her. When put down for her nap, she slept soundly and the adults were able to enjoy their raucous conversations without interruption. They even had a sing-along that didn't wake Emma. She was up in time to see the guests off after another round of being passed from person to person.

Jack and Maddie were pleased Emma was so sociable. Because of their line of work, she would be exposed to a lot of people and they were happy she appeared to enjoy it. She fit right into their lifestyle.

# *CHAPTER 49*

Emma became a seasoned world traveller at a very young age and she seemed to love it. Bob and Jack's tour schedule still required them to be away from home for up to three weeks at a time. Not wanting to miss any of Emma's growth milestones, Jack brought Maddie and Emma along on tour. He had missed Maddie terribly when he was on tour and she was home with the baby and he wanted what he had come to think of as a 'normal' family life – all of them on the road together. Maddie was certainly pleased with this arrangement. She hated being home for extended periods without Jack. Even with Emma and their houseguests there the house had seemed empty.

When there was one of the backstage crew they trusted with Emma, Maddie would sing and dance with Jack on stage, but she insisted her highland dancing days were over. Although sorry, Bob and Jack did not attempt to change her mind. They had decided not to hire another dancer.

Emma's first birthday occurred when they were all on tour. Because she wasn't aware of dates, Jack and Maddie decided they would celebrate it when they got home. On the day of her birthday, Emma got several phone calls. She wasn't quite sure what was going on. She heard voices she recognized, but she couldn't see the people that went with those voices. She seemed to think they were playing games with her and she was happy about that, giggling and laughing every time Maddie put the phone to her ear.

Once home from the tour, Maddie and Jack planned a small party for Emma's birthday. The guest list was short, as Emma didn't know very many people. Siobhan, Charlie, Bob's and Jeannie's families came and a few of Maddie's church friends, Gemma, Judy and Lynn and their families. As usual, Emma was excited and happy to see the people. She didn't really care about her birthday gifts. She was more interested in the guests and the cake.

The first few years of Emma's life were spent on tour, but when she was three, Jack and Maddie decided she should start to make friends at home. They signed Emma up for a play group so she could meet other children. Other than her cousins who were all older than her, she had been with adults all of her short life and they wanted her to learn to play with children her own age before she started school. Although she didn't like Daddy being away, she adjusted well to the other children and soon had a little 'boyfriend'.

Maddie, on the other hand, did not adjust well to being at home all the time. She had loved being on the road. She could deal with not being on the road, but the stay at home mom job did not suit her. She and Jack had agreed once Emma started school they would have a second child, but in the meantime, Maddie was going crazy. She needed something to occupy her mind.

Jack didn't want Maddie going out to work but she needed to do something. When, after some discussion, Jack suggested she go back to school to work on a master's degree, she agreed immediately. She had always loved school and it seemed like a good way to keep her brain from atrophying. Once again, because they lived in Prestwick and she was going to the University of Glasgow she was going to take as many of her courses as possible off campus. It would still involve one or two days a week in Glasgow, but she would be home with Emma most of the time.

Maddie and Jack interviewed fourteen women for the position of part-time nanny before they found one they both agreed was perfect. Mrs. Brown looked 'grandmotherly'. She was average height and not thin, but not fat either. She had grey hair and a round, rosy face that seemed to have a permanent smile. She had raised five children of her own and had also worked for one of their showbiz friends. She certainly had a lot of experience and both Jack and Maddie liked her when they met her. She had a friendly open manner about her. When introduced, Emma really liked her too, climbing up on her lap and asking for a story. Instead of putting the child off so she could talk to the adults, as some of the other interviewees had done, Mrs. Brown immediately started telling a story about a princess who looked very much like Emma. Satisfied with the story Emma got down to play with her dolls and the adults resumed talking where they had left off. Mrs. Brown was hired for two days a week and all were happy with the arrangement. If Maddie only went to Glasgow one day a week, she would have another day to work on her studies. Although she really missed Jack when he was away, life was good again.

# *CHAPTER 50*

At forty-four, Jack was a very handsome man. While Maddie knew he would never stray from her, she often teased him about the female fans that had crushes on him. There was scarcely a week went by that some enamoured woman didn't write to him with protestations of undying love.

When not away on tour, Bob and Jack would often do dinner theatre shows at local clubs. They enjoyed the intimacy of the smaller venues and smaller audiences. Often Maddie would join them and Mrs. Brown would stay with Emma.

One Wednesday night, Maddie had joined the boys at a club in Monkton. Watching the audience, she spotted a young, blonde woman who couldn't take her eyes off Jack. Maddie thought that she would be the source of the next fan letter. She was even more sure when the woman came backstage after the show. Pushing past Bob and Maddie, the woman shook Jack's hand a bit too long, reluctantly letting go and begging him for a kiss.

Driving home to Prestwick that night, Maddie was teasing Jack about his new-found admirer. He told her the same woman had been admiring him at several other shows too. Neither of them noticed the red car following them.

The following Wednesday, Mrs. Brown was out with Emma in her pushchair. They had stopped at one of the local shops and Emma was refusing to get back in the chair when they left. She wanted to walk. A young, blonde woman approaching asked if she could help Mrs. Brown. Thanking her politely Mrs. Brown said no she would let the girl walk a bit.

On the following day, they again met the woman, this time at the park. While Emma played in the sandbox, the woman sat and chatted with Mrs. Brown.

Friday morning Maddie took Emma to the park. A young, blonde woman walked up to them and started to talk to Emma. She exchanged greetings with Maddie then walked away.

*That was odd*, Maddie thought. Emma seemed to know her and she had called Emma by name. She looked vaguely familiar, but Maddie couldn't place her. *Must be one of the other girls' mothers*.

They didn't notice the red car that parked down the road from their house for a week.

# *CHAPTER 51*

Ann was an attractive woman. She was thirty-two but looked younger. Of average height and thin, she had blue eyes, short blonde hair and a pixie-like face.. She had recently divorced her husband and moved to Prestwick from Ayr. Coming out of the divorce very well-off, she got enough money to buy herself a nice little house and enough to live on for a few years before she had to get a job. It was her ex-husband's, but she took the car anyway, saying she had been the one who made the payments on it. He didn't care. He had his sporty little convertible, the one Ann called his 'mid-life crisis' car. The red sedan had been paid off last year and since there was nothing left owing on it, Ann didn't bother changing the registration.

Thursday morning Ann got into the red car and drove off. She had some errands to run and then she had a job to do. Having finished her errands, Ann pulled into a parking spot on the road in a nice neighbourhood. She took her map out and spread it across the steering wheel. She'd lived in Prestwick for less than a year and she was still finding her way around. This was a neighbourhood she wasn't familiar with, but that wasn't the reason she needed the map. She intended to sit in the car for a long time and wanted the map as a prop in case somebody saw her there and questioned her.

What Ann was really doing was watching Jack and Maddie's house. Not sure where they lived, she had followed their car home from Monkton the previous night. Without being obvious, she couldn't see exactly which house they went into, but she figured if she watched for a bit she would see one of them come out of the house.

Ann sat parked there for about four hours then figured she had better leave in case someone was watching her. She didn't want to attract attention. In all that time she had not seen Maddie, Jack or Emma and still didn't know which house was theirs.

Ann returned home more than a little frustrated. How could she put her plan into action if she didn't even know which house Jack lived in? There was nothing more she could do today. It would have to wait till tomorrow. She made herself some supper and fell asleep in front of the telly.

On Friday Ann had no errands. She intended to sit parked in the road until she saw what she was looking for, someone coming out of Jack's house. Once again she spread the map across the steering wheel. After two hours she thought she ought to move the car. She drove around the block and parked again. She was further away from the houses near where Jack and Maddie had stopped on Wednesday night, but she had her binoculars and at the first sign of activity she would use them. Not wanting to arouse suspicion she would wait until there was movement at one of the houses to take them out.

At about 12:30 a dark green sedan pulled up to one of the houses. Ann thought it looked like the car she had followed on Wednesday. She crouched down in her car and picked up the binoculars. Sure enough Jack, Maddie and Emma got out of the car. She now knew which house to watch. Satisfied with her progress today, Ann went home. She still had work to do.

Saturday dawned rainy and cold. Ann thought there wouldn't be any point in watching Jack's house in this weather. She didn't feel like going out on a day like this and she didn't think too many other people would either unless they had to. Besides, she had other things to do.

The weather on Sunday was a little better. It was still cloudy and grey, but at least it wasn't raining. Ann drove to the neighbourhood Jack, Maddie and Emma lived in, and drove slowly by their house. Not seeing anyone about, she went around the block and drove past it again. The houses were in a single row, the front facing one road and the back facing another road with no houses between. Ann thought she might be less likely to be noticed if she parked on the back road. She had her binoculars and she had time. She knew Jack and Bob were heading to the US on a tour starting Wednesday. She didn't realize Jack would be leaving today, thinking he would go Tuesday.

Ann thought she had the house pinpointed and was watching it carefully, binoculars hidden under the map that was spread out on the steering wheel again. A door opened and she whipped up the binoculars, ducking down to make herself as inconspicuous as possible. When a woman came out the back door, Ann realized she had been watching the wrong house.

*It must be the one on the other side,* she thought.

That was even better. She was one house further away from her target.

Ann had been sitting in her car for about two hours when the sun came out. There was no shade where she was parked so she drove around to the front of the house and parked under a tree almost directly across the road from Jack's house. She mentally kicked herself when she pulled up to the house. The car that had been in the drive was gone. She'd been sitting at the back of the house when the activity was at the front. She waited a little while, hoping the car would come back, but after an hour with no traffic or activity on the road, she thought it best to leave.

Now that she had the house pinpointed Ann thought she'd try and get closer. She wanted to see what was going on in the house. To be honest, she also wanted to see what the house looked like inside. Jack's house had some shrubbery around the window of what appeared to be the kitchen and Ann thought she might be able to see what the family was doing without being too obvious to the neighbours. Monday at suppertime, cursing the long days with daylight lasting late into the evening, she took a chance. After some thought, she took a dog lead with her. If anyone questioned her, she was looking for her dog. They needn't know she didn't have a dog. Luckily for her, instead of fences Jack and most of his neighbours had hedges around their yards – perfect for small dogs to hide in.

Ann parked three houses away from Jack's. There was no one around, but to keep up appearances she went into the yards of two of the neighbours first, finally working her way to her target. She made her way to the kitchen window, thinking it was a good omen that the window was open. Maddie and Emma were sitting at the table. There were two McDonald's bags on the table and Emma was saying, "Can I tell Daddy we had McDonald's just because we wanted too?"

"Of course you may."

"He'll want to know why." (McDonald's was always a treat.)

"Tell him we miss him and we had to cheer ourselves up."

Ann was impressed that Emma, at three years of age, was speaking in complete or almost complete sentences. Maddie must have been working very hard on the girl's communication skills.

Ann was disappointed to see the inside of the house. It was tastefully decorated and looked very cozy. Creamy coloured walls in the kitchen gave way to light sage walls in what appeared to be a sitting room. It wasn't easy to see the sitting room from her vantage point, but the impression Ann got was of a comfortable room with overstuffed furniture. Nice as it was, she was sure, with Jack's money, she could have created an even nicer home.

Keeping up her ruse, Ann bent over as if she were looking through the shrubs. She could hear the conversation through the open window.

"When is Daddy going to call?"

"Pretty soon. Let's look at the clock. When the big hand gets to twelve and the little hand is at six, he'll call. That's in ten minutes."

*Damn*, thought Ann. *He's already left on his tour.*

Thinking she had been there long enough, even though there was no one around, Ann left. Tomorrow she would come a bit later and listen to the conversation. She hoped it was something that happened the same time every day. She wouldn't hear Jack's side but she could listen to Maddie and Emma talking to him.

The next night Ann parked further down the road from Jack's house. Once again there was no one out. Hardly surprising, it was pouring with rain. She hoped the window would still be open. When she had worked her way around to the back of the house, lead in hand, she was pleased to see the window was open, not wide but wide enough for her to hear through. Emma had just finished saying, "Look, Mummy the big hand is on twelve," when the phone rang. Ann's guess had been right; the call was a regular occurrence. Emma picked up the phone.

"Hi, Daddy. I miss you. Are you coming home soon? Mummy misses you too." The little girl paused for the person on the other end of the phone to speak. "Yes, Daddy. I'm being good. You can ask Mummy." A pause again. "No, we didn't have McDonald's today." Emma was quiet for a minute. "What did you do today, Daddy?" Emma was quiet again. "We went shopping. Mummy bought me new clothes." Another pause. "Yes, Daddy. How did you know they were pink?" Emma laughed and said, "Mummy wants to talk to you. I love you too, Daddy."

Ann risked a look in the window as Emma passed the phone to Maddie. She listened for a minute then decided she didn't want to hear Maddie telling Jack how much she loved him and missed him. After another quick look in the window she left.

While it was still dark Wednesday morning, Ann parked four houses down the road from Jack's. She thought it would be less suspicious if it appeared she had been parked there all night. This time she was close enough she didn't need the binoculars. She spread the newspaper across the steering wheel. If anyone asked her what she was doing there, it would look like she was waiting for someone.

About 8:00, just when Ann was thinking she should move, her patience was rewarded. An older woman pulled her car into Jack's drive then went into the house. Ann drove around the block twice then parked further up the road from the house. An hour later the woman she had seen earlier came out of the house with Emma in her arms. She went into the garage and came out with the child in a pushchair.

Wanting to make contact with Jack's family, Ann followed Emma and Mrs. Brown. It wasn't easy to drive as slowly as Mrs. Brown walked and Ann ended up going around several blocks. As she had done many times this week, she cursed the red car she was in, thinking it was too conspicuous among all the black and grey cars around. At one point she saw Mrs. Brown stopped in front of a shop, lifting Emma out of the chair. This was her opportunity. She was lucky to find a parking spot a few cars up the road from the shop. She waited till Mrs. Brown and Emma came out of the shop then got out of the car and walked towards them.

Emma was dressed in pink pants and a white shirt.

*She's a very pretty little girl,* thought Ann.

The girl had shoulder length curly blonde hair, perfectly proportioned features and peaches and cream skin. And she was petite. Ann thought she'd be small like her mother. Emma also had the most unusual green eyes.

As Ann was approaching Emma and Mrs. Brown, Emma was very vocally refusing to get back in the pushchair.

*Golden opportunity to make contact*, thought Ann. She walked up to Mrs. Brown and offered to help her get the child into the chair. Mrs. Brown politely refused the help saying the little girl wanted to walk and she would let her. Thinking she had accomplished enough for one day, Ann went home. She had a lot of work to do.

Thursday morning dawned bright and sunny. Ann was parked in the same spot she had been the previous day. She hoped if anyone noticed her car they would think she lived nearby. She'd been there for about half an hour when Mrs. Brown came out of the house with Emma. She got the pushchair out of the garage and they headed off down the road. Ann waited a few minutes then followed them on foot.

Mrs. Brown pushed Emma for about three blocks then turned into a small park. Ann came up to them as Mrs. Brown was lifting Emma out of the chair.

"We meet again," Ann said. She also said hello to Emma.

The girl looked very cute today, dressed in blue jeans and a pink shirt, with a matching pink ribbon tying back her blonde curls. Emma said hello then ran off to play with her friends in the sandbox. Ann sat down on the bench next to the pushchair and started talking to Mrs. Brown. Thinking nothing of it, Mrs. Brown sat beside her and they chatted for about half an hour. Ann was surreptitiously pumping Mrs. Brown for information about the family and managed to get a great deal of information about their daily routine.

Mrs. Brown called Emma and the little girl came running over. She got into her pushchair with no complaints and she and Mrs. Brown headed home.

Ann stayed on the bench until she thought the pair would be home then walked back to her car. Jack was away now, but she wondered why she had only seen him once before he left. She also wondered why she hadn't seen Maddie outside except the once in all the time she'd been watching the house.

On Friday, Ann again parked before daylight. It seemed to be a pattern that Mrs. Brown took Emma out about the same time each day. Today Ann was surprised to see Maddie come out of the house with the little girl. She put Emma in the pushchair and headed down the road.

Thinking how well this had worked out, Ann followed them on foot. They turned into the same park Emma had been at the day before. Ann walked up to them when Maddie was taking Emma out of the pushchair. She spoke to Emma, calling her by name and telling her what a pretty pink shirt she had on.

Emma replied, "Pink is my favourite," and ran off to play with her friends.

Ann exchanged pleasantries with Maddie then walked away. Satisfied with her progress, Ann left for the day. She still had some work to do and not much time left to do it.

On Saturday morning as Ann watched, a teen-aged girl came out of the house next door. She walked up the path to Jack's house. Before she got to the door, a pink blur came hurtling out and into her arms. Ann was delighted. It was someone else with Emma today and she would be able to talk to the girl again. She had come prepared today.

Putting Emma in her pushchair, the babysitter and the little girl went to the park. Ann waited then took her car to the park. When she got there Emma was playing ball with two other girls near some trees. Ann stood behind one of the trees out of sight. She took some tissues and a small bottle out of her purse, poured some of the liquid from the bottle on the tissues and waited.

Emma's babysitter, Jen, and her friends' babysitters stood chatting for a few minutes then the other babysitters walked away, leaving Jen with the three little girls.

Jen went over to where the girls were playing. She spoke to Emma, then turned and walked away. Thinking it was her best chance, while the babysitter had her back turned, Ann walked up to the girls. She spoke quietly to Emma then wiped Emma's nose with the tissues in her hand. Almost immediately the little girl's head began to nod. Keeping a close eye on the babysitter's progress, Ann picked up Emma and ran back to the trees.

Jen heard two voices yelling 'bye' and assumed the other babysitters had returned and one of them was taking her charge home. When Jen turned to look there was no sign of the other babysitters, nor of Emma.

Ann settled the child more comfortably on her hip and walked toward her car. She was not happy to encounter a mother and child. The other woman commented, "Aw, the wean wore hersel' out." She said, "Good morning," to Ann then walked into the park.

Ann buckled Emma into the car seat she had bought and drove away.

# *CHAPTER 52*

Jack was in Los Angeles when the call came. More specifically, he was on stage in Los Angeles. When he returned to his hotel, there was a garbled message from a hysterical Maddie. Worried that Maddie was in such a state, and unable to understand what she was saying, he automatically called her, not even thinking about the time difference. The phone rang four times then was answered by a strange female voice.

Jack had a sinking feeling in the pit of his stomach. His always calm Maddie had sounded hysterical and now a stranger was answering their phone. When he asked to speak to his wife, the voice asked him who he was. Stranger and stranger. Not liking the situation, he nonetheless identified himself. The stranger passed the phone to Maddie.

"Oh my God, Jack. You have to come home," Maddie was crying and her voice kept breaking. "It's horrible. I don't know what to do. Please come home."

"What are you talking about? What's wrong?" Jack heard Maddie crying and then some rustling sounds as the phone was being passed back to the person who had answered. "What is going on there? What is wrong with my wife? And who are you?"

"Mr. Buchanan, I'm Constable Watkins with the Scottish police. There has been an incident here involving your family. It would be of benefit for you to come home as soon as possible."

"What the fuck are you talking about?" Jack rarely swore but he was angry, frustrated and worried sick. "What kind of 'incident'? Just tell me what's happened."

"I'm sorry to tell you this but someone has taken your daughter."

"What?" Jack's stomach did an uncomfortable flip flop and he wondered if he was going to be sick. "Let me talk to my wife." The phone was passed back to Maddie.

"Jack," she said.

"Just what is going on there? Are you okay? Is Emma okay?"

"That's it, Jack, someone took Emma," her voice broke and Jack could hear her crying.

"What do you mean took her?"

"Oh God, Jack, they kidnapped her."

The floor seemed to shift under Jack's feet and he grabbed the edge of the desk to keep from falling. He sat down hard on the chair. "What? When? How? What's being done to find her? Do they want money? What do they want? Is someone looking for her?" Someone had taken his baby girl and he was at least twelve hours away. "Is someone looking for her?" he asked again.

Maddie was again sobbing uncontrollably and the voice that answered him was Constable Watkins.

"Everything possible is being done, sir. We have officers and dogs looking for your daughter. We've issued a media alert. We have a trap and trace set up on your phone in case there is a ransom demand and we are interviewing potential witnesses and neighbours."

"What happened?" Jack asked. The bottom had just fallen out of his world. Although he'd never even imagined this, he was always worried something would happen to Maddie or Emma when he was on the other side of the world. Emma was missing. Maddie was hysterical and he'd be lucky to get home by tomorrow.

"She was taken from the park this morning, sir."

"Taken how? By who?"

"That's what we are working on, sir. We have every available officer searching. At this point it is unclear how or why she was taken."

"I'm coming home. I'll be on the next flight. Find my little girl and look after my wife."

As Jack hung up the phone there was a knock on the door. He opened it to two policemen. After identifying him, they introduced themselves as Officers Smith and Wilson from the Los Angeles Police Department.

"Sorry to disturb you, sir, but are you aware there has been an incident in Scotland involving your daughter?"

"I just found out. I'm sorry to be rude, but I have to leave. I'm on my way home."

"We won't keep you long, sir. The Scottish police have requested our assistance with their investigation. They have asked us to check on you and just make sure the girl isn't here with you. May we look around?"

"My daughter was kidnapped and you think I did it? I don't have time for this. I have to get to the airport." He walked across the hall leaving his door open and knocked on Bob's door. When Bob answered he was shocked by Jack's appearance. Jack was pale and shaking, unable to stand still.

"God, Jack. What's going on?" Catching sight of two policemen going through Jack's room he started to worry.

"You'll have to cancel the rest of the tour, Bob. Emma's been kidnapped and I have to go home."

Bob thought he hadn't heard right. Jack repeated what he had said.

The two policemen, having satisfied themselves that Emma wasn't in Jack's hotel room, were leaving. They stopped to speak to Bob and asked if they could look in his room as well. Bob stepped aside and let them in. He was still trying to process what Jack had said.

"You'll have to cancel the tour," Jack repeated. "I'm going to the airport."

"Wait," said Bob. "I'll call and get us on the next flight."

Satisfied, the officers left after apologizing for disturbing them. Bob dragged Jack into his room and sat him in a chair. He called the front desk and asked them to book a flight for him and Jack. Next he called John to cancel the tour. John had heard about Emma's kidnapping and had been trying to call Jack. He'd also tried to call Maddie. He wanted to tell her he'd cancelled the rest of the tour and Jack was on his way home. He told Bob he had already made plane reservations for them and to just get to the airport as soon as possible. The backstage crew would worry about their luggage.

Bob got their passports and led a still shaking Jack to the elevator. When they got to the ground floor, the hotel staff had already arranged for the hotel shuttle to take them to the airport. They reached the terminal two hours before the flight was due to depart. Jack hadn't said a word since they'd left the hotel and he was pacing the Departure lounge. Bob still wasn't sure what was going on, but he figured he could wait till they were airborne to find out. He thought he must have heard wrong because he thought Jack had said Emma had been kidnapped.

Jack sat silently on the plane, wrestling with his emotions; fear, worry, anger and frustration at not being able to do anything. Once they started serving drinks on the aircraft, Bob got Jack a large whisky and made him drink it quickly. Some of the colour came back to Jack's face and he started to talk.

"They took my baby girl, Bob. Someone took her."

"Tell me what happened, Jack."

As best he could remember, Jack told him about the phone calls and about the police checking on him. He really didn't know a lot. Although they'd been in the air less than an hour, Jack kept looking at his watch and out the window. Bob got him another drink and one for himself. He wondered how Jack was going to handle the three hour layover in New York.

The trip seemed endless, but eventually the plane taxied to a stop on the tarmac at Prestwick International. Bob and Jack were fortunate the Customs and Immigration people recognized them. They had all heard the news of Emma's kidnapping and cleared the boys quickly. John was waiting for them outside Customs. There was a police constable also waiting for them. Both had come to drive them to Jack's home. They went in John's car with a police escort.

The car had almost stopped when Jack jumped out and ran to his front door. Totally focussed on his house, he didn't notice the police cars parked on his lawn, the group of curious onlookers or the news vans parked in the road. As he reached the door, it opened. A uniformed policeman was standing there. Jack rushed past him into the sitting room. Maddie was sitting on the settee, pale, teary and unmoving. Betty was sitting beside her with an arm around her. There were three police officers in the room, one woman and two men.

Jack knelt in front of Maddie and took her hands, "What's happening, luv?"

Maddie looked at him blankly.

"She's been sedated, three times," said Betty.

Jack turned to the officers. "What's going on? Somebody please tell me."

The officers explained what was being done. They had officers going door to door to see if his neighbours had seen anyone suspicious hanging around. They had officers tracking down people who had been in the park, trying to find someone who might have seen something. They had officers with dogs scouring the park. They had issued a media alert requesting anyone with any information to contact them. So far there had been no ransom demand. At this point they didn't know if Emma had been targeted or just convenient.

Once he'd been caught up on progress, or lack thereof, Jack went back to Maddie. Betty got up and went over to Bob, while Jack sat down beside Maddie. He put his arm around her and pulled her into his chest.

"Oh, Jack. Thank God you're home."

He was going to take her upstairs and put her to bed, but it seemed like a better idea to keep her with him. He settled her on the settee with her head in his lap. She stopped fighting the sedatives and she was asleep within a few minutes.

# *CHAPTER 53*

Jack was finally able to get the whole story or at least as much as was known.

As happened frequently on Saturday mornings, Jen, the teenager next door, had taken Emma to the park. Emma was playing ball with two other girls her own age. Jen had gone to Emma's pushchair to get her some juice. She'd only had her back turned for a minute, but when she turned back, there was no sign of Emma. When she tried asking the other girls where Emma was, they just kept saying 'blue lady'. The other girls' babysitters had taken a break, leaving their charges with Jen, and hadn't seen anyone. Jen was running around calling Emma and looking under bushes and behind trees. Some other women started helping her look and one went to a phone box to ring for a policeman. Within five minutes there were six constables on the scene and a dog and handler unit on the way.

Three of the constables started looking for Emma and the other three started interviewing the people there. Neither group turned up anything useful. The dog handler and dog arrived and went to work. The dog walked back and forth between the pushchair and the area where the girls had been playing. He could find no other scent.

At this time a media alert was issued. The media broadcast a call out to anyone who might have seen anything. A forensic team scoured the park. All they found of interest was a handful of tissues that smelled like chloroform.

At the first sign of trouble a constable had gone to inform Maddie. She had insisted on coming to the park. The constable had brought her and she and Jen sat holding each other both in tears. They were taken home by the same constable. He made sure someone was home with Jen then waited with Maddie until a trap and trace team arrived along with a female constable to sit with her. The phone had started ringing before they had the tap on it.

The female constable answered. The first call was from Betty. She had seen the alert on the telly and was calling to see if it was true. After Betty had identified herself Constable Watkins let her talk to Maddie. Maddie was borderline incoherent and Betty said she was coming right over. Within half an hour she was arguing with the policeman at the door. She said, "Just tell Maddie I'm here."

Betty came into the sitting room. Maddie was sitting on the settee with her arms wrapped around herself, rocking, a vacant look on her face, tears rolling down her cheeks. Betty gathered Maddie in her arms. Realizing she wouldn't get answers from the woman who was almost catatonic in her arms, she addressed the police when she asked what was happening.

Maddie became aware enough of her surroundings to realize Jack wasn't there. "I have to call Jack. Oh, God. How am I going to tell him?"

When Betty offered to call him Maddie insisted she had to do it herself. Betty supplied the name of the hotel in Los Angeles and one of the officers tracked down the phone number and dialed. He spoke to the desk clerk who answered the phone, requested Jack's room then handed the phone to Maddie. Shaking, she waited while it rang, then went to an answering machine. "Jack, call me. Something terrible has happened. You have to come home. Please. Call me." Her words were garbled and punctuated by sobs. Betty took the phone from her to try and leave a message, but Maddie had already broken the connection. Betty too was crying, but trying to hold herself together for Maddie, who had dissolved into wracking sobs, her whole body shaking.

Mrs. Brown had heard the news and arrived at the house, only to be prevented from entering by the constable at the door. She wasn't working that day but had come to offer support and help if she could. Betty had the constable let her in. Maddie was so disconnected from the events surrounding her she thought Mrs. Brown had brought Emma home. She jumped up from the settee and ran to hug Mrs. Brown.

"Thank God you brought her home. Where is she? Did she have fun at the park?"

When Maddie realized Mrs. Brown didn't have Emma, her legs buckled and only the support she got from Betty and Mrs. Brown kept her from falling to the floor. With Constable Watkins help, they got her back onto the settee. When Constable Watkins suggested a doctor, Mrs. Brown found the number for the family doctor. Constable Watkins called the doctor's office, identified herself and spoke directly to the doctor. When she rang off, she told Betty the doctor was on her way to the house.

When Dr. Carson arrived, Maddie was aware enough of her surroundings to be arguing with Betty, Mrs. Brown and the police officers. She was determined to take Betty and go out looking for Emma. After talking to Maddie for less than a minute, Dr. Carson removed a syringe from her bag and loaded it. Betty distracted Maddie while Dr. Carson administered 2mg lorazepam, explaining it was a sedative and should calm Maddie without causing loss of consciousness. Although it had been agreed Constable Watkins would answer any ransom demand, they needed Maddie awake to answer potential questions from the kidnapper(s).

Dr. Carson left, saying she would drop in every few hours to check on Maddie.

The phone rang constantly but the calls that were coming in were mostly from the press. Some family friends called offering help. Gemma, Judy and Lynn, three of Maddie's friends from the church arrived with food. They weren't allowed in but the officer at the door assured them Maddie would get their contributions. Several of the neighbours also came over with food.

When Jack phoned, Maddie tried to talk to him, but it was Constable Watkins who explained the situation. Following Jack's call, Maddie became hysterical. She shook off Betty and got up to pace the floor. She tried to physically remove the constable from the front door in an attempt to go out searching for Emma. Dr. Carson had returned, and decided another injection was required. Another 2mg lorazepam was administered. Maddie refused all suggestions that she should go and lie down in bed, but did lie on the settee. Betty sat in a chair beside her holding her hand. The time dragged by with no ransom demand. Maddie was fighting the sedatives and by the time Jack arrived home she had had 6mg of lorazepam. She was still awake, but calmer. Sobs still shook her body but the wild attempts to get out of the house had stopped.

# *CHAPTER 54*

Maddie was still asleep on Jack's lap when the detective inspector investigating the case returned. DI Edwards was in his late 50s. He was a solid man of average height, not exactly fat but much thicker around the middle than he had been in his younger days. His grey hair was thinning and he wore it combed back from his face. His pleasant face masked a very sharp mind and his brown eyes did not miss anything. He had been to talk to Maddie before Jack got home and had not had much success getting information from her. He thought he might have better luck talking to Jack. When Edwards walked into the sitting room, Jack demanded to know what they had found out. There was little news. Almost twenty-four hours had passed since the little girl had disappeared. There had been no ransom demand and they had opened a new line of enquiry - the possibility that someone they knew had taken Emma.

Jack gently woke Maddie so DI Edwards could speak to her. He asked her several questions, including whether she had noticed any strangers hanging around or following her. Concentrating on the detective's questions, Maddie's fuzzy brain reengaged with the situation. With surprising strength, she pushed Jack away, and ran to the door, attempting to push the constable out of the way. When she returned, Dr. Carson administered another 2mg of lorazepam. Eight mg in twelve hours should have been enough to knock Maddie out. It did calm her and make her thoughts fuzzy but she still refused to go to bed. Once again she lay on the settee with her head in Jack's lap. He thought she looked stoned.

Edwards did not attempt to ask Maddie any more questions. Instead, he turned his attention to Jack. Jack could offer no leads on anyone who might have been following or watching them.

Edwards had not realized who Jack and Bob were, but once that realization dawned, he had another angle to pursue. Had they noticed any fans behaving strangely?

"Jack," said Bob. "Remember that woman in Monkton who insisted you kiss her? She must have been at a dozen shows in a row sitting in the front at all of them." Bob turned to the detective. "This woman came to all our shows and sat in the front row. She came backstage to see Jack every time and I was teasing him about his new groupie."

Edwards wanted to know when and where they had seen her. As well as eight venues in Scotland, Bob remembered being surprised by seeing her in New York at three shows. She hadn't been in Los Angeles.

Detective Inspector Edwards finally thought he might be getting somewhere. How many celebrities had had rabid fans stalk them? Someone who had apparently followed Bob and Jack from Scotland to New York could definitely be classified as a rabid fan. Between Bob and Jack, Edwards got a good description of the woman – medium height, thin, short blonde hair, blue eyes, maybe thirty . The question now was how to find her. Even if she wasn't involved, she might know something. He thought it unlikely she wasn't involved.

The eight venues in Scotland did not narrow down where the woman lived. The venues were all in different cities, and New York had how many million residents? Thinking he had gotten as much information from Bob and Jack as he could, Edwards took his leave of them. He wanted to get back to the station to see what the officers canvassing had found out.

# *CHAPTER 55*

Back at the station Edwards found an incident room had been cleared for his investigation. Tables, blackboards, white boards and corkboards lining the small room made navigating it difficult. There were three officers answering the tip line phones. Photos of Emma, her parents, their home and the park were pinned to the cork boards. Someone had started a timeline on one of the white boards. Edwards tried not to think of the statistics he had read of the number of children killed within the first twenty-four hours of being kidnapped.

*That was in the US*, he reasoned with himself. *It's a much more violent society*. Emma had been gone for twenty-three hours.

Edwards read through the reports the canvassers had left. The 'blue lady' the girls in the park had referred to appeared to be a lady in a blue dress. Of all the people they had interviewed in the park, only one woman recalled seeing a lady in a blue dress. She was carrying a small blonde girl who appeared to be asleep. The description of the woman could match the description he'd gotten from the girl's father and uncle. Unfortunately, it could also match half the women in the country.

Information from the neighbours appeared to be more helpful. One neighbour recalled seeing a strange, youngish blonde woman looking for her dog. Two others had noticed an unfamiliar red sedan in the neighbourhood several times in the last week, with a blonde woman in the driver's seat and a map spread out in front of her. They had thought the car belonged to someone who had just moved into the neighbourhood. After a moment's reflection, they both realized they hadn't seen the car since Emma disappeared. One of them had the first three digits of the registration. It wasn't much to go on but it was more than Edwards had had an hour ago.

Edwards checked with the very new computer squad to see if they had run the information against the equally new motor vehicle database. They had more than two thousand hits of those three numbers belonging to a red sedan registered in Scotland. He asked them to run the numbers again, looking for those registered to car rental companies. There was no guarantee the woman lived in Scotland, and maybe she'd had to rent a car. It was a long shot, but it was a place to start. He returned to the incident room and started going through the reports again. Surely there was something there he had missed. He read and reread the reports until his eyes blurred.

Two plain clothes detective sergeants walked into the room. DS Morgan was a very large man. He was well over 6 feet tall and must have weighed about 300 lbs. His hair was carrot coloured and freckles covered his face and arms. His partner DS Flynn was an average sized woman, about 5'6" and wiry. Her rich dark brown hair framed a pixie-like face. Edwards knew them both, but he hadn't worked with them before.

"The super asked us to work with you. Apparently this is a high profile case." Morgan tossed three newspapers onto the desk in front of Edwards. All three of them had similar headlines 'Daughter of Jack Buchanan Kidnapped'. He scanned them quickly, looking for new information, but not finding any.

Edwards had the feeling there was something obvious he was missing.

The two detectives sat down opposite Edwards and waited expectantly for him to bring them up to speed. Edwards told them what they had so far. Not a lot.

He asked, "What are we missing?" but they had no answer.

One of the computer guys came in with the report on rental companies with red sedans. There were forty-three registrations that started with the three digits of the registration they had. There were none in Prestwick but eight in Glasgow and two in Ayr, the cities closest to Prestwick. With no better ideas, he went to his superintendent to ask permission to bring in the Glasgow and Ayr police. This was a high profile case and the super was fielding calls from the press, outraged citizens and, worst of all, the chief super. He didn't care if they wanted to bring in MI5. He just wanted it solved and quickly.

Edwards wasn't sure yet if it was worth the manpower to have the police forces in the other cities interview car rental companies.

## *CHAPTER 56*

Edwards sent Morgan and Flynn to Ayr to interview the two car rental companies there. He himself went to Glasgow. He had called ahead and they were expecting him. A young female constable by the name of Gracie Wyatt had been assigned to him and she met him with a map in her hand. She had taken the eight Glasgow addresses he had given her and marked them on the map.

They went out to visit the car rental companies. Edwards wasn't sure it would be terribly useful; they had a six month window of time to look at. How many people would have rented those cars in that length of time?

The rental companies were all anxious to help. The news of the little girl's kidnapping had spread across the country, but she was a local. Bob and Jack were legendary, unofficial ambassadors of Scotland worldwide. If someone hurt them, it was an attack on all Scots. Each of the companies supplied lists of customers who had rented red sedans in the past six months.

Edwards and Wyatt went back to the station to study the lists. They were not sure what they were looking for, but started by trying to compare names across the lists to see if anyone was on more than one. That turned out to not be the case, but what they did find of interest was a name that was repeated three times on one list. Another list had a name repeated four times during the period they were looking at and yet another list had a name repeated twice. Edwards began to think maybe they were getting somewhere. The next step was to interview those three people.

# *CHAPTER 57*

Emma woke up in a strange room. She didn't feel so good, her head hurt and everything she looked at was fuzzy. There was a lady in a blue dress sitting beside the bed smiling at her.

"How are you, baby? Did you have a good nap?"

The girl didn't answer. Her parents had taught her not to talk to strangers. Looking closer, Emma realized the lady wasn't a stranger. She'd seen her lots of times before. She just couldn't remember where.

Still not saying anything, Emma looked around the strange room. The walls were pale pink and the floor had a dark pink carpet. The bed she was lying on was white wood and had a thick pink feather duvet on it. The pillows had pink ruffles. It was a very comfortable bed, thought Emma, but if her head hadn't hurt so much she would have gotten out of it. She could see a small white dresser with a large mirror on it and a large white table with chairs. There were colouring books and crayons on the table. Emma also saw a small white cupboard with shelves above it. The cupboard doors were closed, but the shelves were lined with toys of all kinds: dolls, stuffed animals, games, books, puzzles. There was a small television in one corner of the room. There were dark pink curtains that matched the carpet on two walls and the light on the ceiling had a pink shade.

*It's a nice room*, she thought. Emma loved pink.

"I know your head must hurt," said the lady helping Emma off the bed. "Come over to the table and have some juice and cookies. That will make you feel better."

Emma sat at the table and the woman gave her some apple juice and a plate with three chocolate chip cookies on it – they were her favourite.

"Where's my mummy?" the little girl asked.

"I'm your mummy," the lady replied.

"No," said Emma. "My mummy has red hair and it's long."

The woman had short blonde hair. They had not attracted any attention when she had taken Emma. The little blonde girl had looked like she belonged to the blonde lady.

Emma started to cry. "I want my mummy," she repeated over and over.

"Stop it," said the woman. "I'm your mummy now." Emma cried harder. "If you're just going to cry, you can sit in here by yourself," said the woman. She held a small bottle up to Emma's nose then left.

Emma was scared. She didn't like being alone in this strange place. She went over and moved one of the curtains so she could look out the window. There was no window, just more wall under the curtain. She tried the other curtain, but it was the same.

Not knowing what else to do and not feeling very well, Emma climbed up on the bed. Her head still hurt; she was scared and she wanted her mummy and daddy. She started to cry again and cried herself to sleep.

The woman was angry. After all the work she had done to create a nice room for her, the little brat had said she wasn't her mummy and then started to howl. She climbed into the red car and slammed the door. It was rush hour and tourist season and the streets of Prestwick were crammed with cars. That didn't improve her mood any.

# *CHAPTER 58*

Edwards and Wyatt had interviewed the three people who had rented the red cars and found nothing that sent up red flags. Two of the women had been dark haired women in their 50s; the third was a diminutive Oriental lady. None of them came close to matching the description Edwards had of the woman he was looking for.

Back at the station, Edwards and Wyatt sat morosely drinking bad coffee. Edwards was wracking his brain. He again had the feeling he was missing something obvious. With nothing else to do in Glasgow, he headed back to Prestwick. Halfway there he realized what he was missing. Suddenly in a hurry, he turned the flashing lights and siren on in his unmarked police car and sped to the station.

Almost running, he went into the incident room at the station. Flynn was taking a turn at the tip line and Edwards nearly pulled her off her chair. "Concert tickets," he said to her. "Most people buy concert tickets on the phone with credit cards." Flynn looked confused. "Call the theatres and get their credit card receipts." Edwards was thinking so fast Flynn had trouble keeping up. "The theatres they saw the woman at. Call them and ask for a copy of their credit card receipts," he repeated running out of the room.

He went into the huge computer room looking for Smith who had run the red car against the motor vehicle data base. "Smith, can you print out that list of red cars and their owners? Leave out the rentals."

"Aye, sir, I can print the list but it will take until tomorrow for the whole list to print. Even without the rentals there are over two thousand names." The massive new computer was efficient, but it wasn't fast.

"Then stop wasting time and start printing. I need it in alphabetical order. Can you do that?" Smith nodded. "You work on nothing else till it's done. I'll clear it with the super," Edwards added as an afterthought. He realized that wasn't all he was going to have to clear with the super. The theatres were not going to be pleased about having to produce six months' worth of credit card receipts.

In the super's office Edwards was talking so fast, Superintendent MacLeod couldn't follow him.

"Slow down, Edwards. You're not making any sense. What happened in Glasgow?"

"Dead end, sir. But we're looking at this all wrong. What we need to do is look at the theatres' receipts. If the same name appears on all of them then we have her."

The super started to smile. "You, Flynn and Morgan work on nothing else. I'll find a couple of constables to help go through names."

John had given Edwards a copy of the tour schedules showing the dates and names of theatres Bob and Jack had played at. As expected, the theatres did not want to give up their lists. They only had to produce the receipts from Bob and Jack's shows, but there was still some resistance. There was no issue of confidentiality. It was just an awful lot of paperwork. Edwards asked the super to enlist the local police in each city. With a little persuasion, the theatres complied. Each of the police stations reported that a list would be forthcoming. The only problem was that it would take a couple of days to produce. Manually going through that many receipts would take some time too. The receipts would be forwarded to Edwards and his team would sort through them matching each theatre's list to the others.

It was a lot of work, but true to his word, the super had scrounged four constables to help. The receipts started coming in on Monday night. Edwards arranged with Smith and the four constables to input the names into the computer as soon as they started coming in, then try running names from each theatre against the names from the other theatres. Edwards tried to think what he could do in the meantime. Emma had been missing for three days.

First, he should go and see the Buchanans. It was only common courtesy that he let them know they had a new lead. Those poor people must be going crazy. Edwards knew if his daughter was taken he would be. Jack had called six times, looking for information on what was happening. Edwards had had little to report. He was pleased he now had something positive to tell them.

# *CHAPTER 59*

Edwards approached the house. There were still, or again, people gathered in the road watching the house. Although not as many, there were still news vans in the road too. With very little activity, most of the news teams had been pulled to cover other stories. There was a flurry of activity from those still there when Edwards got out of his car. They rushed over, pushing microphones in his face and throwing questions at him.

"I have no comment. Speak to the department's press officer."

The door was opened for him by a uniform. He was glad to see there was still a police presence there. The trap and trace team had been pulled after two days with no ransom demand. The woman had taken the girl for another reason. At least he hoped she had. The alternative was too ugly to consider. That the little girl might already be dead was on everyone's mind but no one was even suggesting it.

Jack, Maddie, Bob, Betty and Mrs. Brown were in the sitting room and there was a different constable standing by the door. Maddie was sitting up straight on the settee clasping Jack's hand in a death grip, a vacant look on her pretty face. She was stoned. Dr. Carson had paid several visits over the last 48 hours. Each time she had sedated Maddie. The twice the sedative had worn off between visits, Maddie had tried to get out of the house to look for her daughter. Each time she had dissolved into hysterics. She looked like she hadn't slept at all. In fact, they all looked like they hadn't slept.

With both hope and dread on their faces, all but Maddie stood up when Edwards walked in.

"I'm sorry," he said. "There is no news yet.' The group was unaware that police and volunteers had been searching local woods, fields and farms, expecting to find a small body. "However, we do have a new line of enquiry. Because there has been no ransom demand, we believe the woman (he was sure now it was the woman from the concerts) took Emma for another reason. We don't yet know why." He explained how they were trying to find her. He knew he shouldn't be discussing their ongoing case, but he felt very sorry for them and wanted to give them some hope. He asked Bob and Jack if they could narrow down the dates or places they had seen the woman. If they could reduce some of the paperwork, they could move faster. Bob and Jack tried to remember, but they couldn't narrow it down any further. John's copy of the touring schedule was the shortest list they were going to get, but at least they knew which theatres and dates to ask for receipts from. Still, it was going to take time, and not knowing why the woman had taken Emma, they didn't know how much time they had.

# *CHAPTER 60*

Emma had been sleeping a lot. Each time the lady left, she had the girl sniff a small bottle she had. Emma didn't know what it was, but it smelled funny and it always made her sleepy. For some reason every time she woke up in this room her head hurt.

This time when Emma woke up her head didn't hurt as badly. She was hoping it was breakfast time because she was really hungry. She looked around. The lady wasn't there but there was food on the table. Fish sticks, chips and chocolate milk. It was an odd breakfast, but the lady knew what food Emma liked.

Emma didn't like being left alone in this strange room. She wondered once again where her mummy and daddy were and why they hadn't come to get her. With nothing else to do when she had finished eating, Emma walked over to the shelf of toys. There was one doll she really liked so she took it off the shelf. Not knowing what to do next, she went back to the table. There were colouring books and crayons there, so she climbed back up on the chair. Asking the doll if she wanted to colour too, Emma sat her on the table and gave her a crayon.

When the lady walked in the door Emma was colouring. She looked up and asked the lady where her mummy and daddy were. The woman had cooled down after her previous hasty exits and she was ready for the question.

"Your mummy and daddy don't want you anymore so they gave you to me." Emma looked incredulous then she started to cry again. *Christ*, thought the woman, *this child cries a lot*. The crying wasn't as annoying this time. There were no sounds. Large silent tears ran down Emma's face.

# *CHAPTER 61*

As the credit card receipts started coming in, the massive job of matching names began. The constables worked on the lists, beginning with the two smallest theatres. Four names the same showed up on their first pass through. The names were matched to the list of red car owners to obtain addresses. If there was no match on the red car list, the credit card company would be contacted for an address.

Once again Edwards enlisted the help of police forces in other cities for the job of interviewing the people who showed up on multiple lists. There were a surprising number of people who had gone to more than one show. Edwards thought maybe when this case was over he would take his wife to one of their shows. They seemed pretty popular.

Edwards took Flynn and they went to interview the local matches. The first two women were older ladies, grandmotherly, thought Edwards. The third person they went to interview was more promising. When they knocked on the door, it was opened by a woman with blonde hair who could have been anywhere between thirty-five and forty-five. The detectives showed their warrant cards and explained what they wanted and the woman was very forthcoming. She explained she had gone with her husband who had been travelling on business and she had been looking for something to do. It was just a coincidence the boys had been playing at two of the stops they had made. Having enjoyed the first show, she had bought tickets for the second. She had invited the detectives into her home and they saw no indication that there was a child there. Still Edwards asked Morgan to check out her story.

The fourth name on the list was a man. They spoke briefly to him, at this point not totally ruling out a male kidnapper, but nothing aroused their suspicions. They thanked him for his time and left.

Checking in with the office from a call box, Edwards was given another three names and addresses. Once again, the first name on the list turned out to be an older woman probably in her sixties. Her husband had also been travelling on business and she had been looking for something to do. Edwards wondered if the two husbands worked for the same firm. Morgan was asked to check out her story.

The second name on this list seemed a bit more promising. There was no red car in the drive, but the garage door was closed and it could have been in there. The woman who answered the door was about thirty. She had short blonde hair. Edwards and Flynn showed their warrant cards and explained why they were there. The woman introduced herself as Ms. Johnson and invited them into the house. She said she had seen the news about the little girl and would do what she could to help, but she didn't know what that might be.

Edwards' nerves were on edge. He was sure he had found something important. Ms. Johnson was too eager to help and she was asking too many questions about what was being done to find the girl.

Flynn picked up on this and said to her, "What a lovely home you have."

Before she had time to ask, the woman offered a tour. Edwards was disappointed. The little girl was obviously not here.

Ms. Johnson said she had been travelling on business and had just happened to be in the cities where Bob and Jack were playing. At loose ends in the evenings, she had bought tickets to their shows. Frustrated, Edwards and Flynn took their leave of the woman, thanking her for her time, and went on to the next person on their list. He again asked Morgan to check on the woman's story. Something didn't feel right about her.

The next woman was a Ms. Airdrie. She was also blonde and about thirty but she was not as friendly as Ms. Johnson. She didn't invite them into the house. Her answers were short and abrupt, seeming to indicate the detectives were wasting her time. Edwards had an uneasy feeling about her too. She also said she had been travelling on business and just happened to be in the same places as Jack and Bob. A long-time fan she had purchased tickets to every show where their paths crossed. Once again a call was made to Morgan to check out the woman.

Having reached the end of their list, Edwards and Flynn returned to the station to discuss the morning's work and to get another list from Smith. Both of the last two women they had interviewed had said they'd been travelling on business and had just happened to be in the areas of the shows. Edwards thought it odd that two women had said they were travelling on business. Not very many women did, so even one would have been questionable. Both women had been to the show in Perth, but the other shows each had attended were in different cities. Edwards wondered what kind of jobs they had that would send them out of town on business but not have them in the office on a Tuesday morning. He was sure one of them was somehow involved. His money was on Ms. Johnson. She had been too eager to help and too curious about what was being done. Flynn, although less certain, could see his point.

Armed with another list Edwards and Flynn headed out after lunch. They were both frustrated with the length of time this was taking. Although they didn't say anything to each other they were both worried about how much time little Emma might have left, if they weren't already too late.

# *CHAPTER 62*

This time when Emma woke her head didn't hurt and the lady was sitting beside her bed. Emma was glad. She wasn't sure if she liked the lady, but she knew she didn't like being left alone in the room.

The lady had brought them both lunch from McDonalds. Emma was delighted. She loved McDonalds and it was always a special treat. The lady certainly knew what Emma liked to eat.

This time the lady had also brought Emma some new clothes: bright pink pants, a pale pink T shirt and a pink dress with lots of ruffles. Emma thought it was the most beautiful dress she had ever seen. The lady must know her favourite colour was pink. She put on the dress and felt like a princess. The lady said she looked like a princess.

Emma had been in the room for four days. She wanted nothing more than to see her mummy and daddy and go outside. The lady had said her mummy and daddy didn't want her anymore, but Emma didn't believe that. She had learned though, not to cry for her parents. When she did that, the lady got angry and left her alone in the room.

The lady seemed to be in a very good mood. Today she had brought two books and read both of them to Emma. When she went to leave, Emma started crying and begging to go with her. Having had such a pleasant visit, the woman considered it. These were tears of misery, quite different from the angry tears that she hated.

Not liking to see Emma so miserable, she told the girl they would go out for ice cream. Emma was beside herself. She didn't know how long she'd been in the room, but she knew she wanted out. She also thought the lady must be okay to take her for ice cream.

When they got outside, Emma looked around. This was a very strange road. The houses all looked the same and none of them had any windows. They all had really big doors. There was no grass around any of them.

The lady seemed to drive for a long time before they came to the ice cream shop. Emma enjoyed the drive. She didn't realize how long it had been, but it seemed like a very long time since she had seen outside.

Emma and the lady were sitting at a little table in the ice cream shop when another lady came over to talk to Emma's lady. They talked for a minute then the other lady left. Emma finished her ice cream and they got back in the car.

The lady was worried about something and didn't talk much on the way back. She went into the room with Emma but said she couldn't stay, she'd be back later. After she left, Emma cried herself to sleep. She had thought things were getting better, but now she was alone in the room again.

# *CHAPTER 63*

Morgan was answering phones on the tip line. There weren't as many media alerts as there had been but the alert still ran after each newscast on telly and there was always a flurry of calls. The one he had just taken seemed more promising than the others. The caller had just seen a woman she knew at an ice cream shop with a little blonde girl in a pink dress; a woman she thought had no children.

This time Morgan went out with Edwards. Flynn had been sent to talk to the people at the ice cream shop. Edwards had checked the address Morgan had and found it to be just down the road from Ms. Johnson. In an unmarked police car, they went to interview the neighbour. Edwards brought along a picture of Emma. The neighbour, a Mrs. Wilson, identified the photo as the little girl who had been with Ms. Johnson. She hadn't seen the girl in the neighbourhood before, and she was pretty sure Ms. Johnson had no children. Ms. Johnson had lived there less than a year though and was something of a recluse. Mrs. Wilson rarely saw her outside so she couldn't be sure. She told them the girl had appeared to be fine and enjoying some ice cream. They thanked her and left.

Anxious to re-interview Ms. Johnson, they went back to her house. They rang the doorbell and knocked on the door. There was no answer. Unsure if the woman was there and not answering or if she was indeed not home, they looked around her yard. She must be keeping the girl somewhere else. There were no children's toys in the yards, front or back. A quick look in the window of the garage showed no car, red or other coloured.

Believing they had found their woman, Edwards arranged for a constable to stay out of sight and watch the house until Ms. Johnson came home and to follow her if she left again. Mrs. Wilson was happy to help and let the officer use her garden to watch from. Edwards was going to see if they could find a judge who would give him a warrant to search Ms. Johnson's house.

Edwards and Morgan went back to the station. The super was in his office and Edwards wasted no time bringing him up to date on their investigation.

While the super wrote the warrant, Edwards checked his messages. Sure he was on the right track, he looked for Ms. Johnson's name on the new lists the computer team had left for him. She was on both the list from Aberdeen and the one from Inverness. It had taken three days to get the receipts from the theatre in New York, but they had finally come in. Ms. Johnson was on that list too, three times. Sure now that they had the right person, Edwards told the super, who had just finished writing his search warrant. With the additional information he knew he would have no trouble getting it.

Ten minutes later, Edwards, Morgan and Flynn were out the door of the station on their way to Ms. Johnson's. Two police cars with uniformed constables met them there. While they were waiting on the porch for an answer to their knocking, a forensics van arrived. There was no answer so Edwards had one of the constables force the door.

Inside, the house was immaculate. There was a framed picture of Jack on the mantle and another one of Jack and Emma.

Edwards looked at Flynn. "Those photos weren't there before."

"No, Guv. They weren't."

The constables began searching, checking the other rooms for signs of the child. The forensic team started looking for fingerprints or other clues. Morgan, going through the desk, found something of interest. It was a file containing four receipts from a storage company. With no sign of the little girl at the house, they called the super for a warrant to search the storage locker.

Ann had come back to sit with Emma. After seeing her nosy neighbour at the ice cream shop, she was worried. She didn't spend much time outside at home, so she was hoping the neighbour didn't know the child wasn't hers. Nonetheless, she had to find someplace else to go. She couldn't go home. When she had come back into Emma's room, the little girl had thought they were going out again. Worried and with her thoughts elsewhere, Ann had snapped at Emma. Not used to such treatment, Emma started to cry.

Once at the storage company, the detectives noticed a red car parked in front of one of the units. Afraid of spooking the owner of the car, they parked at the office and sent the panda cars around to the back of the facility. They had one of the storage employees accompany them with bolt cutters, however, the cutters were not needed. When they arrived at the locker, the door was unlocked. Beyond the large door there was a four foot space then another wall with a standard house sized door in it. The door was closed but they could hear voices on the other side. Flynn tested the door and found it unlocked. The woman had her back to the door and was yelling at the small girl who was holding her leg and crying.

Emma saw Flynn first. Not knowing she was a police officer Emma thought it was one of the lady's friends. She backed into the corner of the room, tears still flowing. Noticing the girl looking beyond her, Ms. Johnson turned. Pushing past Flynn she ran out the door and into the waiting arms of Morgan.

Edwards was on his way to the Buchanans'. They had found little Emma and she was still alive.

# *CHAPTER 64*

When Edwards arrived at the Buchanans' all was quiet. There was one news van sitting in the road and no neighbours standing around. The door was opened by a constable and Edwards charged into the sitting room. The scene was not much different from what he had seen the last time; tired, worried people sat with tired, worried expressions. The only difference was Jack up pacing the floor.

They all looked up when Edwards strode into the room. He had a huge smile on his face. "We've found her!"

They looked at him, not comprehending at first. "Is she okay?" Jack asked.

"They've taken her to the hospital to get checked out, but she appears to have been well looked after."

"I want to see my baby." Maddie's faint voice came from the settee.

Although she was still sedated and required considerable assistance to get up and walk, Jack had no intention of leaving her at home while they went to get Emma. Edwards drove Jack and Maddie to the hospital and on the way Maddie made valiant efforts to try and shake off the effects of three days of sedatives. Although still requiring assistance to walk, she had managed to clear her head slightly. As they walked into the ER they could hear a child crying.

"That's Emma, where is she?"

A small pink shape came rushing out of a door and launched itself at Jack. "Daddy, Daddy, Mummy," the tears were streaming down her little face. Maddie had dropped to her knees and Emma ran into her arms. Jack knelt down and put his arms around his two girls. All three of them were crying tears of joy.

Emma was the first to pull back. "The lady said you didn't want me anymore."

Jack said, "The lady told you a lie."

In Emma's world telling a lie was the worst possible thing a person could do. "Is she in trouble?"

"She is in so much trouble ye wouldnae believe it," Jack answered. "We love you and we would never give you away."

The hospital staff was concerned about the state Maddie was in and suggested admitting her. Jack finally had his family back together and there was no way he was leaving the hospital without either of them.

Edwards drove them home. Mrs. Brown and Betty had straightened up the sitting room and were warming some of the food the well-wishers had brought.

Once again news vans lined the road and people stood watching; most of them neighbours who had been praying for a successful outcome. When Emma got out of Edwards' car they all cheered. Questions from the news hounds peppered the air.

Leaving Jack to take his girls into the house, Edwards turned to the press. "I have one statement to make. We have found Emma Buchanan. She is safe and well and has now been returned to her parents. Any further information will come from our press officer." With that, he turned and went into the house.

Maddie and Jack were sitting on the settee. Emma was partly on Maddie's knee with her little arms around Jack's neck. Bob and Betty were crouched on the floor in front of them. Mrs. Brown was in the chair beside the settee. Emma was telling them a garbled version of what had happened to her.

Betty and Mrs. Brown set the food out on the dining room table and asked Edwards to join them. Seeing his best opportunity to talk to Emma, he agreed. None of them had realized how hungry they were and other than Emma chattering away, they ate in silence. Even Maddie, stoned as she was, managed to eat something. It seemed to ease the clouds around her mind slightly.

After dinner they returned to the sitting room. Emma sat on her daddy's knee. Maddie, on the verge of collapse, leaned against Jack, holding Emma's hand. Edwards sat in a chair next to the settee. He took a deep breath and asked the little girl to tell him what the lady had been like and what they had been doing for the last few days. At three, Emma was unable to tell the story, but with gentle questioning Edwards extracted the information he needed. They were all relieved that Emma had been treated so well. The only complaints the girl had were being told her mummy and daddy didn't want her and being left alone.

After Edwards left, Jack phoned Siobhan and Charlie to let them know Emma was home. They had wanted to come to the house to sit with the others and wait but Jack had said no. He didn't want the press making a connection between the girls and him. It was the only way he could think of to keep them safe. They contented themselves with calling several times a day to see if there was any news. When Jack phoned them they were very happy that their sister was home safe and insisted on coming over to see her. This time, Jack said yes.

# *CHAPTER 65*

Ann Johnson had expressed surprise when the police had come to get Emma. Having convinced herself that she and Jack had been involved at one time, she was equally certain Emma was their child. Ann had had a stillborn daughter three years previously but believed the people at the hospital had lied to her and had stolen her child. She had been fixated on Jack since before her daughter was born and had convinced herself that Jack was the father and he had thrown her over in favour of the dancer. She was sure Emma was their child and Jack had taken her. She had done nothing more than take back her own child.

Ann was taken to the police station, but after an hour of questioning, it was determined that she was unable to grasp the reality of her situation. She was transferred to the NHS mental health facility for assessment. She would be kept on a locked ward and treated there until her court date.

With treatment, consisting of antipsychotic drugs and psychotherapy, by the time her court case came before the judge, Ann had come to realize and admit Emma was not her child. She expressed remorse for having put Emma's family through such trauma. Her solicitor argued that during the time she had Emma Ann was suffering from untreated mental illness and should be found not guilty of kidnapping. She needed treatment not prison. He emphasized her lack of subterfuge and the ease with which she was discovered were indicative of a lack of understanding the situation and an indication of her mental state.

The Procurator Fiscal saw the case differently. He believed Ann's remorse was not sincere. The woman had been aware enough of the situation that she knew not to take Emma to her home. She had taken a great deal of time and trouble to create the pink room for Emma, the location of which indicated forethought and planning. Her credit card receipts showed she had purchased the materials to outfit the room and the furniture over a period of three months. She had rented the storage unit four months prior to Emma's kidnapping. She had stalked Jack for nearly six months before that and she had then spent days watching the house. She had made contact with Emma, so the girl would recognize her and not make a fuss when Ann approached her. The photos of Emma and Jack had not been on her mantle when the police had come to interview her, indicating she expected a visit from them at some point. All of this indicated a great deal of forethought and planning not consistent with a plea of mental incompetence.

After a battle of expert witnesses and psychiatrists on both sides, the court agreed with the Procurator Fiscal. Ann Johnson was found guilty of kidnapping and sentenced to ten years as a guest of Her Majesty's prison system. She would still be receiving treatment for her psychosis, but would no longer be at liberty to repeat her actions with Emma or with any other child.

Maddie and Jack kept a close eye on the legal progress of Ms. Johnson, eagerly sucking up the information provided by the media and by DI Edwards. When the verdict came down, they heaved a collective sigh of relief. It was safe to go on with their lives again without constantly looking over their shoulders. They were still cautious, realizing there could be other rabid fans. Anytime Bob and Jack saw the same person at more than one show, they were going to make careful note of the date and place.

# *CHAPTER 66*

It had taken Maddie three days to recover from the effects of the sedatives. During that time she had refused to let Emma out of her sight. She had even insisted a small bed be brought into the master bedroom so Emma could sleep with her and Jack. Maddie had wanted Emma in the bed with them, but Jack had refused.

Emma really liked sleeping in her parents' room. The lady had told her her mummy and daddy didn't want her anymore, but this proved they did. For the first few nights she had nightmares about being given away but with the constant attention and reassurances from her parents the bad dreams soon went away.

For two months, Emma slept in her parents' room. At Jack's insistence she was finally moved back to her own room. The first few nights the nightmares returned and Maddie spent those nights sitting in Emma's room. After a week, Emma had settled in and the nightmares ceased.

Emma would be starting school in September and Jack was anxious to start trying for a second child. When he had finally convinced Maddie to return to their bed, they began to work on it. At first, Maddie was distracted and not able to give herself up to their lovemaking like she had before. She was constantly listening for Emma's cries. As Emma settled into her own room, Maddie began to enjoy herself more. Jack worked hard to please her and it wasn't long till their lovemaking returned to the experience it had been before Emma's kidnapping.

As the months went by life returned to normal. Jack started touring again and Emma started school. There was still no sign of a second baby. Jack suggested a visit to the White Stag Inn. It had worked once before, maybe it would again. They had one child and no reason to believe they couldn't have a second.

Mrs. Brown was enlisted to stay with Emma. Maddie and Emma were both a little unsettled at being apart, but Emma was staying in her own house and knew her parents would be coming back. They told her they would. Maddie trusted Mrs. Brown to keep the girl safe.

Jack and Maddie had a wonderful time at the White Stag. It was the first time they'd been away together in a very long time. The separation from Emma was relieved by a telephone call every morning and night. It was winter in the highlands and Maddie and Jack spent their days snowshoeing and relaxing by the fire. Maddie tried to ignore the stags' antlers hanging on the walls in the lounge and enjoy the fire. She and Jack spent the nights making love. Both were hoping for a pregnancy, but there was no pressure and they enjoyed one another. In the relaxed atmosphere their lovemaking took on the same magical quality it had when they were first together. Even after so many years, they were still finding new ways to please each other.

# CHAPTER 67

In March, Jack and Bob had a short tour in Ireland. Since their trip to the White Stag had worked out well, Mrs. Brown was again enlisted to look after Emma and Maddie went on tour. For the first time in over a year, Maddie sang and danced on stage with Jack. The audiences loved it. Betty had come along too and after the tour, they spent a few days in Dublin. On their last night, Maddie and Jack had room service and a nice romantic dinner in their room. Although it was too cold to go out on the balcony, they stood at the door and admired the sunset.

With a mischievous grin, Maddie handed Jack a stick. It was a replay of that night nearly five years ago when she had told him she was pregnant with Emma. Maddie had waited nearly two weeks to tell Jack. The temptation to tell him sooner had been almost unbearable, but she knew it would be sweeter to tell him the same way she had for Emma.

Jack had wondered why Maddie hadn't had any of the Irish coffee she loved on this trip but he hadn't said anything. He wasn't completely surprised at the news, but he was thrilled. Peppering her with the same questions he had the last time, he got some answers that worried him. Maddie had been sick several mornings, but had managed to hide it from him. She'd also been very tired. He had noticed she'd been taking more naps than usual and had even fallen asleep on the plane, something she never did. Concerned about her, he scooped her up and took her to bed. That night they made love three times, each time sweeter and more tender than the previous time.

At breakfast the following day, they told Bob and Betty, making it real. Bob ordered orange juice for Maddie and mimosas for the rest of them. The short flight home was a jolly affair. It was a beautiful sunny winter day, with no turbulence, for which Maddie was grateful. Bob and Jack continued celebrating.

When they saw John at the airport to meet them, Bob and Jack groaned. Sure enough, John had arranged a mini tour of the east of Scotland for them the next week. He drove them back to Jack and Maddie's so they could go over the itinerary and sign the contracts. The last time they had toured eastern Scotland Maddie had sung and danced with Jack. John had negotiated the contract with this in mind, hoping to get Maddie back on stage. It took more than a little persuasion, but eventually she agreed to do this tour with them, although she insisted she was not going back on the road.

John wondered if he should tell them about the tour of Canada he had booked for the three of them in May. He figured it was far enough away he could wait. Maybe the showbiz bug would bite Maddie again.

Maddie wondered if they should tell John she was pregnant so he wouldn't book her on any more tours.

# *CHAPTER 68*

Maddie was on her knees in front of the toilet, resting her sweating head against her arm. Jack was getting her a glass of water.

"This one has got to be a boy," she said. "Boys are always trouble."

Jack was slightly offended, but didn't say anything. Maddie had been sick most mornings with this pregnancy. They had not said anything to each other, but both were remembering the first pregnancy that had ended in heartbreak. In another three weeks they would be past the point at which they had lost Jamie, and once again not saying anything to each other, they were both counting the days.

Jack helped Maddie back to bed. The green was fading from her face. It was bad enough when she was sick at home, but it seemed more miserable when they were on tour. He took her in his arms and they lay there both thinking.

Finally Maddie said what they were both thinking. "Jack, this is the same as the first time."

Jack hugged her tighter and said, "That doesnae mean it'll have the same outcome."

Maddie didn't say anything. She had been trying, unsuccessfully, not to bond with the child growing in her. They both desperately wanted this child. Maddie's body had forgotten the physical pain associated with the loss of Jamie, but her mind remembered the heartbreak.

Although they had intended to tell no one other than Bob and Betty until after the point at which Jamie was lost, they had had to tell John. The showbiz bug had bitten Maddie again, but both she and Jack agreed there would be no highland dancing. It required too much energy and took too much bone jarring work for a pregnant woman.

They had compromised with John and as Maddie had when pregnant with Emma, they all agreed she would sing and dance with Jack, but that was it. John stopped negotiating for Maddie, but she continued to perform periodically with Bob and Jack.

Maddie always enjoyed the tours of Canada, largely because she and Jack would add a few days to the end to visit her family in Ottawa. On this tour, they had decided to bring Emma with them for three reasons. They thought she would get more of an education from travelling than she would in school. More influential though was their reluctance to have her apart from them for nearly a month. She still had the occasional nightmare of being abandoned by her parents. Mrs. Brown had become like a grandmother to Emma, but Jack and Maddie didn't think it was fair to the child to leave her for that long. Anyway, they wanted Emma to spend some time with her mother's family.

Emma had been too young to remember her previous trips on tour so this was a whole new experience for her. She loved flying and she loved being backstage while her mummy and daddy were performing. She had made friends with one of the 'roadies' and always had a backstage babysitter they all trusted.

As had become the pattern, the Canadian tour started in Victoria and worked its way east. John had been able to renegotiate the contracts with some of the Canadian venues to give the group more time off between performances. This gave them some time to show Emma the local sights. She was captivated when they went to the top of the Husky tower in Calgary, but the trip to the top of the CN tower in Toronto amazed her. She couldn't understand how all the other buildings had turned to toys and the people on the ground to ants. She thought it was magic.

The visit with Maddie's family was enjoyed by all. Once again they stayed on the farm with Beckie and Ben. Emma fell in love with the animals. There were lots of cats, a dog named Beamer, cows, donkeys and bunnies, but what she really liked was when the wild racoons and skunks came to eat. Her mummy and daddy had said they couldn't get a racoon or a skunk, but they promised her a kitten when they got home. Emma went upstairs to pack her suitcase. She wanted to go home right away.

Beckie and Ben went with Maddie and Jack when they took Emma sightseeing. They showed Emma the local sights they thought she would like, including the barns at the Experimental Farm, the Museum of Science and Technology and the Parliament Buildings. She was too young to really understand what happened in Parliament, but she liked the sound of the carillon. She just called them the bells. She also really liked the petting zoo they went to. They had pony rides there and Emma couldn't stop talking about 'riding the big horse'.

Maddie had told Beckie she was pregnant but had not told her family. She was still sick nearly every morning and had wanted to wait until they were past the point in her pregnancy when they had lost Jamie. That monumental day was passed when they were in Edmonton. Now they would tell people.

When Maddie included both her mother's and father's sides of the family, the group was too large for anyone's house. Instead, as had become their custom, they rented the party room of Maddie's favourite restaurant. The announcement was made at the family dinner. They let Emma tell everyone she was going to have a baby brother or sister that was growing in Mummy's tummy. Emma felt very important when everyone started congratulating her on becoming a big sister.

As with the shower and stag for the wedding, Beckie and Ben had planned a surprise shower for the new baby. When Maddie, Jack and Emma left Ottawa they had to buy a new suitcase to hold all the gifts they had received for both Emma and the new baby.

Life was good again.

# *CHAPTER 69*

Jack was asleep, but Maddie lay in bed wide awake. The clock said it was 5:23. She felt as large and graceful as an elephant wallowing in a mud bath. She had known this baby was a boy, and the ultrasound had proved her right. She had been sick most mornings for the first four months of the pregnancy. She had been on bedrest for nearly a month after the tour of Canada. During that time Siobhan and Charlie had been constant visitors and of enormous help with Emma and the house. They took turns babysitting and cooking. Maddie was relieved Jack wasn't cooking the whole time. There were a few things he made really well, but otherwise although he tried, cooking wasn't his forte.

Maddie was always tired and she was unhappy that she and Emma couldn't travel with Jack and Bob. As of today the baby was two weeks overdue. She was getting impatient. She was going to be induced on the 27th if the baby didn't make an appearance by then. It was only the 23rd.

Maddie was tired and grumpy but she couldn't sleep. Jack's snoring wasn't improving her mood any. She managed to get out of bed without waking him and waddled down the hall to Emma's room. She looked in on the little girl who was sound asleep, her orange and white kitten, George, curled into a ball beside her. Not wanting to disturb anyone, Maddie went downstairs.

She and Jack had been discussing the idea of moving to a larger house. With the impending arrival of the new baby, the spare room had been converted to a nursery, leaving them without a room for guests. Neither of them liked the idea of visitors having to sleep on a pullout couch in the office. They had also discussed the possibility of building an addition on the house. This was Maddie's preference. They had so many happy memories in this house she didn't want to leave it.

Jack had made the same arrangements for help with the new baby that he had for Emma. Beckie had already been there for two weeks of the four she was staying and Maddie was beginning to think she'd be gone home before the baby arrived. At this rate, Jack would be off on tour again when the baby made his appearance. John had given the boys six weeks off for the new baby, but three of them had already passed.

Jack came down the stairs, concern clouding his handsome face. "Are ye a'right?" he asked Maddie. He had woken up at 5:47, alarmed to find himself in bed alone. He too was a little edgy waiting for the baby, and he'd rushed downstairs only to find a grumpy Maddie in the sitting room. He sat on the settee beside her and put his arm around her.

She leaned into him saying, "I'm so tired of being kicked in the stomach."

He could see the ripples rolling across her belly. He put his hand on her. Although he enjoyed feeling their baby move, Jack couldn't even imagine what it felt like to be kicked in the stomach from the inside. "Stop kickin' yer mummy," he said to her belly.

The feel of Jack's hand on her belly was comforting to Maddie and it also seemed to comfort the child. The constant kicking stopped and with only sporadic boots, Maddie felt a little better.

"You see, luv, boys aren't all bad. This one listens to his daddy."

She smiled. "I'm sorry I've been so miserable the last few days," she said, "but I'm really getting tired of being pregnant."

"We're all anxious for our little Sandy to make his appearance," Jack said. Once they had found out for sure it was a boy, they had named him Andrew and were going to call him Sandy.

"Shall I make some breakfast?" Jack asked.

"Make yourself some, luv. I'm really not hungry."

"You both have to eat," he said. "I can make your favourite."

Maddie's favourite was cinnamon waffles, one thing Jack made well. They were also Beckie's favourite. Beckie normally didn't eat breakfast, but she could be tempted with cinnamon waffles. Despite years of Maddie's irregular meal schedule, Jack still wasn't used to people skipping meals. He especially didn't like their houseguests missing meals. He thought it made him a bad host.

He had just finished mixing the batter when Maddie called him. "You'd better wake Beckie. I think little Sandy is going to put in an appearance today."

"Really?"

"I'm pretty sure."

Jack was uncomfortable with the idea of getting Beckie out of bed, but there was no way he was going to make Maddie walk upstairs. He came downstairs with a sleepy Beckie right behind him. She was definitely not a morning person and it was only 6:30.

“Is it time?” she asked.

“Pretty soon,” Maddie said. “I’m just so miserable right now I wanted to share. Seriously though, I wanted to give you some warning that you will probably have to get Emma ready for school.”

“I can do that.”

Maddie inhaled sharply as a strong contraction rippled through her. “I don’t think this guy is going to take as long as Emma did.”

Jack went to get Maddie’s bag and put it in the car. “Do we need to leave now?” he asked.

“Not just yet, but soon.”

Jack lifted her legs and put them on the coffee table. Maddie asked Beckie to bring her some clothes from upstairs. She didn’t want to go out in her jammies. It took the three of them to get her dressed.

“Jack it’s almost time to go. Would you get Emma up? I want to talk to her before we leave.”

As usual Emma was a bundle of energy when she got up. She gave her daddy a hug then raced downstairs to see mummy, George right behind her. It wasn’t all that easy to give mummy a hug these days. Emma couldn’t get her arms around Maddie’s belly and Maddie had trouble bending over so the little girl could hug her neck. Maddie asked Emma to sit beside her.

“Emma, Mummy and Daddy are going to the hospital now. Remember we talked about Mummy being away for a day or two when your baby brother comes? It’s time for Daddy and me to go and get him. Mummy won’t be coming home tonight, but Daddy will. When Mummy comes home I’ll bring baby Sandy with me. Aunt Beckie and Daddy will look after you while Mummy’s gone.”

Emma was so excited she started bouncing on the couch. Leaving Emma with Beckie, Jack and Maddie headed to the hospital. Her contractions were strong and Jack half carried her to the car.

They had been at the hospital for about six hours when the doctor made the decision to do a C-section. Maddie was suffering very strong, painful contractions, but the baby wasn’t moving and appeared to be in some distress. Jack wasn’t sure he wanted to stay in the room, but before they put Maddie under the anesthetic, she asked him to watch their baby being born. Reluctant as he was to see Maddie cut open, he could never refuse her anything. The room seemed to spin a bit as Jack watched the operation, but it was over quickly and his head cleared at the sight of his son. As he had with Emma, he did a quick inventory: two legs, two arms, ten fingers, ten toes. He was perfect. By the time the doctor had Maddie stitched up and the nurse had the baby cleaned up, Maddie was starting to wake up. Baby Sandy was laid on her chest. Jack kissed her then as he had with Emma, he laid his head on the pillow beside hers and they studied the tiny human being they had created. Sandy was not as tiny as Emma had been. At 9 lbs 9 ozs it was not surprising Maddie had needed a C-section.

Because of the C-section Maddie had to stay in the hospital for three days. On the second day, Jack brought Emma to see Mummy and Sandy. Emma felt very important bringing Sandy a gift. She was so happy to finally have her baby brother she had been willing to give him one of her stuffed animals. Daddy said she could get a new one for him and a new one for herself too. That made her even happier. She didn't have to give up her toys. When it came time for her to leave, she wanted Maddie and little Sandy to go home with them. She wasn't too happy when it was explained to her that they couldn't. She was disappointed. She had told all her friends she had a new baby brother and she wanted to take him to school to show him off.

With the arrival of little Sandy, the definition of 'normal' life changed again for the Buchanans. With two small children, Maddie no longer went on the road with Jack. They both missed that. She would dance and sing with Jack when he and Bob were doing dinner theatre shows locally, but her travelling days were over.

Although what passed for 'normal' life for the Buchanan family had changed, life was good again. They had no idea what the future had in store for them.

# *CHAPTER 70*

Maddie and Jack were watching the telly in the sitting room one Saturday evening when the phone rang. Maddie answered it. Jack was listening, wondering who would be calling this late in the evening. It was almost 11:00. There was silence from Maddie then she started speaking Gaelic to the person on the other end of the phone. Jack hadn't known she spoke Gaelic. His Gaelic was very limited and he only caught a few words here and there. Maddie had a strange look on her face. When she hung up, she went straight to the bar and poured herself a good sized whisky. She gulped it all down, then stood at the bar trying to catch her breath. Jack was more than a little concerned. Maddie rarely drank and when she did it was usually gin and bitter lemon, not neat whisky. She had a very odd look on her face too, something between anger and sorrow.

"What is it, luv?" he asked her.

Still trying to catch her breath after the whisky, she sat beside him on the settee. Not sure where to start, she sat quietly for a moment. Jack was getting worried.

Finally, after what seemed like an eternity, Maddie started to talk. "We need to talk," she said. Jack was immediately on alert. This was their warning phrase for life is going to change significantly and it was usually his statement. With the look on Maddie's face he was afraid of what she was going to say. "You know all of my immediate family, but there's something I didn't tell you about my extended family. It seemed so remote a possibility that I never even thought to mention it." Worried now, Jack waited for her to continue. "I'm not sure where to start. My mother's family is descended from the dukes of Morden. You know the duke was my cousin. He was at our wedding. I was $37^{th}$ in line for the Duchy. There has been a horrible explosion at a hotel in Morden. Fifty-three people have died, including the duke and his whole family. Six are still missing. Other than my mother and grandmother all the people standing between me and the Duchy were killed. My mom and nan both refused the title.

Without thinking, because it was so ingrained in me as a child, I responded with the Gaelic acceptance speech without even thinking about it. I'm not sure what difference this will make for us, but I'm now the MacMorden Duke. We don't have to worry about a larger house. We've just inherited a castle; actually, several castles, some of which are inhabitable. I told you as a child I had spent most of my summers with my cousins in Scotland. What I didn't mention is they were spent in a castle."

Jack was stunned. He didn't know what questions to ask first. Realizing Maddie was in shock, he got up and got them both a dram. This one she sipped slowly. He didn't say anything until she was done with her drink, then he asked her to repeat what she had just said. After she had repeated her tale, Jack sat quietly trying to absorb it.

"So basically what you're telling me is you have a new job and we live in a castle."

Surprised by how simple he made it sound, Maddie said, "Yes."

Still in shock Maddie wasn't sure what to do first. It was almost midnight, but no one she needed to talk to would be getting any sleep. Finally making a decision, her first call was to the Duchy's general manager, Archie MacKay, the person who had delivered the news to her in the first place. Shocked beyond thought when he had first called, Maddie hadn't asked him any questions. She called him now, wanting further explanation of what had actually happened. With the arrival of a new duke, there were often massive staff changes. Maddie wanted to make sure Archie would continue to work for the Duchy, which was more like a business than a family. She had been so far removed from it for so many years, and really not prepared for it at all that she wouldn't know where to begin without him. He seemed relieved he still had a job, but he wasn't able to give her many details of what had happened. There had been a gathering of the senior members of the clan at a hotel in Morden. There had been an explosion at the hotel, which the police were treating as suspicious. Fifty-three of the ninety-one people there had been killed outright and another ten seriously injured and not expected to survive. Several others had been injured and hospitalized, but were expected to fully recover. Six people were still missing and presumed dead. It was expected their bodies would be found when the grim task of sifting through the rubble started. Almost everyone else there had suffered minor injuries. Maddie was horrified. With a promise to go to Morden in the morning, she rang off.

Maddie's next call was to the home farm manager. Duncan MacDougall had been farm manager for thirty years and had known Maddie as a child. Although both still in shock, they relieved each other's minds. Duncan was happy he still had a job and Maddie was happy she still had a manager. As she had told Archie, there were to be no staff changes other than replacements for those who had been lost.

The third call was to the Morden police station. Identifying herself, Maddie asked for details of the incident. At this point, they had few details other than what Archie had told her. They did tell her two of the injured had not survived. She made arrangements to meet with the police chief the following day and to visit the scene of the tragedy.

Maddie and Jack sat together for a long time, not talking then Maddie started to cry. Although not close as adults, several of the dead had been good childhood friends. Between the loss of them and the intimidating turn her life had just taken, she was totally overwhelmed. Jack put his arm around her. Still stunned by the enormity of the situation, he had no idea what to say to her. Knowing neither of them would sleep, he suggested, "Let's go to bed. We probably won't sleep but we can at least rest our bodies. I think tomorrow is going to be a very hard day."

Jack and Maddie got up early in the morning. The press had gotten hold of the story and even though their phone number was unlisted, calls started coming in at 6:00am.

Maddie knew Mrs. Brown was an early riser. Although it wasn't one of the days she normally worked, Maddie called her to see if she was available for the day. Mrs. Brown had seen the early news on telly and was going to offer to come over for the day anyway.

Jack had every intention of going to Morden with Maddie. There wasn't much he could do but offer her moral support and she really appreciated his offer to go with her. She would need that support. They made their plans for the day, Jack insisting they both have a good breakfast first. Maddie wasn't hungry, but Jack offered to make his special cinnamon waffles, and she thought she could eat them. By the time the waffles were ready she'd already been through one pot of coffee and had a second pot brewing. Mrs. Brown arrived when they were eating. Her hug and offer of condolences reduced Maddie to tears.

"I hope I can keep these tears under control," she said. "I'm not going to give the bastards who did this the satisfaction of seeing any appearance of weakness."

Maddie dressed carefully in a MacMorden tartan kilt and a black turtleneck sweater. She also wore an old medallion of the clan crest. She didn't have proper Chief's attire, but she thought this would portray her point as best she could. Her point was clan solidarity, strength and respect and grief for those lost.

# *CHAPTER 71*

Maddie was glad Jack was driving. Her thoughts were so scattered she didn't think she would have been able to keep the car on the road. Their first stop was at the Morden police station. The chief was expecting them. Looking like he hadn't slept all night either, he gave them the information that was known.

"It appears the explosion was deliberately set, not accidental. At this point we have no leads as to who might have done it or why."

Another three of the injured had succumbed to their injuries. That made a total of fifty-eight murders. Three of the remaining injured were in critical condition; two more were in serious but stable condition. There were another seven not as seriously injured still in hospital and several had been treated and released. There were still six people unaccounted for.

The first thing Maddie wanted to do was visit the scene of the tragedy. They went in the chief's car. The hotel she remembered had been a large stone structure that had stood for over two hundred years and looked invincible. All that remained of it were two standing walls and smoking piles of rubble and debris. Amazed that anyone had survived the devastation, Maddie couldn't imagine the amount of explosives it would have taken to reduce the once grand hotel to this state. Whoever had done this did not intend that anyone survive.

Maddie told the chief, "Once you find the people responsible they will be tried for murder for each of the individuals who died as a result of the explosion and attempted murder for each of those who survived." She was determined to ensure their sentences were consecutive and not concurrent. "They will never get out." She vowed to herself that clan business would go on as before. The bombers would not have the satisfaction of having disrupted it nor destroyed the clan.

Their next stop was at the hospital to visit the injured. As well as the three in critical condition and the two in serious condition, six of the seven who had been admitted with non-life-threatening injuries were still there. Although she wasn't able to do anything, the injured and their families appreciated Maddie's visit and the show of support.

The local press had been following them since they first arrived at the police station. At both stops they had shoved microphones into Maddie's face asking questions.

"Do you know what happened?"

"Was it accidental?"

"How did it happen?"

"Who do you think did it?"

"Why would someone do this?" The questions peppered the air.

After each question the chief replied, "No comment."

Flashbulbs were popping as the photographers watched the new duke with the police chief. Maddie was glad she had worn a kilt. She intended every encounter with the press would be a show of strength. As well as the local press, news vans were starting to arrive from all over the country and foreign correspondents were arriving from London. This was being proclaimed an act of war on Scottish soil. They didn't yet know who the war was against.

Having done what she could in town, Maddie thought it time for them to go to the castle. The chief returned her and Jack to their car which was parked at the station. He escorted them to the castle to assist with the army of press following them. Although parts of the castle were open to the public, the area they were going to was private. As it was before opening time for visitors, the press would be halted at the doors of the public area.

Jack had been to several Scottish castles, many of them with Maddie, but Morden was one he had missed. Driving up the long, straight drive, Jack felt an air of unreality. The massive pile of grey stone in front of the car was a real life castle and it was now Maddie's and by extension his. It was a fairly modern castle, built in the early 1700s and as castles go, it was quite plain on the outside. It had been built in a square, with round turrets at each corner. In the centre, a large square turret towered over the rest of the castle. Jack thought it looked very much like Inverary Castle, one he had been to. As they approached the castle Jack saw a flag being raised on the pole on top of the tower. Not only did his wife have a castle, she had a flag that flew over it when she was there. His grasp of reality was becoming very tenuous. He wasn't sure if he was in a nightmare or a fairy tale.

When Maddie and Jack first walked into the vast entrance hall, Jack was amazed to see the great sunburst on the wall made of antique swords and the collection of weapons from the past. The square hall was about three stories high and the sunburst covered one whole wall. Jack made a conscious effort to keep his jaw from dropping. When Maddie turned to him and said, “Hey, honey, we’re home,” he didn’t trust himself to say anything.

Archie was waiting for them when they walked in. Jack thought he looked like any other business man. He was about forty, tall, thin and dressed in business clothes. In the castle, this meant jacket, shirt, tie and kilt. When Archie referred to Maddie as ‘Your Grace’ Jack started to realize just how much of an impact this was going to have on their lives.

When Maddie and Jack had gone in the main door, a large and very thick double door made of solid oak and reinforced with iron studs and hinges, the staff was lined up to greet them. Touched, Maddie made a short speech. Although she had nothing prepared, she expressed sympathy to those who had lost family members and friends and reiterated her intention that once caught, those responsible would be prosecuted to the full extent of the law. She also assured them they would all keep their jobs.

Archie escorted them to the administration wing of the castle which included the duke’s private apartments. This whole area was private and when visitors and the press were let in to the castle, there was no sign of Maddie. Disappointed, the press camped out next to the large wooden door marked ‘private’.

The administration wing looked like any other office in an old building. There was a large open area with a reception desk and two secretaries’ desks. Archie introduce Maddie and Jack to the three women in the office, the young receptionist and two older secretaries. Looking past them, Jack could see two office doors with a corridor next to them leading to what he assumed were several more offices.

Archie led them into the room that would be Maddie’s office. There was a sitting area with a green leather sofa and two matching armchairs. Jack thought the massive wooden desk was the size of their dining room table. It was a rich dark wood polished to the point it glowed. The sun was shining in the large windows behind it intensifying the effect. One wall was lined with matching bookshelves. The opposite wall had a stone fireplace. The only modern touches in the room were a large television set and a telephone on the desk.

After determining the office staff was able to maintain the running of the Duchy without immediate input from Maddie, she insisted, “My first order of business is to plan a memorial service for the victims of the explosion. Their families will have individual funerals, but this will be a group memorial." She would give an address to what was left of the clan, and she would put the call out to anyone else who wanted to say something. "I also intend to erect a memorial plaque marking the scene of the tragedy. It will provide a message of support for the families of the victims and hopefully a threat to the perpetrators." The wording on the plaque would have to be carefully thought out.

The next item on her agenda was to speak to Duncan about the home farm. Although he spent most of his time in the farm administration building, Duncan also had an office in the castle just along the corridor from Maddie's, where he was this morning. Archie had him come into the new duke's office. In his late fifties, Duncan was a big bear of a man. Dressed in his kilt, he looked like the highland warriors Jack had seen in films. His dark red hair was peppered with silver, and his complexion was the ruddy colour associated with a life outdoors. Delighted to see a friend in the midst of all the sorrow, Maddie gave him a big hug which he returned, almost squeezing the air out of her, and then she introduced him to Jack. As she had with the office staff, she assured Duncan that all current employees would keep their jobs. As with the office staff, she determined the farm staff was able to continue without immediate input from her.

Jack was concerned about Maddie. She had stoically faced all the day had brought so far and he thought she was starting to appear brittle.

"You need a break," he said to her.

They had lunch served in the morning room of the private apartments, a charming round room at the base of one of the turrets. Its stone walls were draped with rich tapestries and the lattice windows were open to what had turned into a lovely day. The room was tastefully furnished with reproduction eighteenth century furniture. A few modern touches had been added to the furniture, such as extra padding on the chairs, but the overall appearance had Maddie and Jack feeling like time travellers.

After lunch Maddie gave Jack a tour of the private apartments she remembered so well from her childhood. There had been little change over the years. All the rooms except the library were furnished in eighteenth century reproduction furniture with extra comfort built in. The castle maintained its original appearance, but without damage to the artifacts. The library was a comfy room with an overstuffed love seat and two chairs, a large desk and books lining the walls. A large stone fireplace took up most of one wall. The only modern touch was a large television. Jack was delighted to see the apartments had seven bedrooms.

"One for company and three more kids," he suggested.

Maddie just said, "We'll see."

Not convinced Maddie had had a long enough break, Jack suggested, "Let's go for a walk in the private gardens."

Maddie had another idea. "Why don't we take out a couple of the horses?"

They went down to the private stables, a modern addition out of sight of the public areas. Maddie greeted Andy, the head groom. Like most of the other staff, he had been there for many years and remembered 'little Maddie'.

Jack had done some riding, but not a lot. Andy saddled up a gentle brown mare for him. Maddie, wanting to burn off sorrow, anger and frustration opted for a spirited black stallion. They rode sedately up the hill behind the stable. At the top was a meadow that stretched as far as Jack could see.

Saying, "If you don't mind waiting here for a few minutes, I'll be right back," Maddie urged the stallion forward.

He took off at what Jack thought was breakneck speed. Maddie raced him around the meadow twice before returning to Jack. Both she and the horse were breathing hard when they got back.

"I feel better now," she said.

The day had been full of surprises for Jack, some good and some bad. He knew Maddie had done some riding but he'd had no idea she was such a good rider. Together they cantered across the meadow. Through some trees Jack could see Loch Fyne. He looked over at Maddie and was surprised and relieved to see her crying. The emotions she had bottled up since their visit to the ruined hotel were finally being released. He dismounted and went to help her dismount. He stood with his arms around her while she cried for the family and friends she had lost. They walked over to the edge of the meadow and looked out at the loch.

Mounting their horses again, Maddie again asked Jack to wait for her. She raced the stallion around the meadow twice again. When they returned to the stable, she and the horse were still breathing hard.

Andy looked at them, realizing she had been racing the horse, and said, "You're up to your old tricks, Your Grace."

"Guilty," she admitted.

Leaving the stable, they returned to the private apartments.

There was nothing else to be done today, so Maddie and Jack returned to

Prestwick. They had managed to leave the castle unnoticed, but when they got home there were news vans parked outside the house. Maddie gave in and gave them a short statement.

"We have toured the site of the tragedy and the police will be pursuing the perpetrators until caught. I'm asking for privacy for the families of the victims of this cowardly act. They have lost loved ones and should be allowed to grieve without cameras or microphones. Thank you for your consideration. The chief of police in Morden, or I, will advise you of any progress on the case." Having said all she intended to say, she turned and went into the house.

The first thing Maddie did when she went in was hug Emma. Then she hugged baby Sandy. She had a new appreciation of how precious her family was to her. Too easily they could be taken away. She also gave Jack a big hug and thanked him for supporting her all day. Seeing her as part of the family, Maddie gave Mrs. Brown a hug and thanked her for the day.

Mrs. Brown had a lovely supper ready for them. She listened as Jack tried to explain the day's events to her. Maddie was suddenly too tired to even talk. Chasing her and Jack off to bed, Mrs. Brown readied the children for bed. She had often stayed overnight when Maddie and Jack had been out late, and she thought this would be a good night to stay too. The two of them were so tired they probably wouldn't hear the kids if they cried.

# *CHAPTER 72*

The next morning Maddie rang the police chief in Morden.

"Has there been any progress?" she asked.

"The piles of rubble that used to be the hotel are still smoking, so we haven't been able to check inside, but we did find evidence of dynamite where some of the walls had been. Browne's construction site notified us that all their dynamite had been stolen. My men investigating the theft found three sets of fingerprints that did not belong to the workers on the construction site."

Thanking him, Maddie rang off.

Next on Maddie's agenda was ordering a formal highland kit. She and Jack braved the press that lingered outside and went to the kilt maker in Glasgow. Although Jack had the jackets, he didn't have a kilt in the MacMorden tartan. Maddie needed the whole kit: dress and hunting kilts, formal and informal jackets and appropriate shirts and accessories. She wanted the male kit with a few feminine touches. She was going to be referred to as the duke, not the duchess, and she needed to look the part. Jack's kilt would be ready in a week, but her order was going to take longer. Determining an approximate date of two and a half weeks, she could make plans.

Returning home, Maddie called Archie. She set the date for the memorial as the one month anniversary of the tragedy. Thankfully Jack would be home at that time. She was going to need his support. She asked Archie to inform what was left of the clan and invite any who wanted to speak to do so. The next thing Maddie had to do was work out the wording for the memorial plaque. It was not going to be easy to convey the sentiments involved: sorrow, anger, determination. The memorial service was to be in the church and she wanted to dedicate the plaque marking the site of the tragedy on the same day. She also had difficult speeches to write for the previous duke's funeral and for the memorial service.

It was Sunday, and Bob and Jack were to go on tour Thursday. Jack said to Maddie, "I'm going to cancel the tour. You'll need my support." It was only a one week tour of Ireland, but he didn't want to leave her alone in these circumstances.

Maddie wouldn't hear of it. "No, Jack. You have obligations. While I would love to have you here, it would make me feel even worse to have you cancel a tour for this. I'll miss you, but I can handle it."

Despite the major change in her life, she didn't want Jack to have to change his. They still had to discuss whether they were going to move into the castle. She couldn't see not moving, but she didn't want to leave the house with so many happy memories. She was also reluctant to move Emma away from her friends.

Tuesday, Wednesday, Thursday and Friday, Maddie had multiple funerals to go to. She was determined to make an appearance at all of them. Because there were several each day, many of the appearances would be short and at the receptions afterwards, but she wanted to offer a show of support and sympathy to every family that had lost someone. She didn't have her formal kit yet so she dusted off her old velvet dancing jackets, pleased that they still fit her. One of them was black and fairly plain. It lacked the braiding that decorated most of them. With it and her own MacMorden kilt, she wasn't happy with her appearance, but it was the best she could do for now. Jack joined her for the funerals Tuesday and Wednesday. He didn't have a MacMorden kilt, but he did have a selection of tartans to choose from. He went through them and although his dress Gordon kilt was very similar to the dress MacMorden, he and Maddie decided he should wear his own Buchanan tartan.

Because the funerals were all in and around Morden, the family moved into the castle for a week. Emma was absolutely thrilled. She was sure now that she lived in a castle, she was a princess. Mrs. Brown came with them for the week. Although she was sorry for the circumstances, she too enjoyed the castle.

There were five funerals on Tuesday, two in the morning and three in the afternoon. They were all in the same church at different times so Maddie and Jack were able to attend all of them. They were all funerals for more than one person in a family and three of them included children. After each funeral Maddie spoke to the family, finding it harder each time to mask her own sorrow. The desire to appear strong in the face of the tragedy was taking a toll on her, but she knew the press was watching. She assumed the bombers would be watching the news to see the impact of their actions and she wasn't going to show any sign of weakness. The clan would carry on in the face of adversity as it always had, with a show of strength.

There were four funerals on Wednesday, all for multiple family members. None of these four were in Morden, but in four different nearby villages. All were in the afternoon, so Maddie wasn't able to attend them all, but she and Jack went to the first funeral and made an appearance at the receptions of the others. She was glad to have Jack's support. She was sorry he had to leave Thursday morning, but she didn't tell him that. He was still talking about cancelling the tour.

One of the perks of being the duke was having a car and driver. Maddie was glad of it. She was able to hold herself together for each funeral but after each one she was in tears. Especially hard were the ones for children. She managed to appear strong for each family then fell apart in the car.

Maddie survived the funerals on Thursday and Friday without Jack's support. Knowing she would need someone to lean on, he had arranged for Siobhan and Charlie to come to Morden and stay with Maddie till he returned from Ireland. Maddie was grateful for their support.

On Saturday there was only one funeral. It was for the previous duke and his wife and three children. The duke was Maddie's cousin. She had spent many summers with him and had a lot of happy memories. It was actually thanks to him she could ride as well as she did. He was three years older than her. She always wanted to play with him, but he thought she was too young – and she was a girl. He used to go riding to try and escape her but she always followed him. By the time she was ten she was as good a rider as he was. Since she'd moved to Scotland, she had spoken with the duke on the phone several times, but the only time she'd seen him had been at her wedding.

Although not delivering the eulogy, Maddie was expected to say something at this funeral and she wasn't sure she could. She spent two days writing her address and dissolving into tears each time she read it. She was wondering if she would be able to get through it at the funeral.

Saturday morning the phone rang early. It was the Morden police chief with some bad news. "My men and the firemen were sifting through the debris from the hotel and discovered the bodies of the six people who were missing." That brought the total of people killed to sixty-four. The police chief said, "I'll notify their families this morning. If you think it's appropriate, you can tell the rest of the clan at the duke's funeral this afternoon." The job of speaking to the clan at the funeral was getting harder and harder.

As Jack had noticed so long ago, Maddie was very good at compartmentalizing her emotions. She managed to make it through her address and through the reception afterwards. Maddie was touched that three of her friends from Prestwick, Gemma, Judy and Lynn, and several of her and Jack's entertainment friends had taken the time to come to the funeral. Their support and caring during Jack's absence was very welcome. There were also several representatives from other clans. They were all from different places in Scotland and Maddie thought their appearance sent out a subliminal message that all of Scotland was united against the terrorist tactics.

When she got in the car to return to the castle, the tears came. Maddie was sorry for the lost years when she hadn't really talked to her cousin, and sorry she didn't know his wife or children. When she got back to the castle (she couldn't think of it as home) she hugged Emma so tight, the girl complained, "Mummy, you're squashing me."

Maddie was more careful when she hugged baby Sandy. After a gruelling week, she took Sunday off for her family and herself. Jack was still away, but she spent the day playing with the kids and Siobhan and Charlie, really appreciating their time together.

By the time Jack returned from his tour, his family had moved back to Prestwick.

# *CHAPTER 73*

Maddie was in regular contact with the police chief in Morden. When they had anything new, he would call and update her. One morning he called with some news. "We've been sifting through the rubble of the hotel and we found something interesting." Maddie steeled herself. The last time he'd told her that, what they had found had been six bodies. At least now they were going through finer rubble and there was little likelihood of more bodies. Everyone known to be at the gathering had been accounted for.

The chief's news was very telling. "On one of the bricks, someone scratched 'Sinn Fein', the battle cry of the Irish Republican Army. There's nothing to tell us when it was scratched, but it's interesting that it was found near the residue of one of the bombs." He went on to tell her, "Six of the people killed in the bombing were in the same military regiment. They were stationed in Northern Ireland for a year and just returned to Scotland two weeks before the bombing. I think we now know why the hotel was bombed. We just don't know by whom." There were a couple of groups of Irish sympathizers in Morden and it gave him a place to start.

The police had not been able to match the fingerprints found at the construction site to anyone with a known record in Scotland, but they had also found the same fingerprints at the hotel site. There were only partial prints on the autographed brick they had found, but the partials appeared to match the others they had found. There were full fingerprints on the walls that were still standing and some of the other surfaces, notably in one of the outbuildings where the sniffer dogs had found traces of dynamite. With this new information, the chief contacted the Royal Ulster Constabulary's fingerprint division in Northern Ireland. He sent copies of the prints they had taken to Belfast. The police there were able to match the fingerprints to known Irish terrorists. Now they knew who they were looking for. It was just a matter of time till they were caught. The RUC believed the suspects had gone across the border into the Republic of Ireland, but with the situation the way it was, they believed the terrorists would soon come back to Northern Ireland. That was where the fighting was.

A week before the memorial, Maddie picked up her full highland kit. Jack thought she looked fantastic in it. She'd had two jackets made, a dark green one and a formal black one. She'd also had two kilts made, a dress and a hunting tartan. The shirt she wore with the black jacket and dress kilt had some lace around the neck and around the wrists. It reminded Jack of paintings he'd seen of Bonnie Prince Charlie, who he thought looked rather effeminate.

The memorial service for the victims of the hotel attack was held in the village church. It was a long, sad and somber affair. Photos of all sixty-four of the victims were arranged on poster boards at the front of the church. In a show of solidarity, many of the other clans had again sent representatives. There were also local politicians and two members of the Royal Family. Even though Jack was there to support her, Maddie appreciated the additional support provided by Siobhan, Charlie, Bob and Betty and several of their friends who had also come.

Fifteen clan members had come forward and asked to speak at the memorial, including several of those who had been injured. Following them, Maddie had her address to make. It had not been an easy one to write. At the beginning of her address she shared a few memories of childhood with the previous duke. She also expressed her sorrow and shock. Most important though, she wanted to offer comfort to the survivors while also assuring them that everything possible was being done to apprehend and call to account those responsible. She stressed the point that she wanted "justice not revenge" and asked her fellow clansmen to take this stance too. Although her voice wavered a few times, she managed to get through her address without tears. Following her, the pastor gave a short sermon. The final hymn was 'The Lord's My Shepherd'. Most of the congregation, fighting tears, was unable to sing it.

The dedication of the memorial plaque took place immediately after the memorial service. The day had dawned wet and cold, but by afternoon the clouds had thinned and the sun was trying to make an appearance. A large crowd turned out to witness the dedication. The plaque itself was three feet by three feet and was on a post embedded into the rock and concrete in front of where the hotel had stood. There was a large engraving of the MacMorden crest on the top of the plaque. The inscription underneath was in both English and Gaelic and was very simple: 'To the memory of sixty-four MacMordens who gave up their lives to a cowardly act of violence. We will not forget' and the date of the attack. 'We will not forget' was the clan motto. The individual names of those killed were listed on the back of the plaque.

Maddie had planned a reception following the dedication. After the sorrow and solemnity of the afternoon, it was intended as a celebration of the lives of those lost and their legacy. The drinks flowed freely, at the expense of the Duchy. As Maddie had hoped, after a few drinks people began to share stories of those who had been lost. Some of the stories were quite funny and the dark mood that had hovered over all those there began to lift. Not surprisingly, the local press had been following the day's activities. Maddie hoped the terrorists would see this celebration of life and realize their attack had not daunted the spirit of the clan.

A week later the chief of police called Maddie. He had some interesting news. "The Ulster police got a tip about a meeting of one of the IRA terror cells in a local Belfast pub. They raided the pub and arrested four people. None of them were the men we were looking for, but one of them said something that led them to a raid on a home where the rest of the cell was meeting. They arrested five more men there. Two of them are two of our suspects."

Because Northern Ireland was part of the U.K. there was no extradition required. Once they had answered the charges laid by the Ulster police the suspects would be turned over to Scotland to answer for the bombing.

"How long will they be in Ireland?" Maddie wanted to know.

"I don't know," said the chief. "It'll probably be quite a while. They were wanted there for planting car bombs."

Four days later, the chief again phoned Maddie. "The third man we were looking for washed up on the shore of the River Liffey in Dublin. He had a bullet hole between his eyes."

"Rough justice," Maddie said.

# *CHAPTER 74*

Following the funerals and the memorial, Maddie got down to business. She was determined to understand the workings of the Duchy. Politics and accounting were not things she had ever been good at nor interested in, but she sat with Archie for four days while he patiently went over and over the workings of the estate. She was amazed at the size of the estate and couldn't tell Archie often enough how much she appreciated him staying on as manager. By the end of the four days, she had a rudimentary understanding of how the Duchy worked, but she was very glad she didn't have to run it. She was ultimately responsible for the clan, but with Archie to explain and advise on any issues, she was confident she could do the job. She asked Archie to find suitable people to fill the jobs left vacant by those who were lost.

Maddie didn't feel quite so overwhelmed when she met with Duncan to go through the business of the home farm. Not only was it a smaller piece of the Duchy, there were no politics involved. The work of the farm was straightforward. Part of the estate was run as a producing farm, but the larger share of it was let to tenants who paid rent and worked their own land. She could make logical decisions without having to worry about who might be offended by the politics. She also asked Duncan to fill the vacant positions.

Confident the estate and home farm had been, and were being, well run by her managers Maddie did not feel it necessary to step in and take over. They did not require a lot of input from her to maintain the status quo and she didn't feel she had to interfere with what was already functioning well. She gave her managers credit for knowing more about the workings of the estate than she did. There might be changes later on, but for now things would run as they had been.

Ever considerate of Maddie, Jack spoke to her at breakfast one morning. "I think we should move into the castle," he said. "Your office is there and you can't keep running back and forth every day. You're exhausted and we never get to see you. I can work from anywhere."

It was an hour trip in each direction to and from the castle and even though she had a car and chauffeur the double life was wearing Maddie down. She was relieved Jack made the decision. Still not willing to let her position impact his life any more than absolutely necessary, she had been reluctant to suggest moving even though her presence was usually required in Morden.

Sure she was a real princess now, Emma was thrilled to move into the castle. Sandy was too young to care. Mrs. Brown had become like a surrogate grandmother to Emma and Sandy. She was offered the position of full-time, live-in nanny and was delighted to accept. Her children were all grown and no longer lived in Prestwick so she really had no ties there. Her work would not be arduous as Jack and Maddie were raising their children. They needed Mrs. Brown more as a babysitter than a nanny, however the arrangement suited all.

"What are we going to do with this house?" Maddie asked.

Jack replied, "We don't have to decide right away. We can get a caretaker to look after it and I'm sure the neighbours will keep an eye on it."

Maddie was delighted. "We can come back for a few days any time I need a reality check."

Once again 'normal' family life for the Buchanans was redefined.

Jack was pleased that Maddie was able to travel with him and Bob sometimes. With Mrs. Brown in residence, they had no worries about the children. When Bob and Jack had mini tours Maddie would occasionally go with them, but she insisted her performing days were over. She would watch the shows from backstage. Since Maddie had become such a public figure, she would dress more formally for shows than she had previously when she could change into costume.

One night on a tour Jack thought she looked exceptionally lovely in a long tartan dress. It reminded him of the days when they first danced to Bob's playing. When Bob started his solo waltz Jack went over to the curtain to get Maddie to dance with him. As had happened so many years before, she didn't want him to be embarrassed in front of the audience so she came out from behind the curtain and danced with him.

With Jack away on tour so much and the Duchy pretty much running itself, Maddie was looking for something to occupy her mind. With her background in history, she wanted something tangible to display the clan's history. As a youngster growing up in Ottawa, she had been fascinated by Upper Canada Village, a living history museum about an hour south of the city. Several heritage buildings had been moved together to create a small village. Costumed interpreters performed the tasks that people of the 1860s would have done. She was also impressed by Bunratty Folk Park at Bunratty Castle in Ireland. Thinking she would like to create something similar that combined both museums, she started gathering information. If it was going to be done right, it was going to take several years to set up. She would need help and information from both the managers of Upper Canada Village and of Bunratty Folk Park. It would involve some travelling and she could coordinate it with times Bob and Jack were touring Canada and Ireland.

In the shorter term, Maddie wanted to plan a gathering of the clan and asked Jack what he thought of the idea. "I think it would be fun to make it an eighteenth century camp out, everything authentic to the time. We can have games and contests, mock battles and demonstrations of fighting skills, musicians and story-tellers. The food will be traditional and cooked over open fires as it used to be." As she put her idea into words, she got more and more excited about it. "Everyone can wear eighteenth century clothing and instead of cars we'll all use horses. We can have horse races too. What do you think?"

"I think it sounds like fun, a lot of work, but fun," Jack answered. "When would you have it?"

"I'm thinking next October after the harvests are in and before winter comes."

With two big projects to work on and two small children to look after, Maddie was happy. She had found a new purpose in life. It wasn't the same as travelling with Bob and Jack and performing, and she did miss those days, but it had its own rewards. She still missed Jack terribly when he was away on long tours, but with Mrs. Brown living in she was at least able to travel with them on some of the short ones.

One day when they were out walking in the public gardens, Jack and Maddie encountered some tourists and started talking to them. As it happened, the couple (Steve and Barb Smith) was from Morrisburg, Ontario, a small town near Ottawa, where Maddie had grown up. It was also very close to Upper Canada Village. Amazed at how small the world was, Maddie and Jack talked to the Smiths for about twenty minutes.

Maddie said, "We usually have tea at four, would you like to join us?" Maddie led the way to a small patio at the west side of the castle. The Smiths were surprised to see there were no other tourists on the patio. They were about to comment on this when one of the maids came outside to speak to Maddie.

"Your Grace, there is a phone call for you."

Maddie excused herself and went in to answer the call.

Stunned, the couple spoke at the same time. “Is she the duke?”

They had already visited the castle and heard the story of the new duke. With Jack and Maddie dressed casually, the Smiths had assumed they were also tourists. Suddenly feeling very awkward, they apologized to Jack for taking up his and Maddie’s time and invading the private area of the castle.

Jack assured them they were welcome saying, “Maddie and I are really enjoying this visit. Please don’t apologize.”

Maddie returned as Jack was saying this. “Yes, please stay. It’s nice to speak to someone about what used to be home.” She also wanted to talk about Upper Canada Village, superstitiously thinking the fates had brought them together for that reason.

During the course of their conversation, Maddie and the Smiths discovered they had some acquaintances in common, a family that had moved from Ottawa to Morrisburg several years before.

Still marvelling at how small the world was becoming, they parted company, Barb saying, “We really have something to tell our friends now. We just had tea with a duke.”

# *CHAPTER 75*

Just when Maddie thought life had settled into a predictable routine, Jack came to her and said, "We need to talk." In the years they'd been together that had become their code-phrase for let's change our lives. Not knowing what to expect, she led him into the library and they sat down. It was a damp, chilly day and one of the maids had lit the fire. Maddie found the room lined with books very cozy. It was her favourite room in the castle.

Maddie was beginning to worry. With all the recent changes in their lives, she was afraid of what Jack might have in mind. He wanted to talk, but he didn't seem to know where to start and his silence unnerved her. Finally he started hesitantly. "I know we've had a lot of changes over the past year, some good and some not so good. It seems like life has finally settled down. Now here I am trying to stir things up again."

Maddie couldn't tell where this was going and was a little worried. As patiently as she could, she waited for Jack to elaborate. When he didn't say anything, she leaned forward and kissed him. He responded warmly. Sitting back she said, "Okay, you're not going to tell me you're leaving me, so how bad can it be?"

"No, my love. I have no intention of ever leaving you," he said laughing. "Quite the contrary. What I'm trying to do is suggest we have another child. From what I've read, it seems to be royalty's job to have lots of kids and ensure the succession. You don't have to answer me right away, think about it."

"Sorry to disappoint you, luv, but we're not royalty. I don't have to think about it. I love the idea and I love you."

Jack couldn't believe his ears. He had the most amazing wife in the world.

Life was good again.

CPSIA information can be obtained
at www.ICGtesting.com
Printed in the USA
LVHW04s2221181018
594088LV00001B/2/P

9 781912 601158